I0713493

Theodore Tobias Greenwood
A Child Of Grace

David Michael Willson

PUBLISHED *by* PARABLES
Earthly Stories with a Heavenly Meaning

1

Theodore Tobias Greenwood: A Child Of Grace
Written By David Michael Willson

.

Copyright © David Michael Willson
October, 2017

Published By Parables
October, 2017

Unless otherwise specified Scripture quotations are taken from the authorized version of the King James Bible.

ISBN 978-1-945698-28-6
Printed in the United States of America

Readers should be aware that Internet Web sites offered as citations and/or sources for further information may have been changed or disappeared between the time this was written and when it is read.

THEODORE TOBIAS GREENWOOD
A CHILD OF GRACE

DAVID MICHAEL WILLSON

TABLE OF CONTENTS

Acknowledgments
About the Author

First and foremost, I thank The Father for giving me this story. I thank all the children I crossed paths with over the years, both in my personal life and as a professional in schools and various settings. I thank my informal and formal education from my own life to the Friendship House Children's Center in Scranton, PA, to The Children's Home in Tampa, FL and from The University of Arizona to the Hillsborough Community College in Tampa. And finally, from the Florida State University, and a great course on creative writing at Kodiak Community College in AK- thanks Leslie. It was from these experiences I met and learned about children and a bit of writing. Nearly every character has a little bit of me in him or her and I will be honest and tell you it's not only the good stuff. I've always felt things deeply; when I was affected by someone else's pain, when I created someone else's pain, and when I was able to ease someone else's pain. Not an easy way to live, especially the parts where I hurt others. But, I survived and came to know Jesus. Do I still have struggles? Yes, but I no longer feel alone - thanks be to God. And, I must thank my parents, who did their very best with their foursome of very different personalities. I thank my friends, old and new, and I thank the wonderful community of Northeast Pennsylvania for giving me a wonderful place to grow-up and provide for Tobias' stage. Any town here could be Kannot. My life's dream is to matter in this world before I leave. The Father wants to see what we can do here before we enter into His presence in Heaven. I hope I wrote this book in the manner of His desire; to show a Christian life well-lived and the positive impact it can have upon anyone who comes into contact with that life. You won't be reading lots of scripture or hearing a lot about churches, but rest assured this is a Christian book and you will be witnessing one person in particular, behaving as if walking with Jesus. You will see how he builds fellowship and followers, and you will see most of his life unfold in school, where friends, parents, teachers, and the community all have a presence and role.

The story I tell today was the story that came into my heart on one day back in 2003. It really hasn't changed much. Though it must fall into the Fiction category, it comes from some incredible observations and experiences I've had with children throughout my career. And strangely enough, I was not a practicing Christian when I began, but I believe Tobias walked me into it. This book changed me; it was a slow change and a slow process only because life kept happening. The book and my characters would rest at times, sometimes for several years. I'd wake them up and they would excitedly be waiting for me. By 2016 and the beginning of 2017 I was ready to bring this book to a close and then a funny thing happened --- I realized the story can never end. When something changes you in such a way you just keep paying it forward. And that is my intent --- to tell you there are truly Tobias Greenwoods out there and/or people/children who want to live as Tobias lived. What a gift these Godly creatures bring to us and how fortunate I have been to have walked down a Novel's path with Jesus growing in my heart and really writing the story with me. I remember seeking the Holy Spirit and asking if it was OK to put some things in this book that seemed a bit rough, and the response,

"That's life David, bad things will happen and evil will enter at times. Let's see what you can learn from it, so even the normal growing up stuff in this beautiful, crazy, and often unpredictable and predictable world, is fair game. And, have you read The Old Testament

lately? I'm here all the time, through all the trials and tribulations so if you are a good learner, or if the readers are good learners, things about a Godly life will be learned. Though scripture is really helpful, a Christian life well-lived can be lived without the obvious presence of scripture. It will always be about ME dwelling in you and how you express that to the world around you."

Well, that is the way I felt HIS answer and I cannot apologize for that.

Sincerely,
Thank You Jesus, Thank You All
David Michael Willson

Introduction

How the Story Came to Be

A rough start to the life of a little boy. He has been touched by God and walks with Jesus, yet he doesn't seem to know it himself. His friends notice his peculiarities more than he. Life on earth with all its challenges for a boy like Tobias. He sees horrible things, he acts and doesn't act on them, he teaches his teachers, he loves others, he loves the girl, he feels others' pain, he experiences life in the many typical ways of just growing up. People want to be around him for he has lessons to teach, yet one hates him, a community nearly prejudges him to jail, he'd lay down his life for any other, he's funny, he's serious, he's playful and mysterious. He has heroes too. And he has dreams. A Christian boy to a Christian man with very little interruption. How will his life affect his relationship with Jesus, his family, friends, community, or even the world?

CHAPTER I

A LIFE GOING TO BE CHRISTIAN LIVED

At the end of one's life, how does a life well-lived matter? How, and to what degree, can the human condition of those exposed to such a life be affected? Can a story like the one to follow change people and even the world to become a better place; a place where it matters worth living a life well? --- where the masses can see the benefits of goodness and the repercussions from badness and with no confusion about what is good and what is bad. How does one determine truth in such a story? Questions to ponder followed by a search for their answers should we have the desire to **MATTER.** Regardless of by whom and why such a journey is undertaken, it is the journey that matters more than the outcome because there is no pure or last outcome as the circular movement of life is perpetual. We are born, we grow up, we die and through this process, we live, we learn, we teach, whether we actively choose to engage in these processes or not. The impact of lives upon one another is never linear, it never finishes; there are no end results; it is a forever movement. My friend knew this. This is his story --- the story of Theodore Tobias Greenwood and the cast of characters that surrounded his life.

I still don't fully understand it all, but the impact from being exposed to Tobias is often not easily described but always felt. When we were young I found him strange, but always wanted to be around him. As I got a bit older I found many of the things he did and didn't do oddly interesting and still wanted to always be around him. Another bit older and I became fascinated by what he was able to do, and older still, amazed and never stopped wanting to be around him.

I began to realize the gift of this friendship over the years and now I am deeply touched, grateful and inspired by the impact Tobias' life had on me and our little community in Kannot, Pennsylvania. I choose to believe it was all related to a higher power – one of love, one of free will and one who I believe we will all answer to one day. Tobias knew the Bible and went to church every Sunday though he would rarely mention an organized religion. I believe he had a very close relationship with God. For those who don't subscribe to God, or any higher power, for that matter, I think they can look at Tobias and still be in awe of the manner in which he lived his life. On this earth, I think I have been as close to what my God wishes me to represent as anyone ever. I believe I grew up being exposed to his love and grace through Tobias. I would try to have such discussions with Tobias but he would only say I'm being weird. I think that was just something he was programmed to say to provide cover for his heavenly motives. He simply lived by example; he did not have to preach one word about a religion or his spirituality. He was a beautiful child who remained a beautiful man.

Tobias usually brought out the best in people, yet oddly at times, the worst as well. Lessons would be learned from Tobias and from events that took place throughout his life. He would say we learn goodness from each other, or not (there was always an "or not"), either way we will learn something. He rarely bantered about things. His communication whether it be verbal or nonverbal always seem to have a direct point. Only the love of his earthly life could alter this communication style. The essence of Tobias manifested in all his relationships; with caregivers, elders, teachers, children, clergy, employers, classmates --- everyone.

Nearing Tobias's final year, he began laying much confidence in me, this friend since childhood. The one most thought my mind as quiet as my speak --- but on the contraire my mind was always working and taking in things and I now realize Tobias knew this about me. He knew no matter what he shared with me that I would have some reference to what he spoke. He would tell me things as if in chapter form. The mystery of himself now to align with the mystery experienced by so many others --- it began to hit him too. When he began sharing how he remembered these stories he would say,

"When I tell you my last story it will all come together and you will know".

He would say this as if I were a part of his puzzle, while all along I thought Tobias was a piece to mine and everyone else's puzzle, but in reflection there is no way we could not be pieces to each other's puzzles and no one being the primary. I learned to not question Tobias' insights and words; I was humbled by the invitation into his world. Nonetheless, I still had to ask,

"Know what, Tobias?"

"I'm not sure, but you and I will know together" he said.

The day he contacts me to share his final chapter, I come to his bedside. He seemed so much at peace. He had been in so much physical pain for so long --- two months for this latest period of burn/grafting and infection. But this was his day; he owned it and he ordered a pain free day; a day with his friend. He somehow received the answers he sought and they seemed to bring him joy and peace and he wanted to share these with me. And still his hand lays there in that position again; and he admits to me he knows it; reminding me again he is never alone and never was. I did not have to ask for any clarification.

He began to speak of his mother and father and what he remembered of them. My goodness, he was only two and a half when they left this world and he yet had things stored in memory and could put language to them. I wasn't sure if this was possible, but with Tobias I had to believe it was. He stated how much he loved his Aunt and Uncle, his adoptive parents. They saved me he would say. He told me of a recent conversation he had with his Aunt with such a profound, yet comfortable look on his scarred and beautiful face --- the comfort and peace that seemed to wash away the scars. His Aunt, apparently understanding Tobias' need for truth as he always requested, confessed to him the addictions of his mother and father and that their substance abuse was the reason for the accident. Though it was not truth for his sake he was seeking. He knew by unburdening his Aunt and Uncle of such a secret would bring them more peace when he was gone.

At the time, they questioned themselves and the professionals what best; raising this young life with the open acknowledgement of this fact, or raising the child who had positive roots minus such parental vices. They opted for the latter and when the professionals stated the appropriate time to have such a discussion, ongoing hesitation/discomfort simply moved time past them. Tobias, spoke about this with such love for his Aunt and Uncle --- not the animosity typically heard when such truths are unearthed later in one's life. He truly knew their decision was based in love and that was all he required. When he discussed this with his Aunt, she confessed it all, as I learned in later conversation with her, Tobias smiled and simply said,

"Thank you for doing that for me", with glistening, sparkling eyes --- followed by "I love you both so much".

Tobias remembered some events of his life with his mother and father. He stated remembering his parents being surrounded by bad people at times but that they always tried to protect him. He took great pride in this memory yet said The Father always had one of my hands. Tobias said his Mom and Dad had experienced very tough lives and were very young. They were touched by the evils of this world and moved away from family and friends. He talked about the impact of bad things that happen to people and children and would then say such things do not always have to end badly. It is not a given that anger, resentment, hatred will take over the heart of those mistreated, even the very young. And then there was Raymond; a question to which so many needed an answer and when it came, it came hard.

But now, he wants to share his peace with his friend who never heard him utter, infer, allude to anything about his roots. And the only time this friend and many others saw him lose his sense of peace and grace was at that football game on that night in 1976. Even though this event shocked so many, most came to the understanding it was probably necessary and worked out for the best, but I am still not sure Tobias felt the same way. When I asked him about this he was not able to provide another way of handling such a situation. He could only say "other" feelings overtook his heart on that day. I could only posit this may sometimes be meant to happen. He said this with uncertainty as if this was the one question he will not have answered on this earth, but still he did not seem to mind. He did not seem to have a need to know this. Throughout his years of intermittent healing and relapse and so much pain, I've not witnessed the calmness I see before me now, yet the ongoing familiarity of his grace has always sustained.

The doctors had long stated the terminal nature of Tobias' wounds. His timeline for passing appeared to be approaching with certainty. His wife, children, relatives and friends were as prepared as anyone could be, especially with the help of Tobias. He would remind everyone, "at no place in the Bible does it say we will live a pain or grief-free life", yet he would go on to say, "the Gifts and Graces will far exceed such pains --- if you learn". His last words to me were that I tell his story and MC the next 'Person of the Decade' event in the year 1993 --- a Kannot, Pennsylvania thing. They started this with Tobias after his heroics in 1982. He had such a prideful look on his face when he made this request. He smiled and stated this would also help me make more sense of all this. It was my pain and loss he was now caring about. Tobias was at peace and had all the answers he required to move on, but he knew my mind processed information on a constant basis, so much so that a sleep disorder manifested over the years.

Trying some comic relief, "Thanks, now I'll have this to ponder for 9 more years and during the middle of the night too. I thought things were supposed to start making more sense to me now".

He could only smile; he knew I'd make it and he knew

I needed a lot of time. And with that, I needed to leave the room as his wife and children and some others sat in waiting outside. Tobias had words and messages for them all and one by one they entered and departed; later to tell me their experience at Tobias' request. And finally, his children, with PJ's packed and ready for a nighttime story with their Daddy and Mommy. It would not be long now. This would be the last time I would see Tobias in this world as he would pass the next morning. Let us all not forget he was so right all along about Ramona and to remind us all about those times he would say,

> "Faith, Hope and Love my friends and the greatest of these is Love," with that precious and most sincere smile one could ever see.

Oh, the things most of us just cannot see when we are young. He was right all along about so many things. He offered his grace and love for all and especially noticed during our school years. 'No bullying of anyone because they were different! Didn't matter' he would say about color, religion, sexual orientation, etc. 'Jesus simply wanted us to love our neighbors; he didn't tell us to pick and choose. Faith, Hope and Love and the greatest of these is Love', he would say again. He was saying these things at a time when the rest of us didn't understand ourselves. I'm just so blessed.

So here I am tonight, October 1st, 1993 in this auditorium, renovated since our high school days with more seating and comfort. The much carved in wood rests professing the love of this one to that one with occasional profanities professing the disdain of this one to that one long gone. I was asked to do this a couple years ago. Since then I have felt this would be one of the most important moments in my life. I had so many thoughts and feelings about it. I've been preparing for this speech for many years and not always on a conscious level. My family --- I've tried to share so much with them over the years. They eventually seemed to know what I was going through and provided even more love and comfort especially during the last year, the time I became actively engaged in the planning of this event and my speech's development. It feels very right tonight --- to honor the spirit of Tobias and to celebrate the recipient of this award. And the secret committee --- they know who's in the running, but until the sealed letter is broken on stage only the ballot counters know for sure, and they have sworn a vow of secrecy.

As for the planning of this event; most pointedly, I was asked to seek "those in high places" that would consider attending. High dollar plates were requested to raise funds for several charities the new recipient wishes to champion. This was a kind of media event. Knowing how to accomplish this while sharing such an event with the local community was a tall order. Money for the charities was most important so we decided upon a free community event the following weekend where the community would take joy in this celebration and they would learn of the amounts raised for the charities. With this in mind, the community backed such an event and tried to help connect with any celebrity, politician or well-to-do that would pay the $1,000 seat. It was a great photo op for them. Since the inception of this award for Tobias, the exposure of his life and accolades on at least a regional level, this event would receive much media attention --- and for charity --- one could not look better. The eight hundred seat auditorium would bring about a nice dollar amount and rumor had it again there were several donors ready to match whatever sum raised. When Tobias received the award, it was reported to be the largest amount donated to charities per capita in the country. There were now articles stating the concept of this award ceremony was beginning to take hold in other areas of the country. Some thought Tobias' event was just a passing moment in history, but nothing associated with Tobias was ever just a passing event. Despite the limelight, motives would not be questioned tonight as love long sustained for, and through Tobias, would be in this house. The artists, musicians, and writers touched by Tobias' life would return along with local, state and other political leaders. And per the spirit of Tobias' life, tonight's award winner will come to share many of the qualities one would expect of the one to take this center stage.

For many years, I was an observer of Tobias, a listener of stories told by and about Tobias, and was directly impacted on many occasions as a friend of Tobias. This story will speak to you and it may answer some questions you have about living life as a Christian if you choose to let yourself imagine and consider the possibilities. Through Tobias' Christian life, his ongoing friendship with Jesus continues and his love and compassion for others will be shared. It is a story about the faith and wisdom of a child and what we can learn from such children. And it's a story about how our lives impact upon each other. I've heard there may be others out there like Tobias; some call them Old Souls or Wisdom Children. Most people don't make the Faith connection until they are older. I wonder why it is so hard to see such Faith and the Christian possibilities in these children.

This evening, I reflect upon Tobias' life as I sit with my family and friends in the Kannot High School auditorium recognizing the Person of the Decade. Tobias, being the last recipient, and since passed from complications resulting from his wounds, a more fitting tribute cannot be made. But, I have a need to tell you how we got to this place today. I offer this story of a special person's journey, a task I began many years ago. But it cannot be just Tobias' story, for individual lives and the decisions made impact upon each and others - for better or worse, and to varying degrees. What would happen if we truly understood this? Just a little hint; when musical selections present themselves, if you have the music play it along with the scenes. This boy knew how to have fun and live!

Chapter II

Through the Child,
He Makes His Entrance

Jonathan and Maggie Greenwood were frequently caught up in impassioned discussions about their future. The Greenwoods had been married for two years, and though trying, pregnancy was not coming. Despite their youth, they seemed to well understand the need to be ready and willing parents. They met in college and once graduated, married. While dating they discussed their future together and they discussed having children. They talked about the things we wish everyone to talk about before marriage and certainly before children. Where will we live? What if one of us cannot find a job? How would we raise a child? Do we connect with a church or religion for spiritual guidance? How will we know how to discipline a child? They asked each other if their child would be the most important thing in their lives. What roles do we want our parents, siblings and friends to have with our child? In other words, they pretty much drove each other crazy with the questions they pondered before actually living their lives as parents. Then they took the discussions out of their private communications and began grilling their parents, siblings, friends and pastors. They talked with strangers and teachers and passing preachers, yet what may be most impressive is that they did this with such sincerity and passion. Those questioned would never forget them. After their first year of marriage they were ready. They found a peace with all the questions posed and answers given and gained. These two loving people were ready to bring a child into this world.

By accounts of all those around them, Jonathan and

Maggie Greenwood were supposed to be parents and they would become so to a boy named Theodore Tobias. As sometimes occurs, a child is born with a first and middle name and within a very short period of time the family realizes the child IS the middle name and so it was with Tobias. Something not explainable; it just happens. They would teach Tobias through Gospel messages, modeling of work ethic, loyalty, responsibility, compassion, passion, patience and most importantly love. Jonathan and Maggie were still quite young so there was a wonderful balance and blend of innocence, naiveté and all the active learning avenues they traveled. No one could know how Tobias would evolve yet all certainly knew he would be OK. There was no way anyone could know Tobias would become the person he did and touch the lives of so many and the manner in which he would do so. Despite all the incredible efforts of these parents, their beautiful personalities and their drive to be the best parents they could be, questions would continue to present about Tobias' gifts. Tobias' goodness, in and of itself, was not the mystery. It was the way he interacted with the world that perplexed so many. Tobias would teach lessons to people and through so many means that simple connections to Jonathan and Maggie's efforts could not be the sole explanation.

Tobias was born on October 1st, 1959, yet he and the Greenwoods would not meet until June 6th, 1962. Tobias would not be born to them. He would enter their lives through tragedy. Maggie's sister and brother-in-law lived in a tiny coastal town in Oregon. Though far apart, Maggie tried to remain close to her sister, Sharon. It was through her sister's world that Maggie's desire to become a parent blossomed thus the intense interest in future parenting. Unfortunately, due to college, career, Sharon and Dale's challenges and finances, Maggie and her sister had not been together since before Tobias' birth. All of Maggie's cooing to Tobias was presented via speaker phone; Tobias likely developed a very comforting relationship with that phone. On June 5th, the call came. There may be no truth more powerful than a loved one telling you another loved one has been killed. A call that sucks life's wind out of you and you can only try to respond by fighting to suck some back in. But you gasp and gasp and feel like you are suffocating. With every attempt to breathe, a little air enters and begins allowing your mind and heart to further process the message. Maggie's father has told her Sharon and Dale have been killed in an automobile accident. The traumatic gasping begins and when some words could find their way through the maze of shock and pain,

"What about Tobias, Tobias!?" she cried out to her father.

"He's OK Maggie, he's OK. He was with a babysitter.".

The next two weeks involved bringing Sharon and Dale's bodies and belongings back to Kannot. Though Dale was from the other side of the country, there were no family members who came forward in grief. He seemed alone in life, except for Sharon, and so too in death. The amount of pain for such a family to function in this way is unimaginable for families like Maggie and Jonathan's so these families took care of Dale; Sharon would have had it no other way. Most importantly to them all, it maintained a paternal historical link for Tobias even though only by grave. It was a period of shock, disbelief, numbness, and intensely sharp pain, sometimes presenting in isolation, sometime mixed together. After the task of breaking the physical connections to their lives in Oregon, and the funeral services in Kannot, they were available enough to begin discussions about Tobias' future. As for Tobias, and who were to be his caregivers, there was no doubt. It was clear in written form that Maggie and Jonathan Greenwood were the chosen ones and when the Oregon Children Services received notification they were ready for Tobias after all the services, he would be brought to them. No family members could dispute the decision.

Many were invested in Tobias' well-being by virtue of his tragic early life and by virtue of experiencing Jonathan's and Maggie's desire to be parents. Most would say it felt like their lives were already touched by the child Jonathan and Maggie would give birth to well prior to their child's actual arrival. So, to this family and this community, Tobias's life began again on June 28th when the formal adoption papers were signed. With this formal procedure ending, this family and the extended Kannot, PA family would be forever changed. The titles of Aunt and Uncle were now dismantled as the professionals at the adoption center cited Tobias' age and other developmental factors as reasons for such a decision. They would be Tobias' new Mom and Dad. This was no easy feat for them as it initially brought forth much guilt. Maggie would state it felt like they unfairly took the titles away from the memory of her sister and brother-in-law. Tobias would quickly help them through this. His understanding of expressive and receptive language was exceptional and perplexing to adults. Within his first year with Maggie and Jonathan he would say he had a Mommy and Daddy in memory and he has a Mommy and Daddy now. Though the Greenwoods used this terminology with Tobias, the manner Tobias would start or engage in this discussion brought much peace to them and helped them move past their feelings of guilt and betrayal to their loved one's lost. They would not be alone though. Tobias had his grandparents; Maggie and Jonathan's parents. As Dale entered Sharon's life with so much secrecy, so too was their secrecy with his family. There would be no biological paternal links for Tobias as they disappeared from this earth as much as Dale did – only a grave site reminder. But, he did have a father. He had Thee Father, yet to be fully understood. But those here, those wanting and needing to be involved, they would all come to dote over him as there were no other children in the family.

Some of the new parent observations besides the fact he was so verbal would cause concern for Maggie and Jonathan.

"Jonathan, do you see how Tobias' hand is positioned sometimes, and not always the same hand?" Maggie asks him.

"What do you mean?" he responds

"One will turn slightly sideways and backwards, not all

the time, but sometimes" she says.

"Well, let's ask him if it's hurt or something? Jonathan tells her

"Good idea husband"

"Tobias, come over here please" she calls

"Yes Mommy".

"Honey, does your hand hurt you?" she asks

"Nope, why?" he asks

"Because sometimes it's turned sideways and looks different than your other hand".

"That nice man holds them sometimes. He used to hold them a lot before I came here" he reports with his smile.

"What nice man honey, there's no one there when we see this" Maggie says with concern in her voice.

"He's just a friend for me Mommy. He told me his name is Jesus. He just takes my hand in his" Tobias proclaims.

"OK Maggie, you can stop there", Jonathan says with alarm.

"Tobias, can we keep your friend a secret just for you, me and mommy?"

"Sure Daddy, secrets can be fun sometimes".

Despite being Christians they had a hard time with believing this child's words and knew most, if not all, others would as well. They could only see problems associated with statements like these. Jonathan and Maggie vowed to keep this discussion between them and they truly believed Tobias would too, but throughout his life, they would see the hand turn and would eventually come to believe The Truth behind the story.

Tobias' early life in Kannot mostly involved him remaining close to home. Kannot lies in the Northeastern area of Pennsylvania's rolling mountains. Many immigrants came to this area in the late 1800's to find work in the mining industry. The Welsh would simply transition their limestone quarrying skills to this darker rock, while the Italians, Irish and many others either arrived with mining skills or developed them, to simply engage in work and engage in a new beginning in this beautiful country. Kannot was a bit different than many other towns in Northeastern Pennsylvania as many were settled by a dominant culture. In Kannot, no one culture could lay claim to Kannot's beginnings and the peace they found with such a balance helped define the future of this community. An inspiring area with distinct beauty for each of its four seasons; the snowfalls of winter, the brilliantly colored leaves of autumn, the blossoms of spring and the excitement of warmth for summer. The column dumps, though not attractive, were an accepted part of the backdrop to the area as they were constant reminders of the hard work of current community members and the ancestral history of the community. The column dumps and old coal draglines really shaped the environment of these mining communities. Though the vast amounts of coal deposits had long been stripped there were still some active coal breakers in operation.

There were some family owned/operated businesses in Kannot but most commuted to the larger areas such as Scranton, Honesdale or towns close to these areas for work. Kannot was far enough from larger populations that it maintained its own identity; one of innocence and a strong sense of security and unity.

The freedom for Tobias to begin playing outside and with other children did not begin until he was nearing four years of age. Jonathan and Maggie were quite protective of the little fella. They were caught up in protecting Tobias by keeping him close to them based on his history. Tobias's distinct physical shape, black wavy hair and green eyes would make him stand out within groups of children. He was also big and quite strong for his age. He could do things, move things, say things and figure out things much easier it seemed than others his age. It was time to begin sharing Tobias with the community, while also affording him the opportunity to begin developing friendships.

His first playmate was Raymond Gilbrandt. Raymond lived next door with his Mom. In the early years there was a man in Mrs. Gilbrandt's life, not Raymond's dad though. Raymond's father had died when he was quite young and there appeared no interest in Mrs. Gilbrandt to have a formal Mr. around the home. Mrs. Gilbrandt never spoke of him. She just seemed constantly grieved and lonely. It was apparent that Raymond needed a special friend and Tobias was starved for such a friendship. Much of the play was outdoors for these little lads. Sandbox play to three-wheelers and eventually by about six, they would be riding their little bikes together.

Raymond's proximity was a geographical blessing, the frequency of play seemed endless --- until of course, either would have to go inside for meal time, bath time, or naptime. Then, as in the minds and hearts of most little ones, it seemed they were never allowed to play, forgetting, and not purposely, they had played together for hours before such rude intervention.

During Tobias' early years with the Greenwoods many other things began to present indicating to them they had a very special little boy in their life. His language skills seemed to develop rapidly, but it was not what Tobias could say, but rather how he said things. He had wisdom. Though his voice in sound was immature, his words rarely were. They described him as an old soul as they began to realize his high level of insight and basic human understanding. By four years of age they noticed he loved shaking hands with people. They noticed he would sometimes make contact with the extended hand and then grab and hold both with his other hand. This is something we see at times with elders, from people who are overjoyed to see someone, or even for those grieving. Regardless of which physical salutation was chosen, Tobias took great pride in making sure whomever he contacted they knew he appreciated and enjoyed the contact. Jonathan and Maggie also noticed Tobias do this with Raymond, the double hold.

"Tobias, why do you shake hands differently sometimes with people? Sometimes it's one hand and sometimes with two?"

"They're fragiles" he says.

"What does that mean?" Jonathan asked.

"They just need it, I can feel it".

"Need what Tobias?" Jonathan asked.

"To know that I really like them".

Being a four-year-old, he was done with this discussion despite Jonathan and Maggie's efforts to hear more.

"I want to watch cartoons now".

"Ok Tobias, you may turn the TV on", Jonathan stated.

The conversation was over. Jonathan and Maggie were left with a very simple explanation. They wondered how a child could make a noun out of an adjective and with intention. They would just have to learn more about this little man through observation. They noticed he prayed every night and sometimes during the day. They figured he was taught this by Dale and/or Sharon. They knew he was special, but were not acknowledging the relationship Tobias stated he had since his days with his biological parents. Tobias and his friend Jesus would remain a secret and interestingly Jesus would not receive much of the credit for a long time. The earthly pull against the Christian heart I guess.

CHAPTER III
THE EARLY ELEMENTARY YEARS (K/3 '64-'68)

Most of Tobias' story revolves around school. As with most children, school becomes their most important social culture. Yes, parents must remain the most important people in their lives but school offers much more in addition to home life for 13 years or so. How to relate to other adults, who are during the day, their bosses. How to relate to other children and lots of them. How to manage inherent conflicts with these adults and children. School will be the only period in life where one will be around so many others of the same or similar age group. The potential for life-long friendships is high. The potential for schooling-length happiness or sadness is high too. It truly does become the center of a 13-year whirlwind. Parents rely on teachers, teachers rely on parents, and the children rely on both to help get them through it all. These reliances will work most of the time for many, and only some of the time for others. The public schooling of children is a Big Deal! Thank goodness for school prayer.

Kindergarten through grade three would not only be Tobias' formative schooling years but they would begin the development of a new and better Kannot School District as well. They could not know this little boy's life and presence would change so many things.

An inherent message that comes through from Tobias is one of time and purpose on this earth. He has flashbacks of his Mom stating this and certainly Maggie and Jonathan too. Jonathan and Maggie's parenting was truly based upon discipline and that would be the true meaning of the word discipline --- to teach. Being practicing Christians they led a good life and were good role models --- they walked the talk. Though Tobias' biological parents attempted to say all the right things they could not model it, but this little fella seemed to have the ability to take them at their word since he came to Jonathan and Maggie with some gifts already in play. "We don't have much time here Tobias so we need to make the most of it, become the best people we can be", they would say. The difference with Tobias is that such messages stuck. He understood them and incorporated such wisdoms at an early age. He was able to adopt such messages in his life better than the wisest of elders. He was a movie of a life playing out in front of you asking, what would happen if a little person were able to understand things, big things? Things and issues that generally come through wisdom and later ages in life. Study in school; Don't hurt others; Time is precious; Difference between wants and needs; Free will and choice; etc. In a two-minute time out given by Maggie when he was five, she began stating,

"Did you know what has happened in the world in the two minutes you sat there? Well, let me tell you, many people made marriage proposals; many people made decisions to have children; decisions that would forever change their lives. There have been terrible accidents that would forever change people's lives; some people lost their jobs and some people got jobs and this would change their lives also". And there's a war going on and people are ….

Catching herself as possibly going a bit too far as this five-year old stared her down,

"Or, you could have been doing something productive for this family like cleaning something or playing a game with someone. So, when you choose to have a behavior that gets you in time-out remember how important two minutes can be. You should be thinking about these things when you are ready to waste some of your time".

"OK, I choose marriage thinking. The next time I sit in time-out I will make my marriage words" he tells Maggie.

"What do you mean Tobias?" she says.

"You know, to say the words so the girl will marry you".

"Oh Tobias! I guess what I'm saying is to be careful not to waste time over things like not turning a cartoon off when I tell you too".

"Alright, but I really just wanted to see if the next one was a repeat".

"And you are talking about a marriage proposal Tobias?"

--- as she finds humor she's in a discussion with a five-year-old in which such terminology is being clarified.

"Head outside kiddo, maybe Raymond's out there". Maggie and Jonathan also recognized Tobias simply loved the outdoors. If there were no friends around he could be seen or found anywhere; sitting in a field, by a stream, on a park bench, etc. Many would say Tobias would look like he was thinking deeply or praying during such times. This behavior maintained throughout his life.

Tobias' Kindergarten year began in the fall of 1964. He was a young Kindergartner as he would turn 5 on October 1st. It did not take much convincing to let him start as the teacher could easily see his high level of communication skills and it was only for half-days, so at four years of age he was in. His unique personality and gifts were now being exposed to teachers and other children. He quickly became the child talked about in the teacher's lounge and the name other kids often mentioned to their parents --- and all in a very good way. When his teacher would call home with "a story" about Tobias, they were initially put off by Maggie or Jonathan's reaction; "Yes, that's Tobias". Ms. Dawson thought this was stated in a matter-of-fact kind of way and thus interpreted they did not truly understand how special this little boy was. And there was some truth to this. The Greenwoods did know Tobias was very different and quite unique from other children yet they had little life knowledge of children in general. What schools must offer parents is not that they should focus on comparing children for comparison sake, but they can identify the variances in developmental levels, especially in Kindergarten. A good teacher can readily assess a child's understanding level of academic concepts like numbers, letters, colors, sizes, shapes and such, while also seeing the level of language and social skills. Tobias was far past the Kindergarten level in his language and social skills. He was operating at much higher level within these areas such as words and meanings, sentence structures, conflict resolution skills and compassion for others. He was on par with most academic concepts though numbers were an area that truly challenged him.

During these early years, a teacher could not have had a better teacher aide in the classroom. The other kids adored him. This is where he began to develop a friendship circle that would be long lasting; Raymond, Wilson, Taylor, Sadie, and Jimmy J seemed to be around him more than most. Ms. Dawson would usually tell their parents Tobias behaved like a loving big brother to them and they received him in the same way. To all, he was like the responsible 5th grader who would come in to the class to help the little ones.

He would always give up his position as line leader to a peer who needed a boost. The teacher learned to let Tobias pick, since he often recognized the child in need of such a boost more aptly than she. He did the same with board eraser, paper picker upper, story picking, or any task a Kindergartner took great pride in when chosen or when their turn came around. He would not only share things, he would model how to share things and he would help resolve conflicts between kids about sharing things. He also seemed to have a better understanding of bullying behaviors than most teachers and he seemed able to distinguish this behavior from simple social development factors. Because of this, most conflicts that evolved were often resolved without teacher intervention. Many of these situations involved Raymond and such situations were sometimes the ones that would rise to the level of teacher or even principal intervention. Raymond would often be able to hear the guidance and compassion from Tobias but not from the adults. Tobias was always at his side and it was well understood that without Tobias, Raymond would not be nearly as successful as he had been.

In sum, Ms. Dawson would say she had the best Kindergarten school year in all her 12 years of teaching. By the end of his Kindergarten year, Ms. Dawson would ask all the kids about their favorite thing learned from being in Kindergarten. She asked Tobias and he says,

"Ms. Dawson, teach us to number our days aright, that we may gain a heart of wisdom".

"But Tobias, I didn't teach that" she says.

"I thought you said this a lot through the school year" Tobias says puzzled.

"Not I my little friend, but maybe you read it in the Bible" Ms. Dawson smiles; probably assuming he's confused some messages from his Sunday school class.

Tobias starts to giggle, "You big silly, I can't read yet!"

"How bout this one Ms. Dawson, did you tell me this one?"

- A day is but a thousand years, a thousand years but one.

"OK Tobias, are you telling me you're reading the Bible?"

"No Ms. Dawson, I can't read yet" he's laughing now.

He just thinks Ms. Dawson is just teasing him.

"Well what do you think these things mean Tobias?"

"Just have to make the most of every day!" Tobias says with the biggest of smiles. "I'm learning pretty good aren't I Ms. Dawson?"

"Yes, you are Tobias, but these … Oh nice job!" she says still puzzled.

Every teacher after Kindergarten would come to realize their best teaching year was when Tobias was in their class too. Ms. Dawson would tell her peers about how much more she was able to focus on learning concepts and how this transferred into her happiest and highest performing students since she began teaching. The social and behavioral needs of the kids were largely addressed by Tobias. To him, this was normal. He knew of no other way to interact with his environment. To Ms. Dawson, she was now a believer in Tobias. She was sad about losing her graduating class. She learned things during this school year she would implement in her classroom for the rest of her teaching career. She would never forget Tobias and how he changed her life as a person and teacher. Her perception of her overall class would be validated by the first-grade teachers. They too, were in awe of what this group of children brought into the first grade. These children came to them with a solid understanding of a positive classroom community; where the words 'thank you', 'please', 'I'm sorry' were practiced consistently and the concept of delayed gratification (wait for your turn, wait for the special event/party) was well underway.

Tobias was a wanted student. Teachers would begin arguing their case for him to be in their classroom for the next school year. The elementary school principal eventually decided upon the pulling of straws as this seemed the fairest way. Regardless of what teacher would receive Tobias, they did acknowledge Raymond would go along with him. It was well known Tobias would look out for Raymond and he could provide the best chance of helping Raymond succeed socially. It was the sum of Tobias' impact upon the entire school environment that Maggie or Jonathan could not know. They could not know just how happy he made teachers and how much he taught them, or just how much he impacted the growth and development of his peers. Unless one had been around many, many children, they most likely could not truly see the gifts this young person was bringing to his world and to the worlds of others. This is a gift the good teacher can offer parents; to not compare children in negative contexts, but to compare to better understand what each child is bringing to the proverbial table of life and formal education.

Kannot's population was about thirty-five hundred people, while the township's population was close to six thousand. It was a rural area yet the main area of town seemed a thriving metropolis for the children who were growing up there. The houses had nice yards between them, not crowded, and all adults took responsibility for children playing in their yards. They could start at one house and work their play several yards down without realizing it. It truly was a shared community. Yes, there were some elders that were a bit more sensitive to the energy level of children, but even they would admit they liked the kids but not the noise that came along with them. They played outside on a nearly perpetual basis. The energy of youth is such a beautiful thing to watch especially so when the innocence of childhood presents with all its wonders and laughter.

Raymond lived with his Mom in a modest home. He never spoke of a father though there was a man who visited quite often. He had minimal contact with all the little creatures that played around the neighborhood. Mrs. Gilbrandt, Raymond's Mom, was a nice lady to all of us though she often seemed sad. She seemed weathered by a hard life and thus presented as an age much older than her actual. Nonetheless, her interaction with this group of bandits was always welcoming.

Per the imagination of children, Tobias and Raymond loved airplanes. Jonathan always had a stash of the flyers he would purchase from the local hardware store. O'Leary's Hardware Store always had that one section reserved for all things children. Oh, the intensity and duration with their play of these planes. Tobias' first serious childhood injury came around age 6 from such play. On a day when Raymond was not playing with him one would think the intensity would have decreased a bit, however, not for Tobias. He strained his developing muscles to propel that plane as far and high as possible and then becoming the pilot as the plane took flight. Up against Raymond's house was a high set of shrubberies that covered the side of the house and windows of the first floor and was attempting to do such with the second floor as well. On one of Tobias' best flights ever, he landed himself on top of the shrubs. Unfortunately for Tobias, a step ladder was left out from previous trimmings and leaned against the back corner of the house. Children and ladders; how many times do we hear these words paired? And there's a reason for such and Tobias is about to learn it. He struggles but he is able to position the ladder to give him his best chance at plane recovery. He had to get it as soon as possible; there could be injuries on board with medical attention needed; he is now a first responder. There's also a reason why one is not supposed to stand on the top of a ladder. Despite Tobias' very good 6-year-old physical development and physical abilities, "the top ladder rules" would still apply. Tobias was a very good learner and doubtful he would attempt such a rescue ever again without calling for emergency support. As he wobbles on the top of the ladder with that plane just a hair out of his reach his life takes a bunch of twists and turns; all occurring while gravity screams him to the ground. The wind knocked out of him and an arm in trouble, he stumbles, crying between gasps of air, to his house. Upon entry, Maggie's immediate reaction was to grab the car keys and whisk the little fella off to the local emergency room. She found some piece when she saw that right hand being held and she would notice it for some weeks ahead.

Tobias with his arm in a cast and a few scrapes would not be the same for a little while. He was ashen in color and very quiet both at school and in the home. Maggie and Jonathan were concerned about a head injury however the doctors ruled this out. "Just the trauma of the fall" they would surmise. To make matters worse it seemed Raymond stopped playing with Tobias, not only because he was playing without him, but he went on a rescue mission without him as well --- both big deals in the minds and hearts of childhood buds. To make the matter even worse Tobias did not get the plane; Mrs. Gilbrant did. Later in the day, when she was made aware of the incident, with much ease she opened a second-floor window, leaned out a bit and retrieved it. One would have to wonder if Raymond had been there would he have gone the route of his Mom. Being young guns, Raymond and Tobias probably would have argued who was going up the ladder. Raymond's relationship with other kids would change also over time as he seemed to choose a different path. He was an angry boy. Tobias was really the only one who knew him prior to Kindergarten. When the school years began, Raymond was not an easy boy to play with, but he was comfortable with Tobias and thus he may have been his only friend well into the first grade. Their friendship would dismantle, while many others would solidify.

Lest one forget the positives of wearing a cast at elementary school. Wow, the curiosity of the other kids about the event, the sympathies of teachers, and all the signatures. All the attention could make one feel like the Kannot Elementary School king. Tobias would not let things go too far but he smiled frequently about such attention. The only one who seemed not to care was Raymond. He must have felt very rejected the day Tobias played without him. Based upon Raymond's behaviors he had probably been rejected many times before, a counselor once concluded. Efforts of the counselor to communicate with Mrs. Gibrandt were also met with rejection. On this day, Raymond's feelings may have been further exacerbated by jealousy for the attention one receives when casted. He was mean to Tobias. It was difficult to know how, or if this bothered Tobias because he did not speak of it. He would just tell other kids to not pick on Raymond. "Raymond is allowed to have his feelings so leave him be" he would tell them. But Tobias would cease moving toward Raymond as Raymond would consistently lash out at him. Raymond would generally stay away from Tobias yet sought opportune moments to verbally assault him. Tobias was now getting what Raymond often presented to other kids yet it seemed even more intense. Tobias would take it and not respond. He would continue to tell others to stand down as well. To most, Tobias seemed to become just another kid to Raymond, but it still seemed different. This greatly surprised and saddened the teachers at Kannot Elementary School and the principal. This would be a pattern that played out for a long time to come.

Tobias always exhibited the capacity to keep moving forward. He was interested to learn something about everything but when he chose a specific interest he really went for it. He loved to be in the kitchen, loved to cook, and loved to watch the shows. Nearing 7 years of age, while shopping, he hands his Aunt a shopping list.

"What's this Tobias?"

"I want to make dinner and this is what I'll need."

When someone would talk to Maggie about cooking she would say, "I don't cook" so all assumed Jonathan to be the cook. This would take an unwitting turn when a discussion unfolded with Jonathan at the supermarket and a question about cooking evolved with him. The community had long been intrigued with Maggie's non-cooking stance and equally intrigued with the assumption of Jonathan's cooking. This was not commonplace in the traditional households of old. "I don't cook" he told one parent and a brilliant deduction process began across the gossiping venues of the Kannot community. "Why do they both tell us they don't cook?" many a person would say. "Which one made the incredible hors d'oeuvres for their party at Christmas?" "Why would they not want to take credit for this?" In reality, Tobias was becoming the primary chef of this family. Maggie and Jonathan did in fact cook, but it was not something they loved so much that either would take ownership for. So, when they began to notice Tobias' interest and skills in this area they were well motivated to oblige his efforts. Certainly, these parents were assisting with the more dangerous aspects of cooking such as knife work and deep frying. They would then become Tobias' assistants.

"Are we taking advantage of this?" Maggie would ask Jonathan.

"Yeah, I think so honey".

"Jonathan, I did not want to hear that".

"I know, but I think it's OK since he really loves the kitchen. He would be hurt to not allow him to continue this".

"So that's how you reason it?" Maggie says with a smile.

Jonathan giggles and kisses her on the cheek.

"We have a little unique fella on our hands and we just have to accept our household is not going to be typical. I think our flexibility with this will help us in matters to come with him".

"But what do you think people will think about this,

Jonathan"?

"First, Magpie, who is going to believe a little boy can cook like this, and second, we can't spend much time worrying about what others think as long as we keep it safe".

Alright, so I guess that means we just don't say anything for now," Maggie says.

"That's right; we just continue telling people you do the cooking Maggie".

"Oops. I've already told a few people at the market that I don't cook".

"Someone asked me last week if I cooked and I said no too" Jonathan says.

"We're caught already Jonathan!"

They laugh, both knowing the community is well underway with their exploration of this matter and they both agree to just roll with it.

"Hey, let's just tell them Tobias cooks for us, Maggie says".

"Oh, that's good Maggie; honesty with mischievous, playful intent".

Tobias' interest in cooking and "knowing things" continued to create ongoing intrigue within the Greenwood home. They remembered it started around age four or five. One of Tobias' favorite shows, besides cartoons, was a cooking show, Julia Child – The French Chef. This brought much humor into the home; the odd appearance of a little boy glued to the TV to watch a cooking show. The Greenwood's initially chalked this up to the mystery of Tobias until he began asking for certain things while on shopping trips with Maggie. He was just learning his letters so he could not write down the items; he just tried to remember them. As time passed and his writing skills increased. he was able to create the shopping list. Maggie, then sensing his sincere interest in this arena, would help when requested.

"Mom, how do you spell spaghetti?"

"S-P-A-G-H-E-T-T-I, Tobias".

"Why is there an "H" in there? That doesn't seem right".

"I know Tobias, but it is also an Italian word so spelling rules can be different than in the English language."

By the second-grade Tobias would bring up other words and say,

"So, what about GHOST? And, then, "Why is the 'G' also silent in Night?" Tobias says. "And what about "knife" and "know"? Where's the "K" sound? And where's the "T" in "listen". The other day my teacher spells C-H-O-I-R on the blackboard and asked for volunteers to make a sentence with it. So, I told her --- I do my 'CHORE' every day --- and then told her she must have misspelled it. Then she says the word and uses it in a sentence --- 'Jane likes to sing in the CHOIR' --- she says. Mom, I thought she was teasing us. I just could not see the word spoken in that way because the word 'church' reminds you twice about the "ch" sound and how many words are better than 'church'?"

"Tobias, it will help you to know there are many rules to follow with spelling and sounding out words but there will be more spellings that seem strange. If you take out those silent letters sometimes the words become very different".

"I guess so." Tobias says and he never presents this argument again.

However, one of his friends, Wilson Willson, could never let such an argument go. These "stupid words with stupid spellings" would forever haunt him.

Where does one start with Wilson. The first challenge in Wilson's life is quite obvious. One would have ask, why did his parents go with this name choice? Seems like they purposely did not give him a middle name so folks could not opt for it to avoid the same-name conflict. Wilson was always ready to do battle with the misspelling of his last name.

"Wilson Willson" he would say with agitation.

"That's the first with one L and the second with two! You're spelling my last name like my first name!" he would proclaim.

And the agitated tone was there whether it was a friend, teacher, or stranger. Unfortunately for Wilson this little spelling mistake was not observed as a major crime by the offenders, only Wilson, so the incongruity with the level of the offense was ever apparent.

This issue with his name seemed to transfer into Wilson's disdain for English language rules, or as he would use in his defense, lack of rules. Though Tobias had many questions and confusions about spellings he could let go and move forward, whereas Wilson became mired in the muddiness of the English language. The issues that would evolve in class with words like 'colonel' and the singular and plurality of a word like 'deer' troubled him so. Wilson simply refused to spell these words correctly and all plurals ended with 's'. A colonel in the army was a kernel in the army and two or more deer were 'deers'. He would always lose points for his grammatical incorrectness and spellings, yet he seemed at peace with the sacrifice. He was taking a chance; he was a word spelling activist and was ready for hard time. A minor loss of points was but a pittance to him. This was very important to him. He chose this stand and maintained it throughout elementary school. These issues would crop up throughout later schooling with Wilson, yet with a more tempered, mellowed, and sometimes humorous response. Could you imagine what Wilson thought when reading musical lyrics?

"Just silly how people could spell words just to make them rhyme; where's the justice!" he would profess loudly.

Wilson had an ever-present resistance to these kinds of problems yet he was most endeared by Mrs. Foster in her second-grade class. Despite his disdain for spelling, he found his way to help little Belinda Smith when spelling tests were on the horizon. Belinda had a very deep, raspy voice for such a little girl and her color changed as the year progressed. She was very different than other kids. Belinda also missed a lot of school. The days she was not at school, Wilson would be the first to recognize her absence and report this to Mrs. Foster prior to role. When she would return, Wilson would ask,

"Why weren't you in school Belinda?"

"I was sick" she would say in her deep, raspy tone and then smile for him as if to say, 'I am OK now'.

This was the extent of the inquiry and response always.

Tobias was a friend to Belinda also, but he seemed to allow Wilson to be her main little man. At a very early age teachers observed Tobias to see things going on around him in ways even they did not initially see. In this case, Wilson also needed to be needed and Belinda would be the one to fit his bill. In return, she had a friend; one of very few children that did not fear her strange tone of voice or her changing color. And she would help Wilson too. The other children simply did not understand her. In their young lives, they had never been exposed to such a child. Their reactions to her were not of any bad intention; they were just uncertain and uncertainty at this age usually translated to being scared. They intuitively knew there was something to be scared about yet they could not know it was something inside her; it was not HER. But she was a sweetheart and because it seemed to hurt her to talk, she mostly communicated with her eyes and her smiles; Wilson understood these communications best. It was Belinda who was able to calm Wilson down when he would get upset. He was easily frustrated with aspects of the learning process, especially with reading and spelling. The slightest of smiles from her or maybe even a certain look of displeasure and he would cease an escalating bad behavior immediately. But he could help her with her spelling and reading without any frustrations. Belinda missed a lot of school so Wilson's peer support meant a lot to her and probably much, much, more to her Mom. Mrs. Foster was known to tell the story of this friendship for many years to come. She applauded the beauty and compassion of children that could help other children in ways adults never could. Both she and Mrs. Foster knew what Wilson offered Belinda was so much more than help with missed work --- it was another child's expression of love and compassion and this little girl was experiencing this during her most difficult times when others kept their distance.

Later in the school year, Mrs. Smith came to the doorway of our class. As Mrs. Foster moved toward her she began to cry. It was a cry the entire classroom could hear and see.

Mrs. Smith helped move Mrs. Foster a bit further into the hallway and then closed the door behind them. Wilson would describe this scene many times during his adult years. Mrs. Foster returns tearful and says,

"Children, Belinda will not be coming back to our class. She is a little angel gone to Heaven now".

Wilson remembers no one asking any questions and then Mrs. Foster began teaching again. It was over. He would remember some of the questions he wanted to ask:

"Is heaven a place by her home and can I visit her there?" "Will she come back for the third grade?" "Why are they crying if she is a pretty angel?" "Maybe Mrs. Foster just meant she won't be back for the rest of this week".

Every day, for the rest of the school year, he thought she could either come back to class or fly back to class. No more talk of Belinda, just an empty seat for the rest of the year. On the last day of school Wilson asked Mrs. Foster,

"How come Belinda didn't come back to school?"

"Wilson, I told you she would not be coming back because she was an angel gone to Heaven".

By the time this last word left her lips she realized the great discrepancy between the adult and child understanding of death. She had never been challenged by such a loss in her fifteen years of teaching and now ponders how her entire classroom room of young children was able to largely fend for themselves about the loss of their classmate. There were no letters home to parents from the school administration or Mrs. Foster. Wilson never told his parents and never spoke of Belinda for many years. He would later say the manner in which this unfolded was so quick, so final, and with such a strong and quick explanation, he was numbed. He did not remember grieving for Belinda until years later, in high school. He wanted to visit Mrs. Smith at that time. He wanted to talk with someone who also remembered this sweet little girl. But, he would find Mrs. Smith had long moved away as her husband's career took him somewhere else in this vast world. He wanted to remember Belinda with someone, but oddly few other kids vaguely remembered her as he did. When he got around to asking Tobias, he remembered Belinda and this would provide some solace for Wilson.

Near impossible to know how such incidents will affect our lives, but little Belinda would have significant impact on the life Wilson would eventually lead. His regret later in life would be that he was not able to tell Belinda's family this, especially her Mom. He forgot the family's last name by high school. This is where Tobias would bring his wisdom back to the table. He would tell Wilson,

"I think it is necessary on many levels to remember this story Wilson, but mostly because it validates the lives of children gone. Knowledge of these little angels' impact upon others --- those outside of the family, during their short time on this earth could help ease the pains of their mothers, their fathers, their brothers and sisters and their grandmothers and grandfathers --- if they could only know".

In the meantime, young lives move forward on earth, school moves forward and conscious attention to such matters dissipates and all seems normal again. For Wilson, it would not be so for the rest of his second-grade school year as his little sweetheart was not there to smile or provide her disapproving look, both of which would have the appropriate or intended effect on Wilson. Mrs. Foster seemed to miss the compassion necessary for him at these times. A little boy left to struggle and grieve without so much as a hug.

Mrs. Foster would hopefully make these connections, but it would be later in her career. She would learn from Belinda. How to move a classroom through a similar challenge; how to help the dying child; how to help the grieving children afterwards. Oh, if she could only tell this to the family too. If we are to be passionate and compassionate learners, the gift this little girl left to this world will never end and we could say, 'Thank you Belinda and thank you Mrs. Foster and family'. As for now, Tobias would be there for the wounded Wilson. He would eventually help him settle down but even he knew he could not fill the void his little friend was experiencing. Emotions unable to be expressed in words at this age, but well understood in heart. A sequence that often seems in jeopardy of reversal in later years yet still with verbal difficulty for many. Wilson had to muddle through the complexities of this without much, if any, adult guidance. He didn't know the questions to ask and, at that age, often the adults don't understand the insights to offer. Tobias would still be there to watch over him as they grew up together. He knew this would impact Wilson down the road and was trusting it would be the right kind of impact.

<u>*1)Tobias Begins Making Music Friends*</u>

Tobias was intrigued by music; not playing it, but the words and the meanings to songs. He became friends with Taylor Hughes and Taylor played music, but even Taylor did not pay attention to the words. Tobias was always asking Jonathan and Maggie what this or that song meant. In school, he would ask teachers. Getting frustrated by inconsistent answers from adults as to the meaning of many songs and phrases within them, he rode his bike to the local music store two blocks away and found the name of the record label to of one of his parents' albums --- The Sounds of Silence by Simon and Garfunkel. He wrote down the name and went on a quest to contact the writer of the album's namesake and of I am a Rock, which was on the album as well. Not only did Jonathan and Maggie love these artists, but Tobias did as well. He was intrigued by the words and what they could mean. He also felt something from the melody that he could not describe. Such beautiful music but he could not always understand their meaning. His frustration with adults over previous searches for lyrical meanings led him to seek "thee" answer directly from the writer. A strategy that would become routine over the years.

The songs were quite popular in 1967. It's a Saturday and Jonathan was outside doing yard work and Maggie was inside doing laundry. This was gender typical of the time, but it was not unusual for this couple to swap or help each other in these tasks as well; when observed they appeared a bit radical for the time. Both being busy, Tobias positions himself by the phone with pencil and paper and calls the number.

"Hello, my name is Tobias and I would like to talk to Mr. Simon".

The secretary, being amused by the sound of this little voice asking to speak with a major recording artist of the time, says,

"What do you need Mr. Simon for?"

"Well, I have to ask him about a couple of his songs".

"Honey, he doesn't really take calls like this and he is only here a couple times a month   at most unless he is recording a new record".

"Yeah, but how will I be able to know what he wants his song to mean?"

"Where are you Tobias?"

"I'm in Kannot, Pennsylvania and its really nice here".

"How old are you Tobias?"

"I'm seven and a half and I am in the second grade".

Feeling the situation too cute to pass off, the secretary is moved to action.

"My name is Ms. Samson Tobias and I will see what I can do for you. I do promise I will deliver your message to my boss but there are no guarantees".

"I understand but I just have to try".

"Can I have your number Tobias to call you back?"

"Thank you so much Ms. Samson", this cheery little voice tells her.

Bored from typical groupie calls, Ms. Samson is uplifted by the spirit and passion of this little boy and passes on Tobias' quest to her boss.

About two weeks would pass before a call would come. Tobias had forgotten about his call for the moment. The phone rings during a typical dinner. Phone calls during dinner were not permissible by the Greenwoods, only if emergency needs were determined. Maggie answered the phone and the voice on the other end says,

"This is Paul Simon; is Tobias there?"

Steadfast to their rules, Maggie states,

"Not only do we not take calls at dinner we certainly won't spend time on a crank call" and hangs up".

"Mom, who was that?"

"Believe it or not Tobias, that was Paul Simon of Simon and Garfunkel fame", she says with a sly/sarcastic smile validating her crank call suspicions.

"Mom, I was waiting for that call!"

"What?"

"Yeah, he's going to tell me the meaning of the songs Sound of Silence and I am a Rock".

"Tobias, do you really think someone like that will call you?"

"Yes, Ms. Samson promised me, well she told me she would really try. She works at the record company and she said she would get the message to him".

Still smiling, Maggie says,

"Well if he calls back we'll talk to him a little more".

After about 30 minutes the phone rings again.

"Hello" says Maggie.

"Hello Maggie, are you finished with dinner? Are you Tobias' Mom?"

"Yes, I am and tell me again who you are and why you are calling".

"Somebody at the record company passed a message on to me from your son and I would love to talk with him".

Maggie, realizing this is something Tobias would do is now taking in the celebrity of the call. For Maggie, this means she has ceased communicating and just hands the phone over to Tobias. She and Jonathan just sit back and listen to Tobias's dialogue.

"Can you tell me what the Sounds of Silence and I am a Rock songs mean?"

Silence from Tobias' end as he listens intensely with an occasional,

"Ohhhh", "ah hah", "cool"!

And then,

"So, the Rock and the Island are what you call a 'meta' what? I need to understand that word because I heard it before and it seems to be big in music", Tobias says.

Silence for a while on Tobias's end. Now Maggie and Jonathan are just staring and waiting for Tobias's every response.

"So, you are not actually a Rock or an Island, but the Rock and the Island are lonely?"

Some time goes by again and Tobias begins shaking his head affirmatively and smiling from ear to ear,

"OK, so being a Rock or an Island is not really a good thing. Ok, I'll work on that 'meta' thing from there, what about Sound of Silence?"

And the process starts all over again.

"People just not talking to or hearing each other?"

Further dialogue continues with an ecstatic Tobias giving profuse thanks and then writing a number down.

"Thank you so much Mr. Simon. I promise, Goodbye".

Maggie and Jonathan are still stunned. They are in a place where they are still trying to believe in the possibility of a crank call, but they know better with Tobias. They know how he can connect with anyone. They know their little boy just had a discussion on the phone at the dinner table about the meaning of songs with an internationally known artist.

"What did you write down Tobias?" Maggie asks.

"Mr. Simon gave me his number in case I have more questions in the future. He even said he would help me contact other songwriters should I have questions about their songs. He was nice but he did make me promise to keep his number private and secret so I am very sorry but you cannot see it".

Tobias' discussion with Paul Simon lasted about 20 minutes and it was apparent this man truly enjoyed talking to Tobias. Tobias made it very difficult for people not to be intrigued by him, even people designated by their abilities as "stars and celebrities". As the years would progress, Tobias would speak to many other artists. He was known as this fun little kid from Kannot, Pennsylvania and they simply loved to talk with him. They would give them their numbers and he in turn would promise their security. He would never break this promise or promises to employers, parents, teachers or friends. If Tobias broke a promise one could be quite sure there was some sort of ethical or moral reasoning behind it. This may be best explained through Tobias work ethic as he always promised his best effort no matter the task. Maggie and Jonathan knew full well the value of a promise as it is a value they put much attention to in the raising of Tobias. They would oblige and Tobias' list of songwriter contacts would grow.

2) Good Work Is Good for the Soul

The second and third grades would pass with Tobias and his friends continuing to find their places in their worlds; experiencing and learning about life through play and incredible wonder in their classrooms and school grounds, their homes, and in the community.

In the summer of 1968, Tobias already had a fierce reputation as a hard worker, both in the home and at school. He was now about to bring it to the workplace. Remember, back in the day you could find many young ones working under the table for pennies. Tobias was certainly one of the youngest but his value as an employee, even though "under the table", he was gaining a historical reputation in this little community. In the home, Jonathan and Maggie became concerned at one point with Tobias perfectionistic behaviors. When he would clean his room, or do one of his chores the result would be immaculate. They consulted with a therapist about this. The therapist said,

"If he is not standing over his work and continuing to go back over and over it, nor exhibiting much frustration or even anger when dirt, dust or disorder begins to present, then I would not worry about it".

"No, he doesn't do that, he just moves on and goes through the routine at the beginning of each week" says Maggie.

And that was that; no disorder, just an incredible work ethic. Nonetheless, he would be teased throughout much of his life by those who could not, or would not, do the kind of job he did. Their scapegoat word was "anal". They used this word to validate their own work ethic limitations regardless of etiology. Meanwhile, his employers never minded or sought reasons why Tobias worked the way he did.

An example of Tobias' work ethic and his reasoning for breaking a promise, would evolve through his work at Larson's car wash. Tobias was the youngest of three kids working there. They were the dryers and the inside car cleaners after the cars came through the wash cycle. Anyone who has ever cleaned the interior of the car would readily acknowledge the disdain of doing interior windows, especially the rear window. Many assigned to this task had fallen prior to Tobias arrival. It was the hated assignment. As things often would go with Tobias, he volunteers for the job of interior windows and would gladly do so by team default. On his first day he says,

"I'll take the job no one else wants".

His co-workers laugh. They know what job he is about to be assigned and they know he'll be gone in a couple days.

"OK, little man. We all love to do interior windows and since we like you we'll give you this job for now. Keep in mind that we could take it back any time we want".

"Thanks guys!"

Being a young one, The Greenwoods would only allow Tobias to work two hours during weekdays after school or evenings and four hours on Saturday. This was enough for Tobias. These fourteen hours would garner him about fourteen dollars a week which was enough for him to have a little spending money and to save a little as well, but this did not include tips and there would be many. This is how he would amass his small fortune; at least for an elementary aged boy. He would also find other ways to make a few dollars; cutting grass in the summer, raking leaves in the fall, shoveling snow in the winter, and helping with spring yard, garage, or attic cleanups.

Tobias' reputation as an employee is unparalleled in the Kannot community. He would state he just wanted to be "pride full" about whatever work he did. Strange he would not say "prideful". It was like he wanted to emphasize the "full". He did this with many words. Some believed his meticulous nature to be a fault; however, his ethic remained in high demand. Wherever he worked, the job was done expertly. He cleaned well, spoke well, and organized well. So well in fact, when a manager, boss, supervisor would state such is not always necessary he would put in his resignation and simply tell them "We are not a good match, but thanks for the opportunity to work".

On his first day of work at Larson's Car Wash Tobias goes to town. All his fellow workers could see were butt and elbows in those cars with the little guy coming out sweating profusely. The summers in Northeast, Pennsylvania could bring much humidity and to make matters more challenging, working inside something, like a car, raised the heat index. Tobias took the job thinking if the boss would keep him he may be able to parlay this job into more hours as he became older. Tobias seemed always able to see the bigger picture, the longer-term picture. Something most peers were not simply able to do, or for that matter, even many adults. Though sometimes the cars would back up, it became a customer jest to try and find an area on the inside of the windows either missed or streaked. Tobias found humor with this as well as he became an expert and took even more pride with the review efforts of his customers. Often, they would yell in apparent delight,

"There, there! There's a spot missed!"

Yet upon review it was always found to be on the outside. With apparent pleasure in Tobias' efforts the customers would then gladly relinquish the larger tip, and to the dismay of his cohorts, their lack of attention to detail was called out. Though this did not feel good to them they were smart enough to realize all tips were shared equally so they opted not to mess with Tobias on this matter. It would not be long before Tobias would convince them of the potential for a total team effort.

"Hey guys, you know I get big tips sometimes, right?"

"Yeah, we see that Tobias, don't have to rub it in. People just find you cute because of your age".

"That may have a little to do with it, but don't forget they are admiring my work and taking joy in trying to find a mistake. And, in the event they do find one, it still doesn't affect the good tip. Did you notice that? It is the quality effort the customers like".

"What's your point little man?"

"Well, I've done a little math and found we could probably raise our tip rate significantly if we all provide a better effort".

"Are you saying we don't work as hard as you!?"

In Tobias' truthful manner, he states,

"Yes, that is why my tips are bigger and you guys get a take of this because I work harder. If we all work harder we all get even more".

Tobias knew if he kept the focus on more money with the boys he was more likely to garner a better team effort.

"Billy, you want a new bike and Sam you're saving for your first car. Let's get them both as soon as possible. C'mon, we can do this!"

Billy and Sam move away from Tobias to have a personal discussion about the current situation.

"Sam, he's making some sense here but I can't help feeling this is weird".

"What's weird? Sam says.

"This is an eight-year-old kid and he's talking to us like he's older than us --- he's not even in third grade yet! And it's not just that, he feels older than us, he makes sense and he does work harder and better than us".

"I know" Sam says. "I just could not bring myself to say what you just said. I say we do what he is suggesting but we don't ever tell anyone why we are doing what we are doing."

"Alright Sam, let's do it".

"OK, little butt face we'll try it" both boys say.

They had to save a little face.

"But, we're not busting our tails if this doesn't get us more money".

It now begins, Tobias' ability to lead, even kids much older than himself.

The strategy did prove successful for this team of motivated youth. So much so unfortunately, that Mr. Larson wanted more. He began pressuring the boys to work faster. Tobias held steadfast to his principals.

"Mr. Larson, I cannot do a good job if I go any faster".

The other boys' quality of work began to deteriorate as they succumbed to Mr. Larson's wishes. After much ongoing pressure to "pick up the pace", Tobias approached Mr. Larson.

"Mr. Larson, I cannot do what you are asking so I am giving you my notice. This will be my last week".

"Tobias, I'm just trying to make more money here. The more money I make the more you make".

"No, you are trying to make even more money and you're assuming faster work will make me more money. In the short run, you will make more money, but our tips will decrease so we make less. In the long run, you will lose customers because they will become less and less satisfied and then we all lose. The better the job we do, the more we make and you still make out really well and people are very happy with your car wash".

"Who are you but an eight-year-old, to tell me how to run my business?"

"Oh, I'm sorry Mr. Larson, I did not mean to say this like I am running your business. This is just my observation and it is mixed with my beliefs about work. Anyway, I wish you well".

With sarcasm in his Mr. Larson's tone,

"Tobias, you don't have to work another week, today can be your last day".

"Are you sure Mr. Larson, I don't want to put my co-workers or you in a bad place by being down a worker".

Mr. Larson simmers his attitude a bit, but still releases Tobias from his employ.

The word gets out, probably through his co-workers, as they came to appreciate this little man and his leadership qualities. They could not openly acknowledge such because their adolescent pride was at stake, yet they would never forget the impact of the lessons they learned in such a brief period of time working alongside Tobias. Later in life they would admit this; much later. Larson's car wash eventually slid into closure. Mr. Larson's own pride would not allow him to learn the lesson Tobias had tried to teach him. He would state for many years that the community piled up against him and stopped using his service because of their appreciation for Tobias, not because of poor service. Mr. Larson was a great example of the human ego in chains. He would choose to lose his business rather than look at facts, service, and customer feedback. Word had it even the older boys tried to get him to rehire Tobias. They could not know that Tobias was not re-hirable. Tobias saw the character of Mr. Larson and knew he would not be able to overcome this man's greed for more money. Mr. Larson would not be able to make the connection with better service and better long-term financial gains. Even if this was possible in the long run, Tobias knew he did not have the gift of time to help Mr. Larson work this through. He would do his best to help someone understand his manner of thinking and approach, but he would not belabor a point or enslave himself to someone else's resistance to learn and grow. Tobias had life to live and would not be mired down by such, yet still, he would never disrespect them and their views. It was never an argument from Tobias' side.

Tobias' understanding of time had him always moving forward. He understood free will and had many things he wished to accomplish with his time on this earth. After the incident with Mr. Larson, Tobias' employability shot through the roof. He was on the look-out for the best opportunity and interviewed with many store/shop owners. Never before, was a child of this age so highly sought after for his employ in Kannot. Heck, never before was an adult in Kannot sought after like this. The smart business man or woman knew Tobias was a great investment and if taken care of and respected he would be a hard-working and loyal employee for many years to come. Tobias' search for a good match was on.

Kimberly's Diner was a local hotspot. The Diner had been a part of the Kannot for many years. The Tims family just continued to train and employ its family members through three generations. At present, it is the granddaughter, Kimberly, who is running the show. She knows Tobias well and when she heard of his eligibility she put the word out for him to stop by. It appears the family's generation pattern has begun to leave them deficit of new blood. All their recipes are secrets and they kept them so because of the pride of the family's trade. Kimberly knows if there is anyone she can trust to work for her it would be Tobias. Granted he won't have access to this kind of information but anyone in the family restaurant industry knows the recipes are always at risk, always in need of protecting.

"Hi Ms. Kimberly" Tobias says.

"Hello Tobias. You heard I was looking for you?"

"Yes Ma'am. A teacher at school told me".

"Oh yes, many of them come in early for a coffee before school so I asked them to have you stop by."

"What do you need Ms. Kimberly?"

"I need a worker Tobias. I need a good worker".

Tobias' wheels start to turn. He had not thought about this possibility before because of the family loyalty of this Diner. No one ever talked about working there. Kimberly and her Mom do the cooking with some help from George Tims, the father. There are several cousins that bus and waitress. That's it. The Tims family is beginning to run low on potential employees. Tobias begins thinking about his interest in cooking and becomes open to the possibility.

"What would you need me to do?" he asks.

"I need someone to come by in the morning just for an hour to help me open up; you know, help set the tables and make sure everything is clean. Then, come by around 6:00 to help clean up and close up by 7:00. On the weekends, I could use you even more".

Tobias knew he needed to talk with his parents about

these hours but he also knew Sundays were out. Kimberly's Diner was one of the few businesses open in Kannot on Sundays, even though it was a shorter day for them. But he had a question about the job.

"Will you be teaching me more about cooking?"

"No Tobias, you're only about 8 so I just need you to do some things that I know you can do".

"But Ms. Kimberly, I can cook".

With a gentle and supportive-like smile Kimberly says,

"I'm sure you can Tobias, but I don't need you for that right now".

And with those final two words Tobias found hope.

"When do you think you might need help with cooking" he posits.

"I don't know Tobias. I have not really thought about that".

"But at some time you will need help with cooking?"

"Yes, but I don't know" and she is interrupted abruptly

"OK, I'll talk with my parents about the hours. But you must promise to teach me stuff about cooking too. Saturdays for a few hours but no Sundays --- Can't work on Sundays. When the summers come, I can work more too".

Kimberly enjoyed the passion of this little man. She thought she could keep him interested enough with little lessons scattered about over time. She would agree to these terms. She could not know that he was already aware of many of the foundations and basics of cooking and, in fact, could already put together some hors d'oeuvres, sandwiches and meals.

Tobias approached Jonathan and Maggie about the offer. Tobias already gets up early so the morning hour was not a problem.

"But Tobias, you do things with some friends after school and you have your homework too".

Tobias knew he could make this work. He would just shuffle a few things around. If it became a problem he knew Jonathan and Maggie would notice it immediately. He wanted this badly. He was so motivated by the opportunity to learn more about cooking, baking and serving. What a passionate interest at so young an age. With parental approval, a new path could reveal itself to Tobias.

"I can do it, I can do it. If I can't I will stop" he tells them.

Unlike most family dynamics, Maggie and Jonathan truly knew Tobias would monitor this himself and they also knew he would be loyal to the agreement made.

"Alright Tobias, you can do this, but NOT on Sundays".

"I know Mom. I already told Ms. Kimberly 'no' to Sundays".

Through all the economic challenges of the times, the person never to be out of work for long before being recruited for another job was a young boy. Don't tell Tobias his 'under the table' wages and job was less important than any other job in town. His jobs were as important as many others, but mostly it was important that he made himself, his parents, his friends, and his employers proud --- and probably in that order.

3) Friendships Solidifying - Fellowship in the Making

Tobias' group of special friends and their own personalities were becoming well-defined by the end of third grade, though many would consider him a friend and he them. This group would hold together long after their school days would come to an end. Jimmy J. O'Reilly was the lady's man, or maybe better stated, Jimmy J. perceived himself the ladies' man. We had lots of fun with this over the years. When most boys weren't even thinking "that way" about girls, Jimmy J. was. The laughter, tears and pure entertainment value of Jimmy J's escapades into the life of girls began in the second grade. And I should mention women as well, as they were not off limits to Jimmy J's advances. His innocence and naiveté is what got him out of most jams and he got into many. He truly loved the female and he never did so with disrespect in heart.

Taylor Hughes was rather quiet, but rarely did much slip by him. Remembering things always came easy to him; recalling poems, formulas, and dates without mistake. Music came easy to him as well as he could remember keys, concepts and read/remember music. Piano, guitar, trumpet; didn't matter, he could play them all. He could not understand for a long time why everyone else couldn't. Some teachers said he had a photographic memory. This really made most test-taking very easy. They would tell him how smart he was. Taylor was often uncomfortable with the accolades placed upon him by teachers, especially when they did so in front of others. He did not seem to mind compliments from his peers and they saw everything the teachers saw. He seemed to believe feedback from his peers more truthful for some reason. Tobias did not have a photographic memory or the musical abilities like Taylor but most of the kids viewed him as the smartest person at school. Teachers did not seem to support this view. Funny how teachers and kids see things differently. They were certain Taylor was some kind of genius and they defined Tobias as a "very good boy".

Taylor was also a great example of color not mattering to young children. It's only with age and the muddying of water by adults that it becomes so. Seems there is some link with age and all sorts of ism's. Though our elders can offer so many positives, there is always the latter as they can readily pollute the minds of youngsters as well. This was also something Tobias often spoke of --- opposites. This issue would present with Taylor and a young Chinese boy named Chen. Even in Kannot, this wonderful town with its strength of community, the ugliness of racism would manifest at times through ignorance. It did not appear often since the minority was basically five families, which included Taylor's and Chen's. When pondering the concept of minority, it seems as the minority grows so too does the incidence of ism's as the majority feels more and more threatened. Tobias, and many others found this so disheartening --- that the basis for harms thrown at Taylor and Chen were due primarily to visual variations upon the human condition --- a beautiful and natural variation young children are intrigued by and never fearful of. Here we are today and since the beginning of time still not learning from our children. In Kannot, as most other places, kids like Taylor and Chen would have the stereotype challenge. Chen had to be a martial artist and Taylor an athlete; if they weren't there must be something wrong with them. For all the good the media can do, it also has strong roots in the stereotyping of America and all of its peoples --- the world's peoples for that matter. Tobias would remind people through word or action that children often present the gift of ceasing such negative cycles. He would sometimes be successful, but the stubbornness and ego of the adult mind was a formidable opponent. Whenever someone would go to the racism place in front of Tobias he would be quick to deflate their attempt at viewing themselves and/ or their race as higher than others. He loved being around the varied cultures, yet he found it odd, even in Kannot the only varied cultures they could see were people like Taylor Hughes' family; they were Black, and Chen's family with the slanted eyes. He noticed how most people focus on visuals so he was determined at this young age to learn more about this.

When asked about heroes, Tobias would first mention his parents, and without hesitation proudly proclaim Dr. Martin Luther King as well. He was inadvertently trained by Jonathan and Maggie to not mention Jesus. He loved the stories of Dr. King, the speeches, and the purpose for his being. Townsfolk were intrigued by his knowledge of Dr. King's efforts and further intrigued by Tobias' very open appreciation of him. The adults would ask,

"Why do you need to talk about him so much Tobias?"

"You guys have to get to know him and you will feel the same way!" he would tell them.

As a young lad, Tobias was confused about Taylor's seeming lack of interest in this great leader. Some lessons about racism were yet to be learned but he was willing to learn them. He would never force Taylor into any discussion of this matter yet he felt something different when he was around Taylor's family, but a discussion of Dr. King would evolve. Though Taylor appeared indifferent to clarify this issue, his parents weren't. Tobias would seek some guidance and understanding from them. This was pure Tobias, though he knew much, he knew when he needed to learn more. The lessons he would soon learn will hurt deeply. Tobias' childhood naiveté will be affected by the truths of the adult world, yet despite the hurt, he will become stronger.

Tobias' attention to the matter of race was well formed during his elementary school years. He would conclude people simply opted to go to this ugly place in attempt to raise themselves from their own insecurities in this world --- to put someone else down to feel better about themselves. He went on to notice people did this with each other when visual distinctions were not apparent such as: He's a stupid Pollock; Family full of Whaps; Stupid Republicans; Stupid Democrats. He concluded people will always focus on differences to attack another when the goal is really an unhealthy attempt to raise one's own sense of power. So, if a typical difference was not available to attack someone, a new one would be defined; they're fat, they're skinny, they're cheap. Anyone could be ascribed a negative characteristic. It was not about race or color; it never was. It has always been about one trying to make him or herself more powerful due to their own internal weaknesses. It was, and continues to be, never about the other person. To make matters even worse, when such people latch on to a negative descriptor they will continue to release the angers of their fathers and mothers and likely their fathers and mothers, and they will hand it down to their children and thus, maintain the cycle that perpetuates this ugly, ugly matter. Tobias was invested in stopping this through the power and beauty of children.

Sadie Spagnotti was one of the girls. Jimmy J was the only one who wanted her around all the time. The rest of us liked her, but most of the group generally wanted to be engaged in boy stuff. Sadie was quite feminine yet she really seemed willing to put her femininity aside for the friendship with this odd lot. She was also quiet by most people's standards, yet she had secrets she simply would not share and certainly not outside of her home. We were protective of Sadie, especially after her brother left for Vietnam. Kannot was engaged in the war effort. We had several families who were connected to a plastics molding company in Scranton through their father's employ. These families set up shop in their basements and made inserts for the troops' helmets to decrease shatter effect. Grandparents, young children, friends and neighbors often took part for minimal financial gain. Kannot was well aware of the war, yet most could not fully understand its brutal impact unless they had a loved one involved or lost. Sadie changed and changed even more when Henry returned. Their family was never the same. I think we were her stabilizing force, while her Mom and Dad dealt with the "adult" things. There was much age between Sadie and Henry, probably about twelve years. She always adored him and looked up to him and he returned her favors by being a wonderful older brother. But the damages of war, and maybe in particular this war, would change him. We heard of his aggressive outbursts from others, never from Sadie, but we did see her bruises every now and then. Girls not on the Tomboy list did not usually have bruises. We suspected her parents wore them as well. They were all now part of Henry's battlefield. We heard Henry's unit was attacked at nighttime because some of the young soldiers smoked which made their camp illuminate amongst the blackness of the Vietcong jungle. This was quite a problem at the front end of the war as training and leadership on the battlefield was oft portrayed as negligent. In his unit, Henry was one of eight survivors out of forty-seven --- Henry was a smoker. We could only thank God back then we would learn from this war and would never again send our young people to war ill-equipped from every possible perspective. We took Sadie in on a much more willing and patient basis. Sadie had her passions though very few knew of them as she kept them confined to her home for much of her schooling life.

The last of this childhood troupe was a force of nature to be reckoned with. Collette Adams. See, she even receives such a descriptive stature at the introduction of her name. Collette was a girl Tobias befriended in the second grade. Though Collette was 11, the classroom did not pay so much attention to age. They tried to go by grade levels with these children and they believed Collette understood most things on a second-grade level. He met her in this "special" class he began to his role as a peer helper during his free period. Collette had cerebral palsy (CP). Though most could not understand her, or did not have the patience to try and understand her, Tobias was able to accomplish both. It took many years before teachers, other adults and even most kids were also able to hear and see the beauty of this young lady and sadly this also included her parents. Collette required much patience, and I mean much patience. The time involved to understand, respond to, and continue a conversation with Collette was not on the communication schedule of much of this world and especially for other kids. The typical pace is rather quick when one thinks of it, but I guess the "pace" issue is relative. Tobias both grasped and welcomed her pace and he would sustain his patience and time with her afterschool, on weekends, Holidays, and summers. He just had a way of sharing his time with so many and yet he still appeared available for so much more.

Collette's CP affected her speech and left her with many physical limitations as she was wheelchair bound as well. Tobias' friendship with Collette began in the second grade and strengthened through the years. I cannot present in written form the way Collette sounded to the world. In this story, her words will come through as all others, just remember, the time it takes Collette to get out a question, response or statement, can be multiplied 20-fold from the typical conversation of those non-affected by such a birth defect. This offers the readers a gift; you will experience Collette as Tobias did.

4) A Lesson of Love and Friendship from a Child

The Holiday Season was upon us and what a great age for the excitement of Christmas. Many things became clear about Tobias this Christmas. It really was the first time we celebrated something together. Our parents took us to each other's homes and we visited and shared our Christmas joys, and of course our gifts, with each other. Tobias was reportedly a tough buy for his parents. We heard this directly from Jonathan and Maggie as they spoke with other parents rather openly about this matter.

"Maggie, tell Mr. and Mrs. Hughes what Tobias wanted for Christmas" Jonathan prompted.

"When we ask him what he wants, he tells us 'nothing'. He just tells us to just surprise him. We never hear him say anything about 'wanting' something".

"Yeah, it's weird, isn't it"? Jonathan says to any other parents listening.

He's asking them for their thoughts on this matter.

"I bet when he sees other kids getting stuff he changes his tune" says Mrs. O'Reilly.

"Yeah, that's when the tears come" says Mrs. Hughes.

"Oh right, and this is about the time he realizes he should have given Santa his list" laughs Mrs. Spagnotti.

"That's what we thought would happen when he was four, and then when he was five, and then six, but it never does", says Maggie. "We get him things and you would swear we chose the best gifts in the world for him. He attends to them for a while but most of his happiness and time at Christmas is spent making things and/or doing things for others", says Jonathan. He continues, "Yeah, he makes cards and gives them to people. You'll be getting some I'm sure, just wait for it.

Before their Christmas visit is over Tobias hands out his cards to his friend's parents. The cards would read for example:

'Call me, when you need someone to be with Taylor when you have something really important you need to do"

'Mrs. Spagnotti, I'll help you move some stuff that maybe Sadie can't move; just call me'.

'If Jimmy J forgets to do his chores one day, just give me a call and I'll do them'.

--- and so on.

They're all getting a kick out of this and then Jonathan clarifies further.

"Sure, laugh it off. He'll remember and remind you about this IOU gift card forever or until you use it. With his newly developing skill of writing, he records these in his gift card book".

"That's a strange little fella you got there" was the spoken consensus.

Way back then Tobias's Christmas behaviors and messages were confusing to us. We were young and these actions were beyond our comprehension at that time, but it seemed as if adults had a hard time with this as well. We share these stories to this day and there are many. Though Tobias brought much joy year-round, he touched even more lives with his spirit of Christmas.

In the fall of 1967, while in the third grade, a couple events occurred that not only further defined Tobias, but they also began to define Collette. She was still unknown to most other peers and teachers. Her CP made her personality and her potentialities largely invisible to most others. She was merely known as a child with Cerebral Palsy who was in "that class".

Mr. and Mrs. Adams had a Saturday set aside in town once a month. On this day, Mrs. Adams would get her hair done and Mr. Adams would visit his buddies at the garage at the end of the block. Their routine would often involve from two to three hours. On the other side of the street was Kimberly's Diner. The diner had tables and chairs outside on the wide side walk area. Downtown Kannot was well planned. It was comfortable and welcoming of locals and visitors. Kimberly's was a wonderful part of this town's heart. It was the shop where fundraisers were discussed for hurt or hurting neighbors, where the worried and grieving families of children sent and lost to Vietnam sat for support and console, where couples would frequent and remember the Diner with warmth long after marriage, or of relationships since ended. This was an aspect Tobias was not aware of when he first started there, but would increasingly intrigue him as time moved forward. As true of human nature --- the need and the utilization of such a place, so too were many people's need for a "gossip central" sort of place. This would not go unnoticed by Tobias either.

The Adams' recognized the sense of security associated with Kimberly's Diner from a parenting perspective and they also recognized the canopy of cover out front should it rain. On nice/warm days, they found it to be an ideal spot to place Colette while they went about some business, usually Mrs. Adams for her perm and Mr. Adams' visit to the garage. They could both see her from their respective spots across the street. The Adams' were loving people, though having a child with CP and how best to help her, was something not well understood at that time. They protected Collette, took care of her basic needs, but they did not really know their daughter.

Tobias and Collette, having become friends, discussed this monthly event. It was a horrible experience for Collette as she felt placed there only to be watched. Furthermore, until Tobias entered her world, she really did not know what she had to offer others. Even though she had a wonderful teacher who knew her, cared for her, and attempted to get 'the most' from her, 'the most' was in question as the expectations were quite low. These adults, who loved and cared for her, were simply ignorant to the person inside. On a beautiful autumn Sunday, Tobias knew Collette would have her place under the canopy in front of Kimberly's Diner. He would first go into Diner's for a pack of his favorite gum --- teaberry. Teaberry is not easy to come by these days as its five-minute blast of flavor is out-performed by gums you could chew on for hours now. For the true teaberry lovers, the blast is worth the brevity.

Tobias would show up and sit in front of Collette with

his back to the street, thus his back to Mr. and Mrs. Adams as they would periodically glance across the street at their daughter. Tobias would turn Collette on to teaberry. At first, Mr. Adams went over and asked who he was and what he was doing.

"Son, what are you doing here?"

"Hi Mr. Adams, I am friend of Collette's from school. My name is Tobias".

"You are Jonathan's and Maggie's boy?" "Yep".

"I have heard your name before". So, what are you doing here?"

"Just hanging out with Collette if that's OK; is it?"

At 11 years of age, this was the first time this father had experienced such an interaction --- someone saying they wanted to hang out with his daughter. He seemed ill at ease to ask why knowing inherently such a question would sound terrible.

"What are you chewing Collette?" he states loudly. "Guuuuuuuugmumm", Collette responds in her labored manner.

"Son, Collette cannot have gum" he proclaims loudly to Tobias and he takes it from her mouth.

"Why" Tobias asks.

"Because she can choke that's why. Just don't give her any more sticks of gum".

"Ok, Mr. Adams", Tobias reassures.

He would later figure out very tiny pieces could not choke her, but still give her the teaberry blast and besides he would reason, Mr. Adams said no more 'sticks" of gum. Mr. Adams begins his walk back to the garage, but he was not walking with purpose; he was preoccupied. If a car was coming he would not have known it; he would not have been hit because of a low speed limit but the driver would have been perplexed by a man who did not even recognize he may have been hit if the driver was also preoccupied in thought. Maybe he was joyful inside, maybe he was questioning Tobias' motives, maybe he was wondering what Collette was thinking. Did she know him? Was she comfortable? Who knows, but he was deep in thought. Nonetheless, Tobias was there to stay.

Mrs. Adams watches as well.

"What is that boy doing over there?" she says out loud not seeking an answer from another but from herself. She cannot find one; she gets one from a friend.

"That's Tobias Greenwood. He's a really nice boy so I'm sure they are OK".

"What do you think he's doing?" Mrs. Adams says.

"Looks like he's just sitting there with her; I can only see his back but it looks like Collette is doing something".

When Collette was stimulated in any manner her physical behaviors became more animated thus there was more body jerking, arm and head movements and vocal volume/gesturing. This began to upset Mrs. Adams as she believed Collette was agitated. She walked across the street with shampoo in hair to confront Tobias.

"What are you doing young man?"

"Hi Mrs. Adams!"

"How do you know me? I'm a friend of Collette's. She's told me about these Sunday visits. I just met Mr. Adams too".

"OK, but I think you are upsetting my daughter".

Tobias, in surprised manner,

"Really, why do you think that?"

"Because of the way she is acting".

"Oh yeah, when I first met her at school I used to think that but we talked about it and this just happens when she is excited to say something".

Quicker than anyone could expect, Mrs. Adams went on the attack.

"Who are you to tell me about my daughter's behaviors and what they mean! Who do you think you are!"

These were not questions to which Mrs. Adams wanted an answer, but she would get one. He never seemed scared of anything and in the throes of an angry mother he maintained his fearlessness.

"I am Collette's friend Mrs. Adams".

Unlike Mr. Adams, who had the insight to not further his confusion or speculation out loud, Mrs. Adam states,

"My daughter cannot have friends." Her tone now seemed to lower a bit as if trying to teach and this tone prompted Tobias to continue the dialogue.

"Why?"

"Because she can't communicate like other kids. We just try to keep her safe and comfortable."

Mrs. Adams is now past the initial attack and is sincerely trying to help this young boy understand her daughter. Tobias states,

"Yes, I know she cannot communicate like other kids but she still communicates. We just have to learn how best to do this".

Mrs. Adams, not wanting to have any further discussion with this boy, turns her attention to Collette and asks if this boy is bothering her and if she wants him to go away. Confident in her ability to understand her daughter's "yes and no" responses, she receives a "no" to each response but remained mistrustful of the response. Mrs. Adams' walk back to the beauty shop is abrupt and one of apparent irritation and anger. Though different from the walk of her husband just thirty minutes prior, the possible danger from the street similar. Both parents have just experienced a new birth in their relationship with their daughter, not of nine months but at age 11, and they were not prepared.

"What happened over there Joan?" the hairdresser asks.

"Just a goofy kid trying to pull something; I'll be keeping an eye on him".

Thus begins Tobias' monthly Sundays with Collette. Their relationship has now moved outside the walls of the classroom and school. Tobias's support of her would continue and expand as the years ensued.

Writing was even more challenging than verbal communication for Collette, it simply was not possible at that time. One word written may be deciphered, but beyond that …. Tobias' time with her often involved scribing for her. He would do this during the school day whenever possible and during his time with Collette after school, in the evenings and weekends. Later, Tobias would have difficulty assuring people her written words were "her" written words. Collette also had a crush on Tobias and he well understood why. He truly was the one person who got her. However, Tobias did not feel the same way toward her. Sometimes they argued like a brother and sister. Collette was the only person Tobias was ever heard to argue with. He remained consistent in his messages with Collette when issues of jealousy and such would arise.

"Collette, I am not attracted to you in that way, I am attracted to you as a wonderful friend" he would say.

Tobias' consistency with this message, though sometimes met with anger or sadness, was presented in a gentle matter-of-fact mode. This honesty was no doubt the glue that held their lifelong friendship together. A gentle smile would be cast upon anyone witnessing an argument. He was cautious not to have Collette view him as patronizing. It was as if he was teaching others about the normalcy needed for all relationships, while reassuring them he was not trying to hurt her.

Collette was not an easy person to be around. She was ornery. She often conflicted with the rest of the group, but Tobias held it all together. There would be conflicts about school projects, proms, peers, teachers, and Mr. and Mrs. Adams as well. Tobias would be alongside her through much of them. She was a member of the group, though one could speculate with good confidence her acceptance was in large due to Tobias' guidance and support. Without him, her fiery passion for life, to be heard, and her gifts would likely have gone on tragically undiscovered.

Tobias' own issues and pain took center stage in the spring his third-grade school year. April 4th, 1968 would be the day that would prompt Tobias to seek answers. His hero, Dr. Martin Luther King, was murdered. Tobias behaved like a lost soul that day. There were not many days throughout Tobias' life that his parents, teachers, or peers worried about him. There were not many days in his life where he required console as he was often the one giving it. The school nurse even called home and mentioned concern over Tobias' hand twisting. He was devastated and easily tearful at school and at home for nearly three weeks. He was a grieving child. He reassured everyone he was OK and that it was OK for him to be so sad and hurt. In intense grief, he was still teaching. After a few weeks, he was able to begin picking up the pieces of his heart and mind and was ready to try and understand the ways of this world that promoted such hatreds upon each other. This quest had been building as the Vietnam War was also a constant reminder of confusion surrounding the deaths of so many people and for reasons not well understood. Adults again, arguing and disagreeing, making terrible events even more confusing. He would finish out the school year becoming more of himself though many noticed his ongoing grief over the loss of one of his heroes. He would later recognize he must sit down with Taylor's parents to try and better understand the life and events surrounding Dr. King. The dominant culture of Kannot could not offer him the agreement and peace he seemed to need in order to move forward.

Tobias needed to better understand the word 'racism'. He was always hearing on TV and even in town at times,

"He did that because he is Black?"

"Yes, they all do the same thing".

Tobias remembers a Black woman in Scranton once that wouldn't let him play with her child. She called him a little racist. He just recalled the anger on her face and posture. She's looking at Tobias and notices he doesn't seem to truly understand her feelings. Tobias then says,

"Maybe it's not the color. Maybe some people are just not nice and don't know Jesus".

Just a matter-of-factly communication typical of Tobias. I remember him telling me that story. I always hoped it helped the lady change some of her perceptions that 'all White people are racists'.

"I just hope we can get there someday", Tobias would always say about this 'color and power thing'. I want Dr.

King's family to be proud for what he did for all of us. And for everyone who is different".

Nearing the end of their third-grade school year, the last parent-teacher conferences came about. The dreaded moments for the kids who knew they could be working harder and the dreaded moment for the parents who knew they could be working harder. The kids fearful of the consequences coming from home, while the parents fearful of teacher confrontation of their lack of efforts. Back then it was common for a teacher to take this on and uncommon for a parent to react in a negative manner --- whether rightly or wrongly so, it just was. The challenge at such a meeting was who would be willing to admit so to move forward with better results. The teacher was rarely questioned even if they had personalities not in much favor with kids and even many adults. Students were generally expected to adapt to the personalities and demands of the teacher without projection of blame.

Mrs. Adams entered Ms. Berringer's class as she did with every conference since Kindergarten. Attendance was largely assumed the mother's role. As usual, Mrs. Adams would always place Collette outside in the hall and Ms. Berringer would have to encourage her to bring Collette in where any praises of Collette would be downplayed or disbelieved. Ms. Berringer was a loving person and Mrs. Adams viewed her as a do-gooder trying to make her feel better for having such a burdened child. For the first time, Mrs. Adams would not oblige bringing Collette in the room and began a discussion abiut another child.

"Is there a boy that bothers Collette at school?"

"Not that I've heard of Mrs. Adams and let me tell you Tobias would not allow it".

"That's him! That's the kid I am talking about!" she strongly states.

"Mrs. Adams, what would make you think Tobias is bothering her?"

"He bothers her when we go to town sometimes so I thought he probably does it at school too. He actually tried to tell me he communicates with her and that they are friends".

"Well, Mrs. Adams, he does and they are. Some students are encouraged to have lunch with us and visit with our kids. Tobias offered to begin doing this last year before we asked him. Tobias' lunch period is still a work period for us so he tries to eat his lunch while helping. He helps lots of our kids, but he and Collette really connected. We don't fully know how they communicate as clearly as they do, but we are trying to learn from them. Tobias gets so invested in the tasks he is doing with the class that he sometimes doesn't even eat his lunch. We keep reminding him to eat but he is glowing and his lunch becomes a far second thought. We alerted his parents to this so they make sure he has smaller snacks with him as well. They don't want this taken away from him. It is the favorite part of his day. His afternoon teachers afford him the opportunity to go to the office area to eat his lunch or his snacks. Mrs. Adams, you're not asking me to stop Tobias from helping Collette, are you?"

"Well, I think much of what you said is just silly and I can't believe you are holding weight on teaching abilities of an eight-year-old" Mrs. Adams responds.

"Mrs. Adams, maybe it would help if you come in one day and observe Tobias and Collette working and recreating together".

"Ms. Berringer, my daughter doesn't recreate".

Her tone is one of escalation as she begins to draw back from further discussion on this topic. Ms. Berringer receives the message and submits. She decides to not show examples of Collette's work with Tobias as she believes it will re-escalate doubt and defensiveness. The meeting ends as if off a cliff. On the way out the door, Mrs. Adams states,

"Maybe I will come in at some time when I get a chance" in a calmer, respectful tone.

"Curiosity may have been aroused," thinks Ms. Berringer. Despite the stubbornness of this mother, much of it was borne of ignorance surrounding cerebral palsy and even of well-intentioned loving parents. Ms. Berringer also recognized she knew little of this disability and that is why she chose to try and learn from Collette and Tobias.

With this troupe of exciting little people banded together by Tobias a new phase in our lives was nearing. Entering the fourth grade was more than just a new number and new grade level. We would now be considered "the big kids". A description also fostered by a physical separation (the cafeteria) between the halls of the Kindergarten through grade three classes and the fourth through sixth grade classrooms. But it was more than the physical placement of the classrooms. The teachers were sure to begin recognizing this down the homestretch of third grade and during the front end of fourth. It was very common to hear, "Hey, you're not little kids anymore" the teachers would mantra, an ever-pervasive mantra for all matters pertaining to schoolwork and behaviors. At this point we only heard it said to the "big kids"; soon it would be directed at us --- and we couldn't wait --- initially. But first, we had the excitement of another summer; a time of fun for most kids, a time of vacations with families, and a time to think of the excitement of the coming fourth grade. The summer went by without much fanfare but lots of typical summer fun. By early August most kids could not wait for school to start; a feeling often forgotten by about the third week of September.

Chapter IV

The Upper Elementary Years
(4th/6th '68 -'71)

1) Abilities vs Disabilities

What a wonderful teacher! Ms. Hathway was the new teacher for Collette's classroom. Tobias began the fourth-grade lunch time in Ms. Hathway's class as he did for a couple years prior. Because of Collette's age they moved her up as well. Ms. Hathaway refused to allow the word "can't" in her room. She made it fun to not use that word. You could say, "I don't know how to do this" but it better end with a "Yet". She made sure her students understood they were not supposed to already know everything. Tobias was usually the teaching partner whether directly assisting the teacher with the lesson for kids who were struggling or through more indirect means. Tobias had a way with kids who needed "extra" help. I don't recall much of the language used with these kids but today they call it "special education". There wasn't a kid Tobias couldn't connect with and help maximize their effort and outcome. Most of us realized he was better at motivating those kids than many, if not all the teachers, but the ones who did not realize such were unfortunately many of those same teachers. I think sometimes it was an ego thing, which had to be difficult for the adults but Tobias could work with that too.

Tobias' skills with assisting/teaching the "hard to teach kids" were much more exposed through his work in Ms.

Hathway's class. Despite Tobias' time as a helper, his abilities were not shared with the masses or discussed in the teacher lounge. His peers and even close friends did not know what went on in there. It really was an isolated classroom and maybe in previous years Ms. Berringer felt isolated from her peers also. For whatever reason, she did not speak so openly about Tobias and his work over the course of two years in her classroom. It appears most were afraid to venture into such a classroom, even the school administration. This classroom had a few kids in wheelchairs; one who could not walk, two who could not walk or talk clearly, one kid who seemed to get angry very easy, two kids who could not read, and two kids who could walk and talk but were said to be mentally retarded. I know more now about these kids now, but back then this was how they were described by teachers when asked about them.

He was the one responsible for a major change with one question, "Ms. Hathway, why can't this classroom eat in the cafeteria like everybody else?" Ms. Hathway was surprised by her inability to answer this question in any manner that made sense. She took the question home with her. She thought about the scenario. She pondered the mainstream's discomfort with vocal noises from some her kids, some drooling behaviors from another, and in sum, the very visual nature of some of the disabilities with the children in her class. Yet, she further pondered them being citizens in this country and there was not a place she could think of outside the school to which they were not allowed. So why she thought, why should they not be in the cafeteria with the other kids? Maybe the adults were trying to protect the other students from seeing some of the realities of this world; that some people are born with such challenges whether physical or mental. This pondering did not work for her either, since she had long recognized children to be far more accepting of human differences than most adults. She particularly learned this from Tobias, though she still recognized this as a child-specific gift. By the next day, she was approaching the principal to begin a new and more open schooling experience for her students.

The same questions were presented and processed with the principal, and he too, came to the same conclusion as Ms. Hathway; Why not? Mr. Carson was a good man. He had enough leadership strength to know what to fight for and what not to and he chose to fight for this one. But there would be no fight. I wish this would be the case across the board when these challenges come up in schools, but in the Kannot Elementary School issues of compassion and generally doing right by all children had already been on the upswing --- they were fortunate. This was no accident, yet it was not necessarily occurring through a fully conscious level. They had been watching and telling stories of Tobias since he entered Kindergarten and through this they were growing themselves; becoming better people and better teachers. They were teachers and school personnel willing to learn whether they were actively engaged in it or unknowing of the process. It is the heart that gives the final blessing for this to occur whether the mind is aware or not. And this group's minds and hearts agreed. If a heart is not able to do this the consciousness level of one's mind is moot.

Tobias' efforts in Mrs. Hathway's classroom, mixed with Ms. Hathway's strength and willingness for change, meant big changes. The classroom was separated physically from the main halls of the school as it was located down the end of a corridor that included the janitor's room, a storage room and the nurse's office. It was further away from the populace than Ms. Dawson's classroom. It seemed to me as the kids got older maybe they were perceived as a bit scarier so the leprosy perception was prevailing. Soon after the cafeteria success, and not without some fights I may add, changes were demanded in how the teachers and student population viewed and interacted with the students in this class. In the latter part of the 60s, Kannot Elementary was doing things unheard of with all their students. Can you imagine? All students dining together regardless of physical or mental challenges! What a concept! And, teachers assisting teachers in educating the mass of the student population about the varying disabilities they may see in the school and community. Wow! And perhaps most incredibly, was helping all to acknowledge that the children in the "special" class were at their core children first. Foreign, cutting edge concepts; enlightenment begins! Tobias was ecstatic. He had been so connected with these kids for so long. He felt bad about these barriers and did not want to be associated with them. He set out to prove and model for the potential of a different schooling experience for them while not knowing or even imagining the changes that would begin taking place. As his friends, we knew he was most happy that Collette's life would get better and you could see it in her eyes; there was a twinkle. It was childhood excitement visiting her. The excitement of knowing life will get better, new challenges will come, and new challenges will be conquered. Tobias had a burden lifted. Up until this time, the heavy load of peer support for these kids was largely on his shoulders. No more. There began to be more kids involved and more kids taking ownership of the Kannot School Community. Community meant all for one and one for all and now these kids were included. Kannot was doing radical things!

2) Helping the Bullied and the Bully

Bullying did not seem to exist so much in the earlier grades. For some reason by the 4th grade it was something we would see more of. Not that it was rampant at Kannot Elementary but some kids seemed to be drawn to this behavior. When Tobias became aware of another child engaging in a bullying behavior you could find him near that student before school, at recess and after school. As soon as he would see it he would intervene. "Why did you do that" he would ask the offender. The offender, would often very proudly say something like, "You see how fat he is?" Tobias would say, "Do you have anyone in your family that is not perfect? Anyone? Anyone who is fat? Anyone who is like the boy you now bully?" A blind stare would often be returned or, "Yeah, but not that fat". It was just enough to get them thinking outside of the moment. Remember, every time you bully this boy, you bully that person; the person in your family that you love. This boy has people in his family who love him too. Think about it and tell me tomorrow if you are done with this stuff. Some kids came back to Tobias before the next day and relinquished their bullying behaviors. Some kids came to him the next day to do so and then there were a select few who would tell him to buzz off and attempt to hold steadfast to their right to bully. There seemed a difference between kids that were trying to find their own strengths and abilities and by being around the weakness of another and reminding them so, their prowess would be validated. As opposed to others who appeared simply angry and mean. The former a simpler matter of the mind, education and some time; the latter, a matter of mind, heart and much time.

Just relent the other students would encourage. Give it up; not worth the battle. It will never work here and we want you to be our friend and that means not picking on others. "Screw you!" "Hey, I was you" and "I was you" from two peers. You can do this, just publicly apologize and we'll stand with you". "Never!" After a few days of discomfort and school and peer consistency; "OK, I'm ready", a tearful boy would usually say to Tobias. The bullies recognized Tobias was the one they needed to relinquish their fight to. Tobias, in his uncanny way of understanding the world, knew bullies have likely been bullied themselves. These kids had to feel his true compassion for them and thus were willing to receive his message and his welcome to a school world without such strains. They also knew Tobias was not about dominance or ego. He truly wanted everyone to feel safe at school and truly wanted the bullies to have better lives too --- and once they experienced him, even for a short while, they felt this from him. Afterwards, they would be free to experience the joys of school, of friends, of teacher admiration --- a true sense of belonging --- something they had not yet experienced in their young lives.

Tobias and Kannot Elementary's biggest challenge was Tommy Hollister. Tommy had been recognized as a bully since his family moved into Kannot and entered Kannot

Elementary for the second-grade school year. He was sly. Even Tobias was challenged by his cunning. The teachers and principal knew even less. They heard reports but simply never saw any such incident. Tobias knew and it was still hard for him to see. There were verbal confrontations during the second and third grade but Tommy knew to keep his actions away from Tobias and to keep away from kids Tobias was close to. Therefore, Collette and others he saw Tobias interact with frequently were off limits.

Tommy's bullying behaviors were escalating rapidly at the front end of this school year. It was as if Tommy had a horrible summer and he was going to make others pay and they could be anyone who would exhibit fear. Kids who would be most vulnerable, i.e., smallest, tallest, skinniest, fattest, quietest, kids with disabilities, kids from different cultures, etc. In sum, there were not many who would be off Tommy's attack list. Kids like Taylor, Collette, and Sadie would rank high on Tommy's wish list but they were close to Tobias so they were relatively safe. The frequency and intensity of his behaviors were increasing. He even made some direct attempts at Tobias to see if Tobias had learned about fear yet --- he did not. Tobias must have known now was the time to address Tommy's role as a citizen of Kannot Elementary. He must have known this had nowhere to go but to a really bad place and if not addressed soon it may get ahead of everyone, Tommy included. Tommy was becoming a train with poor brakes and should the brakes give out the only thing to slow him down would involve much damage to others and himself. He was also starting to fill his train cars up with other like-minded or vulnerable kids. Other kids prone to desiring another human being as an outlet for their own pains/issues or for other kids who believed being closer to Tommy would take them out of his sights. The pendulum was starting to swing in Tommy's favor. Issues of privacy and physical development became more a matter associated with the upper elementary school years, thus giving more damaging information and fodder for the bully and his teammates, i.e. the physical development of children or not, the beginning interests in "relationships", hygiene factors, etc. And, if one hones their bullying skills during this period the middle school years become a utopia for them as privacy and puberty enter the life of that age group in significant manner. It continues to amaze me that adults in the school systems still seem to struggle with understanding the totality of this problem. My money was on Tobias back then and it would still be on a similar kid today.

While Tobias was in the office one Monday morning signing up for an off-campus activity with Ms. Hathway's class, Tommy came in per request of a teacher. Students being sent to the office for wrongdoing also had to sign in, that is if they were in the mood to do so. Tommy did not care about this. He was becoming prouder with the sign-in process.

"Hey Greenwood, what's up?" as he signs in.

"Nothing much Tommy, just going with Ms. Hathway's class on Friday to the zoo".

"Greenwood, Ms. Hathway's class is the zoo" as he giggles himself into laughter.

"Not nice, my friend".

"Not your friend Greenwood" he says. Hey, what's this?" looking at the sign in sheet. Your name is Theodore Tobias Greenwood?"

Tobias always wrote his full name. Though his spoken name rarely included Theodore he wanted to recognize his biological parents' full choice of names so he always did so on paper.

"Yes, it is Tommy".

"You're telling me your name is Teddy Tubby!" Tommy pronounces with glee. This sounds like a nickname some kid would give a fat little stuffed animal" he furthers.

Tommy truly did not understand such things did not bother Tobias.

"I guess Tommy, I guess" he stated and then began to leave the office area.

"See ya Teddy Tubby".

Tommy believes he now has the fodder to publicly

embarrass or harass who he has now defined as his arch nemesis. He realizes a victory over Tobias would imprison the entire student population to his terror. He had full confidence the adults would not be able to catch him, he was "Teflon Tommy". He knew his underlings would take most of the hits as they would get caught much more frequently and they would be terrified to expose their ring leader.

Knowing Tommy was going to begin coming after him Tobias began seeking the opportunity to get a step ahead of him and later that day the step came. As he was in the office delivering a message from Ms. Hathway, through the office window he notices Tommy and some of his right hands outside picking up papers. He asks Mrs. Barton, the office secretary, what they are doing.

"That's a part of Mr. Thompson's new way of addressing problems. Don't worry Tobias, you'll never be doing that".

"Only if I choose to, right Mrs. Barton?"

"That's right Tobias", she says, knowing this boy would never be there for a purposeful negative behavior.

"Tobias, I'm in here by myself and need to use the powder room for just a minute, could you stay there and just tell whoever comes in I'll be right back?"

"Sure Mrs. Barton, but where's Mr. Thompson?"

"Oh, he's out and about somewhere".

Tobias' plan was now in formation. He would make an appeal to all students in all classrooms. He just required access and security in which to activate his plan. Being in the office with no adults, locked doors, and access to the classroom announcement system provided the access and security necessary. He knew there would be consequences yet the cause was just.

I'm sure Tobias was very confident in justified civil disobedience, especially because of his admiration and respect for Dr. King. Maybe there are those that would not dare compare this issue with anything Dr. King had done, or with any of his teachings but Tobias would. To be in a school run by bullies; children fearful of using the restrooms, being on a bus, being in the gym locker room; anywhere with lowered or no adult supervision, was a horrible experience. School would no longer be fun or safe for many, many children, especially for those deemed different. And they would not be able to perform to their abilities because their days would be filled with stress and anxiety about what literally lie, or stand, around the next corner. Some children experiencing such fear would wet themselves, while others would lose interest in school and interest in learning. School was, and is in large, the life of a child. This should never be allowed to happen in mass in a school and when it does there is most certainly enough shame to go around for the adults that allowed it to become so. "In the end, we will not remember the words of our enemies, but the silence of our friends" one of many quotes by Dr. King that Tobias would cite in history class, but he really incorporated the spirit of Doctor King's words into his life not as just a timely/required response to a history lesson. How does such a young man do this? Tobias would never allow any of his senses to ignore something that would hurt others and all his senses readily received such information. He knew the level of harm being placed upon children would become worse if not addressed. There is no doubt in my mind Tobias would believe Dr. King would be proud he was able to transfer his teachings into this situation.

Mrs. Barton leaves the office. He gives her a few seconds and then locks the door behind her. He is free to implement his plan and even more pleased as he sees Mr. Thompson's keys on his desk through the open doorway to his office behind Mrs. Barton's desk. And there along the wall above Mrs. Barton's desk are a coupled rows and series of lights and switches looking like the console of jet plane. A flip up opens office communication to an individual classroom and down ceases it. There may have been a master switch, but Tobias cannot locate it. So, it's on! There were approximately 20 switches flipped before Tobias began.

"Testing, testing, 123."

He was not sure this was working until he saw the angered face of Mr. Thompson appear in the window of the office door. Shortly thereafter the perplexed face of Mrs. Barton joined him. He waved to both, tried to indicate a plea for forgiveness through his eyes and then started his speech.

"Hello everyone, this is Tobias. I need your best attention and I need everyone to do what I ask in the coming days. We have a bullying problem here and kids are being hurt. I believe if one of us is being hurt we are all being hurt in some way. I love this school, I love my teachers, and I want this to stop. I need us all to be and to feel safe."

The panicked door banging and yelling has now subsided. Mr. Thompson knows Tobias is now up to good as opposed to bad. He is curiously, yet still anxiously, waiting to hear what comes next while also contemplating the consequence for this behavior. He knew there had to be a consequence, even for Tobias' act of courage for whatever he was about to do. All this going on while Tommy and his boys walked about outside picking up papers, oblivious to the hopeful future being made at this precise time.

"Tommy and some other kids have been bullying many of you. Most of them are outside right now. Some of you are inside and I will ask you to keep quiet and to change your ways today. These behaviors will be stopping in the next couple days. When it does stop, you will want to be one of the students who helped it stop instead of one who attempted to keep doing it. Most of us will be able to forgive now, but there may be some that won't. It depends on you. At lunch tomorrow, and maybe in other places, Tommy will probably start calling me Teddy Tubby. My name is Theodore Tobias so this is what he chooses to call me. It's a nickname he believes hurts me though it doesn't. Anyone else can call me that if you like, it's kind of cool, but it's the intent that matters. I also know this is just one method of bullying and that they use many others too. Anyway, I would like you all to not laugh when he does this. Any agreement to a bully's behavior is like fuel. They use it for more energy. And if other things arise within the next couple days, try to be strong by ignoring and not responding. We can do this together"

The teachers are now aware and all students are now

aware.

"I will also ask the principal and teachers to not allow Tommy and his three friends, whom many of us can now see out on the playground to not be in any unsupervised areas without an adult. Please start this tomorrow. You can do this --- we trust you as we will do our part. Feel free to wave to them; they'll think it's cool and possibly even roll on the ground laughing because they believe they are distracting you from the teachers and your work. And look, Tommy is actually rolling on the ground. Do not mention this or talk openly about this until this is over --- not even to parents. That's all I need to say. Thank You".

This was perhaps one of the best situational examples for one of Tobias' favorite quotes by Dr. King. "A genuine leader is not a searcher for consensus but a molder of consensus".

"Great!" Mr. Thompson says to Mrs. Barton.

"How in the world are we going to do this?"

"Well Mr. Thompson, you are kind of backed into a corner so you better figure it out and soon".

With that final message, Mr. Thompson and Mrs. Barton can only wait until Tobias is finished and opens the doors. He turns off the switches, gets up, walks over and opens the door, and without hesitation or even direction walks behind Mr. Thompson into his office as if turning himself in. The total of this event was around four minutes. Four minutes of time, four minutes of leadership, four minutes of courage, four minutes of civil disobedience for a just cause. He will site Dr. King's work in defense of his actions to Mr. Barton. Wow, how people can change lives for the better or worse in such short amounts of time. A period of time most would have difficult remembering it ever happened. But it was four minutes of a very public Tobias and this was unusual for him --- so all would remember and they would take heed. People listened to Tobias; kids and adults. When he spoke, it was usually so clear and precise in intent and meaning; his was a voice you could not ignore for there was always purpose. He was far from a chatterbox and this is also why most were not only willing to listen to him, but ready to do so. In contrast to the chatterbox that is usually heard, often with irritation, but rarely listened to. There would be the secrecy he requested from all the students and by day's end the following message came over the classroom speakers.

"Mr. Thompson is calling for a mandatory meeting for all teachers after school today. All teachers meet in the auditorium; again, a mandatory meeting for all teachers in the auditorium after school today", spoken in a rather bubbly tone by Mrs. Barton.

Tommy was heard to remark,

"Yeah, they're going to talk about how stupid school is!" He waits for the laughter and support of his classmates near him but it does not come.

"What are you a bunch of idiots" he says, but they ignore.

In and of itself, this does not alert him to any mass campaign. It will come tomorrow.

During Tobias' little speech he used the words 'believe' and 'need'. It's important to understand Tobias's choice of words always exuded confidence thus confidence was given them. I am not sure if I ever heard Tobias say, "I think so, or I think …" To say, "I believe" furthered his certainty. He wasn't just thinking about it; he had already done that somewhere at some time. That's the strange part. He was still so young where did he learn these lessons? A question that may never be answered for curiosity's sake. He truly understood the difference between wants and needs. He seemed to know what he needed materially in this world and he seemed to typically know what he "needed" to say. He would not be heard saying that's all I "have" to say". This would posit the assumption he may be at a loss for some necessary information at the time. When Tobias would say that's all I "need" to say, listeners found peace and resolve that even if there were some other thoughts in there they were simply not necessary or relevant now. Tobias's choice of language, along with the confidence and sincerity of his messages, seemed understood by young and old equally well.

Most adults did not seem able to accomplish this level of communication. If someone could not fully grasp his words, they easily grasped the message through the deeper levels of human communication; the nonverbal and emotional.

School the next day would be different since every student and adult knew of the impending clash. Stress, blood pressures and anxieties were high all around that is except for Tobias. Tobias did not appear to fear anything earthly. I say earthly because that is what I can see. I do not know if he has fear for a higher authority; he never spoke of this topic directly. Tommy is a big kid. He would be considered intimidating by most students' standards and there were even teachers who were hesitant to hold him accountable for the constancy of his misdeeds. They would never admit this and this seems to be what allows bullying behaviors to really take hold in a school. When the bully can feel any hesitancy from adults to hold them accountable bad things begin to get worse. It was so with this case. Tobias had some size to him but remember, his physical stature was misperceived. He seemed slightly overweight, of soft belly and muscle, and small shoulders. This is what perhaps led to the mystic behind his fearlessness. His physical gifts had not yet been recognized on any significant scale. There were some situational occurrences that had his family members, close friends, and maybe a teacher or two scratch their heads like the movement of some furniture Maggie could not move, but Tobias could at age eight. Or, the breaking of a dead tree that both Jimmy J and Taylor together could not snap, or the amount of items Tobias could put in the gymnasium clean up bag and drag across the floor when in first grade. These were all things that received some attention and comment, but would not move beyond the observer's brief intrigue. Probably so since they were only observing isolated events and not seeing the gift in total. Because of these factors, many had a hard time thinking about a fight between Tommy and Tobias. Tobias, fearless and confident, but not known to be a fighter. To even think of Tobias hurting someone was an odd thought, a foreign thought, for his parents, peers and teachers. What would he do if someone tried to physically hurt him? What would he do if someone was being physically hurt in front of him? These situations had never come up in Tobias' young life yet. Then there's Tommy. He seemed to like physical conflict. He was beginning to fight more. He already hurt some kids early in this school year and it was apparent even some adults would do the proverbial 'walk on egg shells' around his behaviors to avoid his arguments and temper.

It was a rainy day. There would be no outside recess or outside clean-ups. Whether behaviors were good or bad, all kids would be inside today. These kinds of days were frequently met with increases in naughty behaviors, especially for the teachers who were ill-prepared to deal with children having pent up physical energies. But this was an issue for the masses and not uncommon. The bullies had more challenges as their primary venue of service, the playground, was not available but this group was opportunistic and relentless. They did not have the positive typical outlets like most other kids, but they still had that "other" negative energy thing going on. This combination raised the likelihood of significant increases in bullying behaviors and they would be even more brazen. On this day, a culmination of so many factors would not go unnoticed for long --- probably not past the second period.

Tommy and his boy bully mates seemed to enter the school invigorated by the concept of a more captive audience today. Their bully diets would be met by more prey frequenting the lavs, locker rooms and hallways during classes as everyone would want to get out of class more. Did they know or discuss this with each other or is this instinctual behavior to the bully? Could it be like the Orcas hunting the seal as a family unit? A pack of wolves surrounding a young moose separated from its mother and father? No, these animals are engaging in such behaviors as a matter of survival and need, though they do sometimes look like bullies to the human. Probably because the outnumbering issue combined with the weakness of the prey. But the human bully has neither survival nor need factors in play. It may feel that way to them, but it is still choice; maybe well- ingrained from caregivers or caregiver issues, but it is still a choice. Today will be the day of resolution. Prior to this rainy day, Tobias had thought this clean-up may take several days. The stars have aligned for resolution on this day and it shall be so.

"Good morning", Ms. Marchetti says to Tommy upon entrance into her first period class.

"I don't think so" he says to her with a devilish smile.

Ms. Marchetti was a soft-spoken nice teacher, but not one to pick up on either the intention of his statement or one willing to confront such an intention even if known. She was not unlike many teachers. There were some teachers who certainly over-reacted as well; this would be Mrs. Bulsavich and Mr. Kramer. Unfortunately, their strong reactions came to both bullies and non-bullies alike. They seemed to thrive on a behavior that had comparisons to the bullying behaviors we are discussing here. Without consistent limits from the teacher forces, the environment was ripe for Tommy's picken, or for anyone who chooses to bully for that matter. This did not always seem the case at Kannot Elementary or could it be they had not yet been challenged by the likes of a Tommy Hollister?

The first period bell rings and class begins.

"Mrs. Marchetti, may I use the restroom?"

He was out of his seat and nearing the door. All eyes were on Mrs. Marchetti and she knew it. She knew what was expected of her but the kids in the class held little confidence. Here it was, just a few minutes into first period and the plan has begun to fail already they thought. Then,

"No Tommy, please have a seat".

A puzzled Tommy and startled class now have all twenty-six pairs of eyes on Mrs. Marchetti. Her directive had some hesitations behind it so Tommy went at her again as he continues walking toward the door.

"Please, please, please, please ….."

The word "no" generates this mantra. The general student population gets frustrated by so many teachers who succumb their limits with bullies. All they could think is "You are not supposed to be afraid of him too!" They just want the teacher to say, "Stop it now!" To say it with confidence and to say it as if a consequence will undoubtedly be given. Remember, the bully is always assessing for signs of weakness. He stops but remains near the door as if to challenge her response as the incorrect one. Then,

"Tommy, have a seat".

This was stated with firmness not typical of Mrs. Marchetti's usual manner. A sigh of relief and no doubt a psychological victory has just occurred for Mrs. Marchetti, the students in the class and Kannot Elementary. Tommy walks back to his seat a bit stunned and still pleading,

"But I have to go".

"You should have gone before you entered the class; we have too much stuff to go over now".

"This is stupid; you better let me go later".

One knew Mrs. Marchetti would be challenged one more time before class was finished. Every other kid who really had to go to the bathroom in the class now knew they could not. They did not want to provide any more discomfort to Mrs. Marchetti as they were incredibly proud of her.

As certain as the geese flying south for the winter, Tommy asks again near the end of the period. Mrs. Marchetti is now appearing a bit more shaken. Tommy sees this.

"You can't stop me if I really have to go!" he states loudly.

Somewhat panicked, Mrs. Marchetti goes to her phone and speaks with someone with her back to the class. Within a minute, Jerry, the janitor arrives.

"Someone have to go to the restroom in here?" he says.

Jerry was the only adult in the school it seemed OK to call by his first name. He was not typically ascribed any authority and was known as a friendly man, not the sort to take on the likes of Tommy. However, Jerry was quite willfully on board with the plan since he long observed the relational stylings of this boy. He knew it was time. "

Yes Jerry, Tommy", Mrs. Marchetti reports.

"OK, young man let's go".

"I don't need anyone to go with me" Tommy states with conflictual intent.

"Apparently, you do", Jerry says.

Unbeknownst to the students until this moment, it appears the school staff decided to be open with Tommy and the other identified bullies about the new rule only applying to them. They did not want to place other kids in jeopardy by maintaining the odd look of this --- a certain group needing escort yet the masses not. It seemed as if Tommy really had to go at this time since he stopped and relinquished his argument for the moment. He nonetheless told Jerry how stupid this was all the way to the lav and all the way back to the class. Tommy re-entered the class in somewhat of a daze. He did not have enough time to process what just happened as the bell rang for the next period and he left quickly. Mrs. Marchetti may not have ever received such gracious goodbyes from her entire class. In their eyes she saw respect, admiration, love. She saw and felt everything. She needed to leave her classroom for the staff lounge for a brief period between classes. Reports had it that she cried in there; that, during the moments of her departing students she felt what they had been looking for from her throughout her entire career. Though she felt shame, she also felt a new classroom and school world had unfolded to her. She was not just there to teach, but she was there to make sure the environment was ripe for teaching and learning; that it was safe. She got it. And so, she would re-enter her classroom for second period, and the rest of her career, a different person. The change would be apparent to all.

During the transition between classes, Tommy hooked up with two of 'his' boys, Carl and Stanley.

"You should have seen what that stupid lady and idiot Jerry just did to me. I had to have an escort to the lav!"

"You too" both boys say simultaneously.

"What the hell is going on?" Tommy questions angrily.

"Are they doing this with everybody?" "No", said Carl. Mrs. Bulsavich let another kid go without calling the office.

When I asked her why Tammy could go without someone and I couldn't, she told me to shut-up."

"OK, I see what's going on. Some babies must have said something about us. Let's find out who during our next class. MAKE other kids tell you. There's no way some other kids don't know what's going on".

Tommy had given his directive. Armed with an idea the three boys enter their second period classes --- all separate from each other, which by the way, weakens the bully. Strength in numbers works for both good and evil.

Tommy now has an idea about what he is up against. Rather than immediately challenge the teacher for a pass to the lav he begins threatening some other kids. Unfortunately, the teacher remains in the hallway for a bit after the bell and Tommy grabs a couple kids by the collar.

"You know anything about this lav pass stuff boy?" he says to one.

"How bout you!" as he pushes another boy into the blackboard.

The teacher enters and the room is pale and silent. A bully has just had free rein to terrorize other kids. It is the first known breakdown in the plan of protection. It is Mr. Loring's class, or Mr. Boring's class, as dubbed by most kids. Mr. Loring did not seem to care for much. He exhibited minimal passion for teaching and even less for behavior management. This was not good. Unlike what had happened in Mrs. Marchetti's class, the opposite is occurring in this one. Tommy threatens others the entire period. He is met by many, 'I don't knows', but you could feel the confidence decreasing. The students do not feel safe in Mr. Loring's class. They hope against hope Mr. Loring will rise to the occasion, but to their sadness he does not. Mr. Loring is not on-board. It was not until the end of the class that Mr. Loring says, "Alright, you may hand in the assignment given by my sub yesterday". In their despair, the students had forgotten Mr. Loring had not been at school yesterday. Even though scared, they are trying to renew their faith in him by his obliviousness to the events of the last twenty-four hours

--- he had simply not gotten the message. This works in their favor as they now believe it will be different for the following periods as all those teachers were here.

What now becomes obvious to Tommy and his friends is that it seems they have an adult near them everywhere they go between classes; janitor, teacher aids, teachers, office staff, principal. Tommy, escalating his defiance, confronts the principal.

"Hey Mr. Thompson, what's going on?"

"Good morning Tommy" he responds.

"You think it's a good morning when I can't go anywhere without a teacher or somebody around me!" Tommy with irritation proclaims.

"Watch your tone young man. I decided the bullying stuff is going to stop".

"Bullying stuff, who's bullying?"

"You and some of your friends, Tommy".

"You can't prove that! Who told you this! Someone lied about me and I'll take care of it when I find out who!" Tommy spouts off loudly so other kids could hear him.

Mr. Thompson pulls Tommy off to the side and says,

"First of all, I'm not playing the 'prove it' game. I'm not compelled to prove it to you or prove it to your parents either. This is not a democracy here. Look at me as a dictator, Tommy. I am making the call on this and I am telling the teachers what to do and what not to do. You and your pals will be escorted and observed until I am reassured you are finished with this behavior. I want you to be a positive part of the Kannot Elementary School community."

Mr. Thompson is on a roll. He knows he too has allowed this to get out of hand. There were reports of Tommy engaging in these behaviors for a long time now and had he done right by the other students it would not have escalated to what is now happening. Regaining his wits, Tommy is well-equipped with the ability to know when to back down and reassess to fight another day, or at a later time during the same day.

"Mr. Thompson, I don't know who is saying this, but it's

not true. I really like being a part of the Kannot Elementary School community, ask Mr. Loring".

He would continue to site the teachers of present and past he had deemed incompetent and easily manipulated. Mr. Thompson knows this. He knows his staff well. He had just not held them accountable for their obvious shortcomings.

"OK Tommy, we'll see. Go back to class and hold it together or you'll be in my office in a heartbeat".

"Sure Mr. Thompson. Hey, I know it's rainy out but are there any areas out there that need to be cleaned up?"

Tommy had a lapse of judgment here. It was simply too soon after such a confrontation to try and smooth the situation over. He knew it soon after he said it too.

"Back to class Tommy".

Mr. Barton moves on and Tommy realizes he must go underground. But he will seek Mr. Thompson's favor soon again and it will not work out the way in which he envisioned.

Periods three and four move on as does indoor recess. Carl and Stanley relinquished to the pressures of the day. They have concerns about parental involvement so they opt to not challenge their current status. Mr. Thompson had a similar conversation with each of them. Tommy had even threatened both at some point during recess. His threats for the main culprit or culprits behind his current ills continued but on a more silent level. A threat whispered is often stronger than one not. The potential for a witness decreases and further places the threatened in a very lonely and isolated place. By nature, children are never supposed to feel alone and isolated. This feeling is a feeling of nightmares made. It is a feeling, if allowed to go on for too long, will bring much damage to follow. Just exactly how much varies. There is no rule. It is different for different ages and it is different for everyone. The experience is child-specific and even the most knowledgeable of child development and psychology will never be able to know when is "too long". And therefore, bullying should not be addressed with any timeline of tolerance.

Later in the afternoon the rain began to subside and by the end of the 6th period it had ceased. Mr. Thompson then decided he would give a teacher and a classroom a break from Tommy by taking him up on his offer for outside clean-up. About the same time Mr. Thompson was planning for Tommy's school community service, Tobias became aware of a situation that occurred during the 5th to 6th period transition. Tommy had gotten hold of little Timmy Timenti, TT as many referred to him. "Tobias, Tommy scared TT and TT told him what you did yesterday, said Jimmy J. "Tell TT it's OK when you see him". Tobias knew the confrontation was necessary and soon to be. As fate would have it, Mr. Thompson sent Tommy outside. Fate would also have Tobias see him out there at the beginning of 7th period.

Kannot Elementary was kind of a U-shaped school. It was made of the small red brick familiar to many older structures of the times. It was known to be a large school at the time. It was the larger feeder school to the Junior High School. There were two other smaller elementary schools in the Kannot School District. There are not many red brick schools left as most had been torn down and replaced since the "Tobias" years. Such schools became synonymous with asbestos dangers and all the fears associated. When you walked into the school it was the middle of the open end of the U. You walked across a large open area and into the main office. Should you turn left or right the hallway width lessened and classrooms ran along each side. To the left were the upper classes grades 4 through 6 and to the right were the classes K through 3. There was only one area without windows on the front western corner of the building; this was the gymnasium and cafeteria. In the back of the school, or at the bottom of the U shape, in full view from the office area, was the playground and recess area. It was there where Mr. Thompson sent Tommy to begin his clean-up.

The 7th period bell rang, Tommy goes outside and Tobias enters his classroom. Before the teacher begins the lesson, a peer points out Tommy to Tobias.

"Mrs. Bulsavich, may I use the restroom?" Tobias

requests.

"Tobias, you just got in here. What's the matter with you boy!"

She was tough on everyone. She just seemed angry; good kid, bad kid; did not seem to matter, at least in the eyes of her students.

"You must have forgotten you had to go and in my twenty-five years of teaching I still don't understand how you kids can forget to do this --- go on boy".

"Thank you Mrs. Bulsavich", Tobias states as he leaves the room.

Within a minute, Tobias is outside approaching Tommy. The class sees this before Mrs. Bulsavich and as if on cue they begin asking questions and volunteering answers like no other day in Mrs. Bulsavich's twenty-five years.

"My goodness, finally! After twenty-five years, I finally get the full attention, interest and cooperation that are due me. I will remember this class forever!"

The scene is playing out like a silent movie from within the building, while reflection and research upon this event yielded the best information about what happened out there.

"Greenwood, I hear you had a talk with EVERYONE yesterday".

"Yes I did", Tobias replies.

"I bet you don't have much to say today do you" Tommy states proudly.

"Nope, not much to say today Tommy".

Tommy is misinterpreting the situation he is now in. He seemed to think Tobias ended up outside by accident, did not know Tobias knew of TT's bullying, and did not know when Tobias said he had not much to say it meant minimal words would be communicated. Then Tobias surprised and confused Tommy with this statement.

"You will stop hurting other kids today; it all stops today".

These would be the last words Tobias would speak until he believed his effort was finished. Tommy moves toward

Tobias in attempts to do the bully chest push. By now the students in Mrs. Bulsavich's class could no longer keep up the front. They were solely focused on the events outside. Mrs. Bulsavich sees the lack of attention and to where it was being directed.

"Great!" she states. "I get your total undivided attention for the first time in twenty-five years and then a fight breaks out.

She then focuses on the identity of the boys.

"Ohhhhhhhhhhhhhhh, this was coming wasn't it".

The students now realize she is not so much out of the loop, yet she still must call the office but is no less fixated on the events.

Tobias seemed to allow Tommy to push him in the chest. Tobias did not budge; he neither moved into Tommy nor did he move backward. It was an odd scene. It looked as if this hurt Tommy more; like he hit a brick wall. Tommy then charged at Tobias. Tobias went into a low blocking position and ceased Tommy's charge rather quickly. Tommy flew upwards and backwards. He rolled on the ground for a spell as if grasping for air. Tobias would just slowly move backward and the pattern would continue. By now, the classrooms on the back western side of the school were aware of the battle. The teachers and principal decided to let it go since Tobias was not overtly fighting back. They reasoned one would step in to break up a fight if both kids were getting hurt or if one was pummeling the other. In this case, there did not seem to be a pummeling going on and both students were not being hurt --- only one, but he seemed to be doing this to himself. Though they could tell Tobias' had the appearance of a brick wall against Tommy's charges and that his blocks were hurting Tommy, they would stick to their reasoning as a reason to not intervene. Slowly, as if by lure, Tobias moved backward around the back side of the school to the front side. He wanted this battle to be witnessed by the entire school and so it was. Charge after charge, punch after punch was met with a seemingly rock solid mass. This, coming from the boy with small shoulders and of soft-belly.

By the time they arrived back to their starting point, Tommy was visibly exhausted, crying and cussing up a storm at Tobias.

"What you're doing isn't fair Greenwood! You're not fighting me and that's not fair!"

All these words between and within sobs.

"Tommy, kind of like what you do to other kids --- they don't fight back either but since you don't have any pain from pushing, punching and kicking them you just keep on hurting them. Do you know what you would look like right now if I fought back with my fists and my feet? I really did not want to hurt you so I let you hurt yourself".

Sobbing and with some blood from scrapes suffered from his falls, Tommy lays on the ground in defeat. Tobias asks him to look at the classrooms. There, lined up across the back eastern side of the school were students and staff watching from their classroom windows.

"They were there as our journey went around the entire school Tommy" Tobias tells him. I invite you now to bully me whenever you need to bully someone and I promise to never hit you back. This invitation is open to you for the rest of our school years together, but you will not bully anyone else but me. Or, you can be my friend and you can be their friend too, as he points to the faces in the windows. You need to tell me in the morning on your next day of school what you wish to do".

And with that last directive, Tobias walks back into the school and Tommy remains horizontal and crying. Not a word is said as Tobias re-enters Mrs. Bulsavich's class, while Mr. Thompson went out to retrieve Tommy Hollister. Tommy could be heard saying to Mr. Thompson,

"You let him do that, you let him do that"

To which Mr. Thompson replied,

"Tobias was doing nothing but stopping you from hurting him Tommy. It actually looked like he spared you much harm".

Furthering the message, he tells Tommy he is suspended for three days for fighting.

"What about Tobias! Tommy yells while still crying.

"He will have a consequence for going outside without permission".

Tommy just had a hard time understanding what had just happened and I suspect anyone under a similar circumstance would too. It was a beating without a beating so to speak. Tommy's father would cry foul as well and his cries would uncover the origin of his son's bullying behaviors. Mr. Thompson remained strong in his decision. The next decision would be Tommy's upon his return to school as he knew Tobias would be looking for him.

During Tommy's three-day suspension Kannot Elementary was a different school. The other bullies quickly fell in line with the new school resolve --- no more bullying. There were heartfelt apologies and some not so heartfelt but simply made to cease any further consequences from peers or school adults. Though the heart-felt apologies were best, the others were accepted with the belief they would come in time as these kids would slowly experience the joys of a safe and fun school and thus see the errors of their history. Yet there were still tensions as most did not know what would unfold upon Tommy's return. All eyes were on Tobias. They just observed him going about his school days in his typical ways of respect, patience, kindness, and a true desire to learn. Most people were aware of Tobias's special spirit by this time, yet most did not know the depth of his strength, confidence, and resolve for such matters as the one presenting them now. Looking back, he was not nervous or tense about Tommy's return because he already had resolved the situation in his heart and mind when he stated,

"I invite you now to bully me whenever you need to bully someone and I promise to never hit you back. This invitation is open to you for the rest of our school years together, but you will not bully anyone else but me. Or, you can be my friend and you can be their friend too, as he points to the faces in the windows. You need to tell me in the morning on your next day of school what you wish to do".

It was as simple as this for Tobias. He was a boy

of his word and when he gave his word there were no hesitations in heart or mind. He would be ready to respond to whatever decision Tommy would make upon his return and he was willing to suffer any consequences that could ensue and he would do so in clear conscience. Remember, civil disobedience; "Injustice anywhere is a threat to justice everywhere", Dr. King would often proclaim in his short time on this earth and Tobias wholeheartedly walked the path of Dr. King's words. He loved this man's courage, strength and peaceful means toward the end-goal. Dr. King and his Dream compelled Tobias to at least do his part.

Kannot Elementary was living an unfamiliar school life the rest of the week. A dark cloud had been lifted and all who had been denied the peace and joy of light are experiencing what a school environment is supposed to feel like. Nonetheless, they wonder if this will last. The only one not wondering would be Tobias. Tommy's return was scheduled for Monday of the following week so this gave rise to even more tension over the weekend for many. Now we know this was even more difficult for Tommy, but at that time no one could posit this as a possibility. It is incredible how stress, worry, anxiety can color one's world. How an incident like this can steal so much from the lives of people old and young alike. How the totals of power --- one positive and one negative and the confidence is laid more in the negative. Very much like the compliments of a hundred being washed away by the criticism of one. If we could all live within the confidence of someone like Tobias. A world where confidence is always placed in the power of goodness, and I believe faith, and the criticism of one is just that and it is digested for some possible learning value and then released. And my suspicions about Tobias and faith will be given an answer in his later years and I will forever remember to my questions about this.

On Monday, October 7th, 1968, the routine of the school day started like all others, yet the tension was in the air. The questions being thought or stated were likely,

"What is going to happen today?"

"Maybe Tommy will not come back to school".

"What is Tobias going to do if Tommy comes back angrier?"

"What will Mr. Thompson and the teachers do if this is the case?"

It was beyond perception to ponder what would happen if Tommy re-entered Kannot Elementary a different boy --- a better boy --- a remorseful boy. This was particularly difficult since many knew Tommy's father had an open confrontation with Mr. Thompson when he came to get his son last Tuesday afternoon. Some kids and staff hearing this and most hearing about this, would draw conclusions that Tommy's father had likely terrorized his school/s during his youth and thus were not able to see Tommy breaking such an ingrained cycle. It was a strange environment to be in on this day. How can one child present so much tension over an entire school?

The bell rang for first period and no Tommy. It was not until the middle of this period that Tommy's father was seen dropping him off in front of the school. And he did just that, just dropped him off. Even the adult bully does not do well when they lose their power of intimidation and apparently, Mr. Thompson's resolve accomplished this goal. There may have been more communication between them over the weekend, but we would never know this for certain. Mr. Thompson believed this was just as well since it may be easier to work with Tommy without such a paternal influence. Tommy entered the office area and signed in late. Mr. Thompson asked why he was late and with tears in his eyes Tommy stated he just did not want to come when all the kids were outside or in the hallways before classes started. Mr. Thompson observed the shame behind Tommy's words and simply told him he understood and that this was OK. Tommy then stated,

"Mr. Thompson, I need to see Tobias before I go to class. Can you help me do this?"

"Absolutely, Tommy. Can I have you boys meet in my office?"

"No, Tommy says. "I would rather we sit down outside somewhere on the playground".

"Tommy, you realize many will be able to see you both out there, right?"

"That's why I want to be out there Mr. Thompson".

Is this some kind of ploy? Mr. Thompson thinks. Does Tommy want to go another round in front of everyone again? With some reluctance, Mr. Thompson takes the risk based upon his observation of shame and pain in this boy's words and face.

"OK Tommy, you can go out there and I'll send Tobias out shortly".

Again, as on last Tuesday afternoon, the classroom on the back side of the school observe Tommy out there. Most, or all eyes, including teachers and administrators, watch the meeting unfold. Tommy takes a seat on a swing with his back facing the school. Tobias joins him by sitting on the swing next to him with his back to the school as well. Both boys are swinging ever so slightly and Tommy says to Tobias,

"I don't want to be like my father Tobias".

Probably the most horrible and painful desire a father can pass on to his son.

"Who do you want to be like Tommy?" Tobias responds.

"I just want to feel better, I just want to be happier, and I want other kids to like me".

"I can help you be that person", Tobias tells him.

"Trust me Tobias, if I can just get a break from the anger of my father some of the time, I will take it. I see myself becoming him".

"How bout we change things at school Tommy? You and me together".

"Don't you think all of the other kids will make fun of me and think I am weak?" "Some might, most won't".

"Most will be proud of you, most will respect you. I know I will and I will forever be your friend. We can take on the kids who think differently about this together --- but NOT with threats".

Tommy becomes tearful. Tobias is patting him on the back. The direct communication about this issue is over for the time being.

"Hey, when was the last time you competed for the longest jump from the swing?" Tobias asks Tommy.

"Great Tobias, you know this is not allowed. So, on my first day back after suspension I get in trouble?"

"C'mon just one jump and I'll get the consequence with you".

Tommy couldn't resist the challenge. With all eyes on them and Mr. Thompson knowing Tobias had a reason to engage in this small act of school rule defiance, they are swinging way higher than typical limits. At their peak, they take the leap. They arrive back on earth with a thud and a roll. Tommy lands a good deal in front of Tobias' mark. The boys laugh together and Tommy proclaims his jump's prowess. Tobias grabs Tommy's hand and holds it up and turns them both around toward the school. The faces in the windows are smiling and clapping, even some teachers. Well, they are smiling but not clapping. They had to place a boundary on their level of approval due to the jumps. Nonetheless, you could see the sincere joy in their eyes.

Tommy and Tobias walk back into the school together and Mr. Thompson greets them both with garbage baskets and points them back out to the playground. With a smile and wink he tells them nice job and to get to cleaning the grounds. The boys understand the meaning of Mr. Thompson's actions and return the smile. The classrooms on all sides of the school would hear of the jump and would see these boys horsing around and cleaning the school grounds together. A new era begins at Kannot Elementary School. There were a few bumps in Tommy's healing path yet they were not due to any aggressions by him, but by some of the previously bullied. With great resolve, Tommy, and the kids who became closer to him, helped him through these situations. He and Tobias remained friends though Tommy eventually moved a little further away into a less direct friendship --- maybe his way of maintaining some pride and saying he could do this without

Tobias. All was good as the school environment was back where it was always supposed to be. This experienced taught so many, and probably mostly the teachers and principal. They would never again allow for such behaviors to get a foothold in their classrooms or school. It was a prideful and joyful place to be, but sadly a place where Mr. Hollister never entered again; not for parent nights, school fundraisers or carnivals, or even for class graduations. Tommy not only elicited pride from his classmates and teachers but he also gained compassion for children. He was now able to see the bigger picture when given the opportunity. Fourth grade would move forward with hearts and minds touched in a very learn-ed way.

3) Young Love

Other changes began to occur amongst the group like active interest in the opposite gender. Jimmy J had such a crush on Betty Lou Harkman. A crush in the 5th grade for a boy was something that would go unshared with most, but Jimmy J was not as silent as most due to his open affinity for the ladies. I know he shared more with Tobias on matters of love, but most of us knew there was more to this with Betty Lou so he was a teased lad, even more so than usual. No more so than the day when his beauty queen accepted the invitation to his house to play a board game. Jimmy J believed this to be the best idea since he heard she really liked board games. Later we came to know she stated board games bored her, but Jimmy J got it confused. The cards were stacked against him from the get go. Since they lived so close together and since all the parents were home on this Saturday afternoon, the invite and the event did not appear to concern anyone.

It was a beautiful late spring day. Flowers in full bloom, birds singing, love was in the air and it had all the environmental stimuli one could possibly take. We set up our perch at the border of the house property. It was the only area where we would have a clear view through the patio window, with binoculars, of Jimmy J's recreation room where these two would play Jimmy's choice of game, trouble. The rest of the property had much visual interference from the orchard which engulfed much of the property. There was just enough shrubbery around us to provide the cover we needed for this surveillance. The best scenario for us was to be able to watch Betty Lou walk to the door, Jimmy J answer the door, and then see them reappear in the game room for the great game of Trouble. We had some dialogue about trouble being considered a board game since it had a bubble in the middle of it, but we conceded the category since we knew of no other.

It was not long before the sequence of events unfolded as we had planned and the two began the game. They appeared to be smiling so Jimmy J seemed to have made a good call. Jimmy J's grandfather had a dog. Since he resided next door the dog roamed Jimmy J's property as if it were his own, and inside as well, since there was a doggy door within the back door. This dog loved to roam the local area probably because of all the kids and attention he would get, but with this group of boys he held a special meaning.

Jimmy J's grandfather loved stinky cheese --- seemed to douse himself in the stuff. His house wreaked of the fragrance. He loved it so much that when he got the Daschund puppy 10 years ago he named him Cheese. The old man could not apparently tell the dog took on the odors of his passion over the years and no doubt due to a stinky cheese diet --- not good for the dog nor those around the dog. This older, overweight dog, had an air to him; when he gassed an even more putrid odor arrived. This would always bring great applause and laughter to young males throughout the community. So, this group of local bandits branded him "Stinky Cheese" and we did so with great affection. We never called him just Stinky or just Cheese. The relationship the little man people in this community had with him required the recognition of both, as it was this dog's fate. All due to the fascination of the fart and an exceptional fart from a dog like Stinky Cheese. The belly laughs from our group could last for an hour before control was regained based upon when, where and whom was present when this activity occurred. There were so many ways we would measure farts --- intensity of odor, volume level, duration of sound, frequency, pitch. Many loved competing with Stinky Cheese because he was the gauge in which to measure most aspects of a good fart. The neighborhood kids and probably the adults knew of this relationship with Stinky Cheese --- major local folklore. The boys held him near and dear, while the girls would run, scream and lash out in verbal disgust. They saw no cuteness in him; instead they saw the vileness of young boys and the disgusting and perplexing nature of boy world.

So here sits Jimmy J and Betty Lou. Seemingly having the time of their young lives. Jimmy J often bragged of his odiferous superiority amongst this club especially when he ate pizza from a certain restaurant. The gastrointestinal chemistry was exquisite. We even attempted to ban him from competitions believing this to be an unfair advantage. He would purposely seek out his posse and/or arrange for certain situations to release his presence, or presents, (both work) to some knowing and unknowing beings. He and Stinky Cheese were equals under such circumstances. For as much as Jimmy J loved the ladies his involvement in this specific activity with the fellas was held in secrecy and fully denied when someone chose to bring it up in public.

As fate would have it no other way, Jimmy J had pizza in this restaurant the night before. His invitation was open ended and it just so happened that Betty Lou picked this day. In his excitement, Jimmy forgot his gaseous ways and patterns.

Jimmy J had pursued Betty Lou's affections for years. He tried the hair tugs, the name calling, and even some chest thumping in front of her to gain her favors. Her psyche seemed impenetrable to these tried and proven methods. We knew Jimmy J was out the night before, yet in our excitement the potential repercussions evaded us as well.

So here we sit, binoculars in hand, arguing and tugging

for turns to watch our hero of the moment. Heck, Jimmy J could go down in history today and be recognized as a man amongst boys thus propelling him to an elite status within our school and community. He would be a man-child. He would be the guy we would all go to for consult on matters all things relationship. He may be the first 9-year-old elected mayor in next month's elections. We also thought it possible the school would decide to move him into junior high school as his maturity level would simply be too high for him to remain at the elementary school level --- he just would not fit in there anymore. We did not know yet, but his status would certainly be propelled.

We watch with astounding focus, the kind of focus parents and teachers the world over attempt to harness. Focus that propels the human condition for great things; full scholarships to college, generals in armies, executive officers in business. Per usual Stinky Cheese finds us and wishes to play a bit, or as much as a little old, fatty hotdog could. We knew when riled up a bit he would start producing his gift so we chuckled and played with him and he broke our focus for a spell. Suddenly, a ruckus is observed among the gaming participants and out of the house Betty Lou Hartman runs. She's yelling about the piggish nature of Jimmy J and that she will never play with him again. Jimmy J remained in the house and we suspected the messages being sent from Betty Lou outside had already been sent inside prior to her exit.

It took Jimmy J nearly twenty minutes to emerge. We were in shock and decided to wait, much like one would do when lighting a delayed fuse with the delay seemingly delayed. Not that anyone one of this group would know anything about this. The wait seemed a life time for this group of nine-year-old bandits. What went so greatly wrong? As he neared, he took a nasty verbal stab at Stinky Cheese and the little old fella scurried off. Jimmy J seemed to have a desire to unleash his ill fortune upon the immediate world around him. We waited and waited for Jimmy J to begin to share the events leading to his trauma. He sat with his forehead resting in his hands and his elbows on his knees. And then

---------- we heard and smelled something horrifically similar. The only difference this time was Jimmy J's lack of joy for his toilet room humor prowess, but we all responded in our typical manner. Jimmy J forcefully yelled at us to stop, stating this was no longer funny. He seemed to start laughing and crying at the same time.

A few minutes later he began to settle down enough to begin his story. He stated when he realized what was about to start happening he would use the popping from the game of trouble as noise cover and Stinky Cheese as the scapegoat. In that moment, he saw Stinky Cheese as the most incredible thing in his life --- his best and most treasured friend. He envisioned himself being forever indebted to Stinky Cheese. He would build him one of the nicest houses ever and he would supply him treats for as long as they resided on this earth together. After his first pop and sound cover up, he said it.

"Oh my goodness Stinky Cheese, where are you? Get out of the house!"

A strategy quite well perfected in boydom --- the sound and origin cover-up. Jimmy J, so engrossed in his new role as "the man" did not see us near the edge of the property nor Stinky Cheese playing with us. He knew we were going to be there. Betty Lou began the typical girl response, yet she was hanging in there with Jimmy J. She is seeing him in a light that was quite attractive to her. He was not engaging in a usual boy response to the problem presenting before them. She too, was focusing on the disgusting nature of Stinky Cheese! He had done it! He'd gotten away with it! And just as he began to revel in the success of his strategy, Betty Lou sees a commotion through the patio window at the edge of the property --- there we are, all of us playing with Stinky Cheese. Her quick change of words and emotions must have been traumatic for Jimmy J --- like a hail of Gatling gun gunfire to which Jimmy J could find no cover.

"You're a pig Jimmy J! I hate you!"

There was no visible blood from his wounds as he came from the house, but the gunfire found its way to his heart

– she was an expert shooter. Just moments before, a man amongst boys, now reduced to a near fetal position with an uncertain future.

"It's over". Jimmy J began to tell us. "My life is over".

He would never again have a girl like Betty Lou consider a life with him. He would not likely return to school nor would he ever marry. Sheer devastation. Tobias signals the posse to move on as he stays with Jimmy J. There is no confusion about laughter or crying now; it's all pure cry. Tobias' signal was an attempt to help Jimmy J maintain a spec of possible dignity from somewhere. As we looked back we could see Tobias just sitting next to Jimmy J. No way to know what was said as Tobias never broke confidences from private moments, but lo and behold Jimmy J was in school on Monday morning. Did Jimmy J have a healing with Tobias? Certainly, one does not recover from such a traumatic experience without some serious intervention. Tobias was the only one any of us would want around under such difficult circumstances. Even our parents would call for Tobias when something bad would happen, especially when need for privacy was involved --- not a typical strong point for this age group. It appeared Jimmy J would live, he would go to school and he would likely marry someday.

Jimmy J was a bit tentative around the girls on Monday --- they all knew. Betty Lou had to tell them. She had to protect them from such potential harms. By Tuesday however, Jimmy J was asking if any of them wanted a sampling and Betty Lou if she wanted another. Though this was not typical of Jimmy J and his relationship with girls, seemed he may have realized under such circumstances he needed the power and commonality of brethren behind him. Jimmy J is back and on the prowl seeking the affections of the girls with renewed vigor. Ah, the Beauty and innocence of such childhood moments.

With so much being experienced during their elementary school years, Tobias and his merry band of varying spirits entered their final year at the elementary school level. They were the BIG kids on the block now. What would they do with this kind of power? The group had begun to develop different relationships amongst itself. Taylor and Sadie began spending more time together since the latter half of the fifth grade. Seemed like an odd pairing of a close friendship but we are starting to learn that some friendships just don't have clear rules and guidelines. Sometimes heart and commonality take over. We just could not figure out what the commonality was. We knew the hearts were there though. What would they do at Sadie's house together, where they seemed to hang out a lot? We did know however, their relationship was not romantic, they just found something about each other that made them happier people. To the absolute shock of many, this would present itself during high school.

We would see Tobias for the first time in a more earthly light through his battle with his academic nemesis --- math, and specifically, 6th grade math. It was the subject that challenged Tobias a bit more than others. On this day, Tobias loudly stated how stupid math is because, as he stated, letters do not belong in math! Tobias' classmates did not know how to react as this was so very far away from their understanding of Tobias and his ways. Some nervously laughed while others remained silent. With immediacy, he observed the teacher to be displeased with the outburst. This affected Tobias deeply and he began to feel quite guilty for what he had done. Mr. Barnes was an exceptional teacher. He was relentless in his effort to find a way into each student's learning ways to put seed the concepts of math; not unlike water with its' constant journey to find cracks in which to continue its' journey. Mr. Barnes would try to do this in his teaching of math; he was a good teacher and a nice man.

The next morning, Tobias would seek out Mr. Barnes. He knew he had an open hour before his 3rd period math class. He knocked and was received.

"What's up Tobias?

With a somber face and head tilted downward, Tobias stated,

"I'm sorry for disrespecting math Mr. Barnes" and tears rolled down his face.

"That's OK Tobias".

"No, it's not! This is your passion; this means so much you chose it as a career and I disrespected it..

"OK, well I forgive you and we'll move forward together. I'll do my very best to help you understand why letters are now showing up in math".

As fate and teacher communication would have it, the teacher lounge had much fun with this story and began to latch onto the statement, "Don't disrespect English, Science, Social Studies, PE", etc. Tobias began to hear this repeatedly. Though he recognized the gentle tease behind the term he also recognized the potential good to come of it. Some of the teachers approached Tobias with good humor and thanked him for birthing this new concept. They felt it helped take the focus off them as persons and placed the learning frustrations more on the subject matter. Now kids were more apt to express their frustration with the subject matter as opposed to conflicting with the teacher. Though not always successful in such efforts, more success than previous methods.

With this last lesson, Tobias and his friends and classmates bid farewell to their elementary school years. Wilson would continue to amuse the masses with his reactions to the English language and its rules or, "lack thereof" he would say. The loud proclamation of, 'first name one L, second name two" would continue and amuse others but never himself.

These were school years that would be remembered many years forward. Some with joy, but some with pain, like the suicide of Sadie's brother, Henry, in May of 1970. Sadie would not talk of it but the newspaper did say Henry's sister found him. The power of the guns he and his Vietcong enemies used against each other he now used against himself. He came to view his own self as the enemy and decided to take action. The family would find some solace in the belief that Henry simply wanted to stop hurting them, especially Sadie. Unfortunately, that may have been his intention, but this family's pain was not lessoned by this action. It was a good thing Taylor had found something in common with Sadie as she needed a closer friend within this group during this time. Tobias would be invited into their secret together and we believed Sadie shared her pains with him; we all did when bad things happened. He was safe, he was comforting.

There was also sadness for Raymond's continued regression into isolation and sadness. I think Tobias took this the hardest. For some reason, Tobias did not seem to have an answer or plan for Raymond. This was so unlike him and it was hard to see him stuck. Though his heart broke for his early childhood friend, he would not talk about this with anyone. Attempts were made, even by Mr. Thompson on several occasions. Tobias would simply say he did not know how to help Raymond and that Raymond hated him. Tobias would sometimes plead with Mr. Thompson, a counselor, the local pastor, or even Mrs. Gilbrandt to help Raymond. They realized Tobias met a human he could not help for some reason and it pained him so. Raymond would hear of these attempts and confront Tobias publicly on many occasions.

"Tobias, mind your own business you idiot! You and I both know you are a fake and an idiot!" Raymond would yell, or sarcastically state.

For all the good to continue around Tobias' life so too would this pain. Yet, this exceptional person would move into another phase of life. One of much continued development for himself and those around him --- finding selves through skills and talents, finding relationships that matter more than usual, and finding increased interests.

Chapter V

The Junior High School Years (7th/9th '71-'74)

1) A Teacher Crush Brings Forth Questions About Sexuality

Seventh grade would start off with a bang as Jimmy J and his raging hormones would tell Ms. Gastin how beautiful she was. She was by the way. Don't know where she came from but she had to be a beauty queen or held some title associated with beauty. Jimmy J always believed his compliments were well- received and even desired most of the time. Our experiences with Jimmy J, however, proved he never truly understood when, where, how, or even why his compliments to females should take place. His impulsiveness in this realm would find him in trouble with female classmates and their boyfriends, however he now embarked on a journey not often walked. Telling Ms. Gastin she was so beautiful and that she, and her breasts, distracted him from focusing on his work; her reaction did not match his expected potpourri of reactions. It probably would have worked if he left out the focus on her breasts. Well, our friend just said what many were thinking but Jimmy J and all who witnessed this got the "boundary" lesson --- boys should never focus on the physical attributes of women, especially their teachers --- openly that is. The consequences were quite severe. The administrators were quite hard on Jimmy J, after all, they needed to rescue Ms. Gastin; an opportunity they all longed for. They should have thanked Jimmy J for the additional time they got to spend gazing and glancing at Ms. Gastin's breasts in close proximity.

The open acknowledgement for the appreciation of the female body seemed a rite of passage at this grade level but only with same agers or maybe upper level classmates. This, even more prevalent now, as the bastions of this male age group were now finding the hidden stash of their father's, grandfather's, or older brother's Playboy magazines. The search for these magazines appeared as instinctual as the newly born sea turtles dash for the waters of the ocean --- both unaware of the challenges that lie ahead. All will not make it to this unknown, but oft desired place. Yes, biology has its place, but culture has been proving fertile ground for how one views others --- in any way. Anyway, for those who succumb to the power of biology and culture seem not able to turn back. Jimmy J fell into this category. He probably found "the magazine" back in the second grade as evidenced by his sincere interest in the female condition.

Despite the gravity of this public compliment, Ms. Gastin would come to find him an interesting and likeable young man, though she had to watch how her affections for him presented. She understood the men of the school over-reacted in tone and days of suspension; much more than bullies got for fighting. Could you imagine --- a flirtatious relationship between a female teacher and male junior high boy? But his close friends saw it. Jimmy J's appreciation for females has now been received by an adult. He is the man to go to with all things female! Nonetheless, Tobias' Christian influence and pure goodness upon us still reigned. We had to be good kids and despite Jimmy J's weakness or strength (depends upon whom you talk to), he was never intending to be disrespectful. Tobias, and all of us, would help him polish his actions and all would be well as we moved Jimmy J through junior high school. He would certainly have some conflicts with other boys, though it would most often be associated with jealousies. Tobias would never need Jimmy J's consult about girls. He was in a world of his own. He had a much deeper understanding of things and what popular culture was spreading did not work on him.

Kannot Junior High is so different, so many more

kids and the differences between kids seem even more pronounced. You can see a little tiny girl walking through the halls holding the hand of a boy who has facial hair. It doesn't look right. Sometimes we see the little boy walking with the girl who is developing in ways Jimmy J, and many others, appreciate. This latter doesn't last long though as the focus of older and older boys, with all of its' peer perception power, become too much and the little guys become part of the patience mandate. They must wait for their own growth to be able to compete within this often cruel but normal social school-wide and school-long process.

Unfortunately, patience is not yet a virtue well understood or wanted so one who is challenged by it can live a slow and torturous life at school --- if this becomes their sole focus. This is a major reason why having other interests such as academics, music, or art can truly be beneficial. After all, most adults don't realize the masses of students observe school as first and foremost a social realm, the intensity of which varies, yet the masses come day in and day out to be amongst their friends not necessarily for learning's sake.

It also is during the junior high years that most kids begin defining themselves by their talents and skill sets: the athlete, the brainiac, the artist, etc. The groundwork of their high school identities, and likely post high school identities, are in great motion for most. The quest to truly begin finding oneself is underway. This is a usually thriving time for bullying behaviors as most humans have an innate calling to exploit the weaknesses of others to validate themselves. Not at Kannot Junior High though. Tobias' influence has been far greater than anyone can acknowledge. His bullying interventions in elementary school have benefitted the entire district and by the time we get to high school this influence would be there too. To have a bully-free junior high school environment is something not previously thought possible. Those who do not know him and have not witnessed his actions have much difficulty ascribing such a feat to a seventh-grade boy. But they will eventually. Almost needless to say, everyone really likes it. There will be some minor slips here and there simply because kids will still make mistakes. I look back on these times and think the adults engaged in more bullying than the kids. We just seem to learn better at times but I couldn't understand why back then.

Not to go undiscussed amongst the boys of the group, was the very private nature of the physical and biological development of boys. Jimmy J's exploits continued to bring this subject up. Oh, the urges! And they could only talk with each other about this for parents were now banned from this kind of discussion despite their best intentions to help them through it. Some parents able to boldly go there, others too scared, and others simply out of touch leaving the little men and little ladies to find their own way. Moms wanted to go there when the Dads did not or Dads wanted to go there when the Moms did not, thus creating even more tension around this topic. Not known or unable to conceive at the time, was that this walk has been made by nearly every boy around this age since, since …. well, a very long time ago. So, the kids find themselves addressing the topic amongst their closest circles through their own compassionate and loving ways --- just kidding. It would not be long before Jimmy J, Wilson and Taylor would wonder if Tobias had such urges.

Tobias seemed the odd man out on this topic. The boys had to know. On a 'boys only' hike to their favorite overlook on Sunset Mountain, named for this beautiful experience on any clear sky eve, they begin to open this proverbial can of worms.

"Hey Tobias, ever do anything with your thing?" Jimmy J asks.

Taylor then jumps on board.

"Yeah Tobias, we need your thoughts on this".

The boys giggle themselves into uncontrolled laughter. After several minutes of prodding and play, Tobias says, "I don't believe this is any of your business". Wilson very quickly deduces this response to indicate Tobias knows of what they speak. Gleefully, Taylor begins chanting in song-like rhythm,

"You did it, you do it, can't quit it, you pull it!"

Then they all start,

"Tobias did it, he does it, can't quit it, he pulls it!"

And on and on the song goes. They sing themselves into laughter while Tobias keeps walking slowly ahead. And finally,

"OK my friends I do agree that I believe ….."

And they all, with eyes seriously and intensely focused upon him, amazed they are about to get a response and it comes,

"You all did it, all do it, can't quit it, all pull it".

Tobias now giggling and singing, the boys are stunned. Tobias has shared a special moment with them. He has affirmed their normalcy; this is what they really sought from him. They knew if Tobias could find some silly with this, they could not be evil or shameful kids. Tobias, recognizing the origin of their needs, shared with them a very human moment, more so for their benefit than anything he needed. As in true Tobias manner, he then gives them a little speech on the privacy of the matter and the inappropriateness to any intent of public humiliation. The troupe gets it. They are joyous as a group and more importantly as individuals, their friend Tobias has validated them through his own humanness. This has not been a side they had yet observed in Tobias. Taylor has to add a final thought on the matter;

"Girls do it too you know".

Jimmy J, the lady's man, explodes into hilarity, while Wilson and Tobias just seem to stare off and seemingly ponder this.

"You're so stupid Taylor, girls don't have anything to pull!" Jimmy J commands.

Sounded reasonable and since Jimmy J was the authority on the female condition at the time, his wisdom would go unquestioned. Girls simply did not, nor could not do it. Tobias' knowledge of the opposite sex and how he presented interest in such, was quite different than Jimmy J's, heck, it was different from any of us. Though he played the fool well, in the end we learned he was always about respect, equality and compassion. He just loved others in an agopic way and

it is about to unfold in front of them.
Tobias Meets His Soulmate

From the first day Ramona Evans came to Kannot Junior High, Tobias had a different look about him. She was a painted girl and it was difficult to see her face behind it all. She got off the bus with a little brother and sister in tow. She would walk them directly to their classrooms. Tobias wanted to learn more of this girl and found where she was living. The family had moved from a neighboring district and rumor had it Ramona got in so much trouble at her previous school that she was expelled. She enters Kannot Junior High after the Easter Holiday break. This was an odd time for a child to leave and enter a school. It reinforced probable problems.

Tobias learned they only lived three blocks from his home. He would walk by her house during the early evening and weekends at times just to see if he could catch a glimpse of her and her family; at times, he did. He would notice her patience with her Mom's yells/directives and her tendency to always be around her little siblings. There was a man in the house, but he seemed detached and did not appear to interact with the family. He noticed Ramona's Mom in town on several occasions and he could see where Ramona got her paint from. He really liked this girl though he was invisible to her. She did not seem to notice many people around her. She just came to class, seemed miserable in there and laboriously communicated with teachers. I heard she was threatened by the principal with expulsion here at Kannot Junior High if she engaged in the "shenanigans" she did at her previous school.

Tobias begins moving closer to her within the school; classrooms, lunch, PE. She was in almost all his classes. At one point, she stops and says to him;

"Do you need something?" It was rhetorical, but Tobias being Tobias,

"Yes I do, it is a pencil, I need a pencil."

"Oh yeah, and do you need the pencil when you are

walking by my house all the time too?"

Tobias, being Tobias again,

"Actually, at those times I need a glass of water so if you would be so kind the next time I walk by to get me one that would be great".

Tobias was so excited she had been noticing him, while she seemed irritated she had to directly address this with him. Observing this discussion, Cindy Palermo had to, and if you knew Cindy you would really know she just had to let Ramona know that Tobias liked her.

"Oooooooooooohhhhhhhhhh, Tobias likes the new girl. No, for real Ramona, he really likes you", Cindy stated like a life-long friend.

Ramona made a disgust gesture and then told Cindy to buzz off and Tobias walked away feeling like a million bucks! He had her attention, she knew he existed. Cindy could not stop there however, as she knew of Tobias' allergy to a specific perfume. She remembered this from third grade. Tobias would begin tearing, nose running and sneezing and once it started it seemed to last throughout the day. They finally pinpointed the culprit; a girl's perfume, but not a common one. Nonetheless, the family agreed to not use it and all became well again. Cindy, wanting a new friend, since she generally exhausts the old ones, finds Ramona at the end of the day,

"Hey, I know how you keep Tobias away from you".

"Are you going to keep bothering me too?" Ramona says.

"No, I'm just trying to help"

"OK, how?"

"Pink Princess perfume; he's allergic to it. Wear it and he can't stay near you."

Ramona sees her brother and sister coming out of the school and leaves.

The next day Tobias begins his routine of being around Ramona and is excited to see how she notices him.

"OK kid, I see you and don't want you near me; besides, I'm engaged".

Tobias is not deterred. By day's end she has decided upon the more drastic action as her words of rejection and relationship commitment do not affect Tobias.

Tobias enters the classroom the next morning and moves by her and bam! As if hit by a bat, he begins the torturous reaction to the perfume. He quickly identifies the source. She smiles and he moves to the other side of the classroom. The teacher asks,

"Tobias, are you alright?"

"Yes, I'm OK Ma'am" --- through the nose wiping, eyes running and sneezes.

At the end of the day he sentences himself to another bout as he is committed to tell her the following.

"OK, I get it Ramona Evans. I know what you're doing. I will keep checking in with you and when I realize you are not wearing it I will ask you out; I promise".

These last two words Ramona knew all too well and simply laughed them off. Ramona says,

"Fine, your choice kid".

He states his name again,

"My name is Tobias".

"Like I said, your choice kid", she tells him.

Tobias walks away sneezing. The teacher and nurse asked her to stop wearing it but she cited her rights and then stated he could just stay away from her. She had her Mom convinced he was bothering her so she supported her daughter's decision to keep wearing the perfume.

Though the physical repercussions were difficult for Tobias, his heart just fluttered for Ramona. He takes advantage of her actions to prove his love for her. He seizes the opportunity to let her know she is worth all of this and more. Nobody could understand what he saw in this girl as she kept everyone else at bay and they gladly obliged. This was like Tobias' growing challenge with Raymond. Raymond was not easy to be around either, but Tobias appeared to have a soft spot for him and never liked it when someone spoke ill of him. This routine continued for the rest of 7th grade. Tobias never wavered. He watched as Ramona had brief relationships with other boys. He heard ugly rumors to which he would address in her favor and every now and then he would just find his way near her and openly suffer the consequences in effort to continue to prove his affections for her. Probably at some point in the 8th grade she began to find some humor and compassion with Tobias.

"Geez kid, why don't you just stop? You agree to stop coming near me and I'll stop wearing the perfume".

"Nope", said Tobias. You stop wearing it and I'll be near you all the time".

Though in front of Tobias she paraded her skills of rejection, he was sensing a new intrigue coming from her. Her look was changing he would tell disbelieving friends. We would all say,

"Tobias, we don't see anything changing man. C'mon there are other girls here".

"Nope, she's the one. She's the one I'll marry".

"Why, Tobias, why"?

"Because you only see her now and I see her everywhere; yesterday, today, and tomorrow. I see most people like this. You guys can't understand this now so you'll just have to trust me. I see her heart just like I see all of yours --- you have to be able to seethe and feel the heart first", he tells us, but it's just too deep for us and our best response,

"You're crazy!" and then go about the serious business of our junior high school years.

The business of farting, burping, discussing their expertise of the female condition, especially the boobies, the business of masturbation and the making of the associative gesture to the other guys were all matters of significance. This really was a club in which all males were welcome --- very serious and time intensive stuff and all the while being plagued by the demands of the more minor inconveniences, like family and school. During all such behavior and discussion, Tobias generally remained quiet unless it led to hurting someone. Other than that, he seemed to find some humor in these things though he did not actively participate. He would just get weird, like the weird wisdom stuff.

"Tobias pulls it?" was the taunt needed to maintain the bond made in the seventh grade as it felt this kept us all "real" with him.

All he would say,

"Do most or all guys at this age and older, do it?"

"Yes", would be the answer to come. "But when you start having sex with girls it stops" says Jimmy J.

The consensus of this brain-trust determined that at some point during high school --- for the luckies - masturbation of the male species ceases forever. Contrary to popular belief, or popular desired belief, everyone in high school was not having sex. It was a much smaller group than most thought. It was simply a statement made in attempt to raise one to a perceived higher level amongst peers. It often worked, but more importantly girls were hurt because at some point a boy would feel he had to state or make an inference to his conquest. Boys would then be hurt by the perceptions made of them for their dishonesty and serious violation into the life of another person --- but it was often deemed worth the consequence. This is perhaps the ugliest side of the maturation process --- the lack of insight into the hearts of others and not always age associated.

During the adolescent phase, insight frequently takes a back seat to no sight and hindsight is not often sought for the totality of a lesson learned. In response to our probes, Tobias would only say,

"OK, you already answered this question".

"What's that mean Tobias?"

"I'm not saying, I'm just saying, you answered your question".

We knew to never do this publicly with him, but we never saw the gentle humor we saw with him on that fateful hike to Sunset Mountain. We found this as odd as Tobias' disinterest in any girl other than Ramona, even though they were not going out and even though some other girls did like him. They would tell him so – usually through someone else but he would soon after approach them and say,

"Thank you for liking me, but I don't not have those same

kinds of feelings, I only have those for Ramona Evans".

They would either tell him he's weird, start crying, or just walk away confused. However, Tobias would never forget their interest in him and he would always be there to help should they need a friend. Oh, and Ramona Evans, hated the fact that Tobias would openly tell people of his affections for her. Even the brief boyfriends, attempting to flex their pre-ad or adolescent muscles would approach Tobias and tell him to stop. Tobias never showed fear from angry threatening adults so same-agers would certainly not elicit it. This reaction kept many an aggressor at bay. Not only would this freak them out, he would then tell them how lucky they were to be with Ramona and congratulate them. They would usually walk away feeling kind of good – kinda. We loved watching him when in such potential conflicts. He was one of the most popular kids, but not by any active desire of his own. Most knew he was just different. He was likeable, a leader through action and less frequently word. He was a friend to all who allowed him to be and the only ones who didn't, Ramona and Raymond.

One would think he would have many girls wanting to be around him, but Tobias's physical presentation was not apparently attractive to many girls. He had a growth spurt, yet his spurt took him from a lanky youngster to a young man with an odd pear-shaped body. His physical presence was one of friendship and compassion not one of mad/ passionate desire, at this age anyway. Most kids could not see the person within; the focus was on the external and though girls frequently take the harder hit on this topic, the boys also had their place in this adolescent storyline. When reminded of this by his concerned friends, Tobias would only smile and say,

"Ramona doesn't care about these things".

We would say,

"Sure she does, look who she dates!"

"Do those relationships last, are they meaningful?" he would say.

"Tobias she's 14, we're 14, what are you talking about"!

He spoke in a different language to us and we did not always understand him. There was no 'Tobias language class' only English, Spanish, and French would be coming up in high school.

3) Friendships Strengthen and He keeps on Trying

Our friendship circle remained strong. We were committed to each other. Sadie was coming out on the other side of her grief. We could see her silent joyous nature coming back. Her smiles began to present in a sincere manner at some time during the seventh grade. Up until that time, she smiled for the benefit of others only. Now, she is smiling again for herself. She is a survivor and she cares deeply for people but she does not ever communicate this verbally. She hurts deeply for pets not well taken care of too. We saw her many times crying over a stray dog or cat and we know there were many times her parents came home to new visitors. They too were good people. They would sometimes take the new pets in and sometimes take them to a vet or animal shelter in the Honesdale or Scranton areas. This family was not hardened by the loss of Henry. They became stronger together and they came out of the sharpest of pain still with love for their neighbors and four-legged creatures. They began spending energies trying to support our young men coming home from war – women were not yet fully recognized for their efforts. The nightly news would present the body counts and the scenes of anti-war protestors pushing and spitting at the young soldiers as they got off buses, trains and planes to come back to their homes. Though nothing occurred on this level in Kannot there were anti-war activists here. We watched all of this. One had to think this kind of homecoming to be a major contributing factor to the many lives of isolation, shame, guilt, and anger, much like their son Henry, succumbed to. This was a family that did not remain silent should they hear of or observe a young soldier being degraded. The anti-war arguments would be better understood if there was a pro-war movement but there were no groups marching with such banners. I guess it's possible, but people who may agree on the necessity of a war may not actually like it. I like the pro-peace agenda and so would the Spagnotti's. I wonder if people would be able to see this in retrospect? But Sadie was probably the closest to Tobias when it came to being able to see and feel hearts.

Sadie and Taylor's mysterious relationship within this group has maintained. The only one not curious was Tobias. That bugger knew everything; I know this for sure. He would just smile when we would try to get it out of him.

"What do they do together, Tobias?" we would take turns asking.

Taylor and Sadie had long ceased with any response to our questions. Tobias would say,

"Is Sadie happier? Does Taylor look happier? Isn't this the most important thing we should recognize about their friendship?"

After all, Taylor's eccentricities isolated him from many peers too. He was so exceptional with his mind and his music, that most peers and adults simply could not connect with him, nor he them. Tobias reminded us that our acceptance of them and their relationship with each other within this group was a contributing factor to their evolving happiness. He cautioned us to not interfere with this because of simple curiosity and that our curiosities would be answered at some time. Our unconditional trust in Tobias prompted our full-fledged support of our friends.

Collette's schooling experience continued to get better. With all the changes and progress made at the elementary levels, the Junior High School teacher, Mrs. Jasper, had a wealth of information and strategies provided to her from Ms. Hathway. Collette was becoming more patient with her peers as her peers became more willing to be around her. Still, no one understood her like Tobias. As a group, we believe Collette knew almost everything that went on within our group and school. Most perceived her as a very good listener since she did not seem able to communicate successfully on the expressive level. Communication with

Collette must have seemed like going to a confessional if Catholic --- peers unloaded on her, yet were given the added bonus of no Hail Mary's. It was a wonderful thing they must have thought. Wilson one day posited to his boy mates,

"You don't think Tobias ever told her about our hike to Sunset Mountain, do you?"

"C'mon Wilson, give Tobias some credit. He doesn't give up private information but I bet she knows a lot more than anyone can imagine" Taylor observed.

"You're probably right, maybe we should learn to communicate with her better. You know, to get an idea of how much she understands about things", Jimmy J follows.

"Yeah", the others state in agreement. All the while they all ponder if Collette knew 'everything'.

The group begins their increased investment with Collette due to their own insecurities but one could speculate her biggest fan, Tobias, did not care why such efforts were taking place only that such efforts were taking place. He knew better than anyone that once people started to understand Collette they too would welcome her into their lives.

The Ramona story was always near. The elementary school was next door so Tobias would observe Ramona with her siblings daily as she walked them to their classes. He would observe the care she gave in the way she held their hands. He would observe the attention she gave when they were speaking to her. He would observe the patience for some naughty behaviors at times. He just totally enjoyed watching her and she was always aware. When Ramona was not at school for some reason, she was very uncomfortable when her brother, Elijah, and sister, Eleanor were not in her environment. Tobias understood this and looked out for them when Ramona was not around. It was a mystery if she knew about this. He would walk them to their classes, hands held and talk with them. He would not tell them his name. He would only say he is the patrol boy, even though he wasn't. Ramona did not miss much school, odd for a girl who was reportedly expelled for behavior problems at a previous school. Was she one of those kids the teachers wished would miss more school? When the kids would go home and speak of the nice patrol boy, it was perceived as something a patrol boy was just expected to do. In practice, whenever this happened, Tobias would get to class late and receive demerits. He'd thank the principal for them and the principal would smile. Receiving a consequence for a righteous action was something Tobias held in high regard. One of his heroes had much to do with this. School administrators and teachers knew they would never add up to a problem for Tobias, but they felt they had to remain consistent with the system. There really was no other student operating on this plane so these actions touched their hearts deeply. They would later proudly proclaim they gave Tobias demerits. It was a way in which they would share a special aspect of their relationship with others about him.

The patrol boy on the bus received a gracious gift of Ramona --- she would no longer give the little man a hard time. That was her way of saying thanks. She never publicly acknowledged him with her siblings and they never publicly acknowledged him to her. All was well in the world when Ramona could not make it to school and this was no small feat for these two little ones, whom also had some behavioral challenges evolving. Ramona always experienced stress and anxiety for them when she could not go to school, but no longer. She was now able to let go, and with the challenges of this family, this was no small feat. Issues of trust, rejection, and desertion abounded. Though she could never see such skills in her daily experiences with this patrol boy, she was comforted he was able to do this when she could not.

Tobias knew that one day Ramona would figure this out, but he thought let that be one day, but for today, while she still rejected or resisted him, it was the patrol boy. The rejection – resistance issue was in constant debate amongst Tobias' friends with rejection winning out, however, Tobias was quite at peace with his resistance stance. But something changed when school returned after the Holiday Season. Tobias made his usual round past Ramona and the allergen impact did not occur. There was no perfume in the air around

Ramona. He was initially surprised simply because of the longevity of his routine; he had just come to expect it even though he knew one day it would cease, he had habitually began reaching for his handkerchief. He was just surprised it was this day and immediately seized the moment.

"Hi Ramona" he blurts out.

"Don't make a big deal of this Tobias and don't talk to me in here".

"OK, see you at recess?"

"Yeah".

This man among boys fumbled about all morning. He was as off task as a kid could be; didn't volunteer any questions or answers, minimal interactions with his teachers or classmates; just out of sorts for Tobias. But we knew what knocked him there. Tobias finds Ramona at recess.

"Hello again Ramona". "

"Tobias, don't make a big deal out of this and don't talk to me too long here either".

"When can I talk to you for a longer time?"

"Well, you know when you walk by my house every evening, well this evening just come into the yard a little bit".

"OK".

And he would.

The "first date", as he called it, and "the meeting", as Ramona called it, was arranged. Tobias had it all planned out, and I mean ALL planned out. He goes to Ramona's house on Friday evening. She lets him in and as the little brother and sister enter the front room they explode in joy to see Tobias.

"Hi patrol boy!"

Tobias awaits Ramona's reaction but what she offers was quite unexpected.

"Think I'm stupid Tobias. They see you walking around the house here too, especially during the Christmas Break --- Twice a day? Didn't you have anything else to do?"

"I was just getting my exercise and I shovel snow for some of the neighbors on your block too".

"I never saw a shovel".

"Well, I assess first and then I go back home for the shovel".

"You're an idiot Tobias".

These two reminded many of us of Charlie Brown and Lucy. Lucy's always picking up that ball and watching Charlie Brown land flat on his butt.

Ms. Evans enters the room and Ramona introduces her to Tobias.

"Tobias, this is my mom, Camille Evans", and then goes back to her room to get ready. Ms. Evans is quite painted; smoking, and staring Tobias down. There is great physical similarity between this Mom and Ramona. There is no father in the picture, nor mentioned since she arrived in Kannot, but there have been men observed at the home, but Ramona never speaks of them. There were rumors of alcoholism in the family; a father who eventually viewed his family as the poison rather than the alcohol itself and a Mom who now seems to drink to numb herself from years on a marital battlefield, one that has left three children in its wake and she seems unable to recognize she now sustains the wake. Ramona, being the oldest, probably took, and takes, the brunt of the parental dysfunctions to protect her younger siblings. These were speculations that moved forward with increased credibility over the years. After an uncomfortable amount of silence, she asks,

"What are your intentions for my daughter?"

"Well, Ms. Evans. I believe we will get through the rest of our high school years strengthening our relationship. There will be some challenging times I'm sure, but as the love grows stronger and the hearts fonder, we will make it. I promise to support Ramona in whatever decision she chooses after high school. I would never hold her back. She will probably get a little nervous during our senior year because she will be thinking I will leave her but let me assure you I will not. I will be a very good chef at that point and will be able to find work anywhere. Marriage could come soon after high school or possibly after schooling or whatever. I would be supportive of what she chooses post high school. And I know you might be a little worried about the grandparent thing, but I am happy to announce you will eventually come to love the role and you will become good at it".

"Kid, what are your intentions this evening with my daughter?"

"OK so you got the bigger picture, as for this evening, we will be right over there at the burger place. I brought these binoculars so you could check on us if you choose. You can see the seat we will be sitting in from your side window; if you want her home earlier than 9:00 here is the restaurant's number. Also, Mrs. Evans, and it may be early to say something like this, but I do believe smoking is not good for you and it is very bad I think to smoke indoors; one for fire hazard and two for the smoke all the kids are breathing in. But just something to think about".

Minimal verbal reaction through the entirety of Tobias' banter but she sarcastically smiles at Ramona as she reenters the room and says,

"Quite different from anything you've ever brought here".

"Mom, I don't bring anyone in here".

"Exactly, probably should have omitted this one too".

The date/meeting seems to go off without a hitch. Tobias just needed to get past this first date. He knew it was all downhill or uphill from there and he was ready for whatever the pitch.

Later that evening when Ramona was tucking in her siblings, her Mom beckons her from the TV room.

"Ramona, tell that kid I want an explanation about the "eventually" comment.

"Eventually what?"

"Just tell him I want to know what he meant by that".

Now, he had the attention of them both!

The next day at school, as if Ramona needed to save face, she begins her perfume regimen again. Tobias sneezes and snots the entire day because he just could not stay far away from her.

"Well, it hurts that you are doing this but it simply won't do it", he says to her.

"Do what?" she says.

"Push me away".

"We'll see about that and don't talk to my mother anymore; she thinks you are strange".

"Please thank her for the honest observation. She meant a good strange, right?"

As school years and summers passed, ninth grade was upon us. Music would play an odd role in Tobias' next effort to bring Ramona 'home' to him. He really did use this terminology. We thought he was losing it. Tobias once told us he learned to dance to some songs by Herb Alpert and the Tijuana Brass and Ferranti and Teicher. One truly should know the kind of music these folks made in order to understand how strange a statement this was. Apparently, he used to dance with his parents to these songs as they were two of Jonathan's favorite artists. From Herb's sparky hip brass thing to Ferranti and Teicher's larger than life musical events like Theme from Exodus. These styles certainly ran the gamut of what one could express in dance ----- though not sure if much of their music was meant to be expressed in dance. Tobias apparently thought so. Jonathan and Maggie were probably being silly with him yet Tobias ended up with a dance style born from these experiences; a dance style he found no ills with; he was prideful of it. It was not pretty to watch and watch we all would at school dances. It was painfully mesmerizing. You just could not take your eyes off him. There were certainly lessons to be learned here, but they were not going to come during the high school years; there was much too much maturity required for this learning process. He would simply tell us,

"You have to find your own dance fellas and when you do you will know it".

The boy could not get a girl to dance with him, though they were mesmerized too, but different from the boys; they loved his joy. There were some boys who would try to mimic him, but they would only try once. The joyful physical self-expression Tobias found was not to be found by others in mimicry. It could not be done and these attempts to copy the master left them walking off the dance floor, heads hanging low and without the silliness and laughter they initially brought to the floor. The strangeness, the uniqueness, the joyful spirit Tobias would prance himself about the dance floor was just for him. We were now certain his joyful and confident nature truly came from within as there was not one thing about the external nature of his dance that could do this for anyone else.

A song by Tommy James and the Shondells would feed Tobias' drive for his newest strategy in pursuit of his sweetheart. It had been around for a while but Tobias had recently begun walking around singing it. He was learning the lyrics. He apparently thought it was a sweet idea to consider the song title words, Mony, Mony as a potential nickname for Ramona. This boy was deeply love-struck. He was willing to make the biggest fool of himself and do it publicly. To add another dimension to this, no one could understand his wisdom within this realm, the relationship realm. We understood Tobias' wisdom surrounded many things, but could not see it in this area. He baffled us. As alluded to earlier, this promoted an appearance of a boy who would soon be placed into a psychiatric institution. We were trying to go along with him and support him, but his relentless, though patient and compassionate pursuit of Ramona, was becoming somewhat unsettling.

Tobias had known Ramona's birthday within an hour after he set eyes upon her. He would present her with a gift and she would leave it in her last class of the day. This was painful to watch, but Tobias never looked pained. Nonetheless, this behavior further estranged us from Ramona, but we could not show this to Tobias. She was not in our hearts and minds in a good way, yet Tobias always tried to keep our perceptions of her in check. "You cannot see her yet as I see her, just hang in there", he would repeatedly say. We all hoped he would come up with something a bit more traditional in expressing his adoration like a box of chocolates, some flowers, or a little card. Even with these things we were in much compromise with our feelings due to rejection's perfection by Ramona. Being in our early teens, May was a lifetime away and maybe if we were to forget about it, the event would not take place. In our hearts, we knew Tobias would not forget. To him it would be just one more opportunity to request Ramona into his life and he had used this term.

Matters other than relationships were occurring as well.

4) Tobias' Physical Gifts Exposed

Tobias had apparently kept a secret from all his friends regarding his physical abilities and capacities. He was enticed into football during our freshman year due to his height and weight. The fact the coach needed more players to meet the minimal league requirements to field a team prompted a blitzkrieg of recruiting before the freshman team began its' games. Tobias was about 5'11' and 190 pounds at that time, but his shape and that seemingly soft belly provided cover for any possible athletic ability. We knew of his strength as exhibited the time we were moving railroad ties for Taylor's father. We were to move the pile from point A to point B as directed by Mr. Hughes. Mr. Hughes seemed to assign this to Taylor and his group of marauders as a punishment of sort for something. Maybe the trampling of his flower bed last week during our game of football in his yard or maybe the broken window in the kitchen that Taylor said was from a rock thrown by the lawn mower. Mr. Hughes would tell us a few times, "Strange boys, never found the rock". Ok, so maybe it was the football, at least we learned Jimmy J could really kick that thing; he just did not have good directional control yet. Mr. Hughes assigned the task and walked inside with a wry smile upon his face. Coming back out 20 minutes later with the apparent expectation of ridiculing our physical limitations, he was perplexed. The entire pile, all 50 ties, were moved and stacked neatly.

"OK, who else helped"? he stated.

"Just us Dad, but actually Tobias did most of it. Show

him Tobias!" Taylor gleefully pleads.

"I'm tired, got to get home" says Tobias.

"Yeah right boys. I'll find out who helped and I may have another task for you all soon" as Mr. Hughes moved back into the house with his suspicions intact.

We knew of Tobias' strength from things like this, yet his quickness and athletic prowess were something else altogether. Knowing Tobias and his commitment to teamwork and doing one's best, in retrospect we should have not been so surprised. When that coach gave his first day of practice speech about teamwork, hard work, always play to the best of your ability, Tobias was all in. These were words and concepts well-ingrained into the life of our friend. It is still odd to wonder why he could not lose that extra weight around the midsection that helped foster the pear shape he had become known for. The shoulders looked smaller than they were and the same for his legs --- all a concert of deception to which opposing players and coaches would initially subscribe to. He just did not look the part. But to see the speed, agility and power this kid could muster during practice was awesome. He did not exhibit his explosive power too much in scrimmage because he did not want to hurt his teammates. He probably gave between fifty and seventy-five percent during practice, but when game day came, Tobias was all business and in the spirit of sport he would play his butt off for his team. Should the team lose, his head was never low. He would say, "Nothing to be sorry/regretful for, I gave it my best, they simply played better today". Then he would ask his teammates, "Did you give your best?" If they hesitated he would then give them permission to sulk. If they said yes, he would say great! He was the optimal sportsman. He never played to beat someone. He played to win. Two different perspectives he would tell us. When you play to beat someone, you are giving away a lot of power, power you need to win and do your best. You are giving away emotional power to strangers, or at least to people you don't know so well. I want to maintain all my power to win for my team, my family, my friends, and our school. Unfortunately, the masses never really latched on to this as evidenced by the 'beat this team or that team' banners that would inevitably present on many a porch, window, and car for game weekend. But he did manage to sway most of his team members and even coaches over the years to his philosophy of sport, which he would always state as the true meaning and intention of sport. We learned these things about Tobias through our community clubs and teams and PE classes. Now he was about to share his gifts on the football field with The Kannot Junior High School Spartans.

5) A Committed Teammate and Friend – And He's Still Trying

The season began and Tobias was devastating to other freshman teams. It almost seemed unfair. He never took his helmet off until the locker room. This, and the fact that the uniform covered much of his physique's oddness, he would never be recognized, nor believed, to be the person they either watched or read about in the paper over the weekend. He was not supposed to be able to do the things he was doing because of his physical appearance. But he was doing it and doing it better than ever seen before in Kannot and maybe the region. Though Tobias had minimal formal understanding of the game, the coach wanted to begin playing him on the varsity team. Tobias refused. I don't think they could do this today, but the rules were different back then; probably vague rules manipulated by coaches and schools for all the wrong reasons. Tobias would have none of it. He said he wanted to play all his football games with his grade level teammates. If expected to play varsity without his classmates, he would cease to play. Tobias did not say things like this in threatening manner. He'd say something like, "No coach, I can't do that. I need to stay with my team here. If you tell me I must do this than I will choose not to play at all. If this happens is there any other way I can help the team?" He was not a penetrable person when it came to his views of right and wrong. He stuck to this even though his freshman teammates told him to go ahead. Ultimately, he remained on the freshman team.

A decision he would refer to during the next three years of varsity play. There was always a lesson. Sometimes he had to walk us through it, sometimes we just listened or watched. We definitely learned things at the time, but we would learn even more in reflection.

The football season came and went and Tobias and Tommy Hollister were front and center in all dialogues about the future of Kannot High School Spartan football. Tommy, long since the days of defiance and opposition, is now an excellent team player and friend to many. He understands Tobias and has learned to follow his attitude toward sports well. However, Tommy looks the part of an athlete. He is six feet tall, 185 pounds and growing. His muscle definition is exceptionally defined for a 14-year-old and he understands the intricacies of sports. Tobias does not yet fully understand the game so Tommy will work with Tobias during the summer because they both are invested in the team. Each would play on both sides of the ball --- not uncommon for teams with small rosters so they knew they needed to be in top shape for the season. They would be guards, linebackers, fullbacks. They would aggress for Spartan kickoffs and punts and block for Spartan returns. They would become the ultimate two-way players, yet life at school and all other places would continue to happen as well. Despite all this excitement, the inevitable came back to haunt us.

Darn! It's May and Ramona's birthday event nears. As fate would have it, Tobias doesn't forget. Nothing different has changed regarding Tobias' feelings about Ramona. We've pointed out all the boys she has "dated" during the year and the rumors. We do this to break him of her evil spell. We do this one day in mass, after school in Sadie's back yard. Collette is the only one not there as her parents remain apprehensive to allow her into this very active group. Taylor, Wilson, Jimmy J and Sadie complete the half-moon shape of the intervention. The meeting is skillfully disguised as a meeting to talk about the school year and discuss summer plans. It's a reasonable and witty cover. At some point, someone will take advantage of a segue moment to move the discussion toward the Ramona birthday stuff. As if on cue, while in her kitchen and near the open kitchen window, Mrs. Spagnotti begins belting out "I Think We're Alone Now, by Tommy James and the Shondells. Is she taunting us? Did Sadie tell her? No, she didn't even know we were out there. It was just happenstance and/or the power of the universe supporting Tobias' musical choice. But, she sounded great. Sadie never spoke of her mother's talent. Back to the matter at hand after the serenade ends.

We are a resourceful and, I might add, a brilliant lot when we put our heads together. So here we go and, as Wilson playfully introduces himself as "Wilson Willson, first name one L last name two", Tobias interrupts,

"Ok, let me try to settle you guys down about my gift to Ramona next week".

With that statement seems I must detract the "brilliant lot" previously stated.

"I'm needing your trust still".

"Tobias, she goes out with other guys", Wilson reports.

"Tobias, she's rejected you for nearly three years now" says Taylor.

"Tobias, I don't want to see you hurt", Sadie states in her gentle compassionate tone.

Jimmy J breaks this brief loving statement with an aggressive parlay of situations over the last three years,

"… these things in no way indicate this girl desires you! Please Tobias, listen to me, I know girls".

"OK everyone". Tobias ceases their intervention. "I know you worry for me so here's my stand: She only goes out with other boys to keep me at arm's length, the rumors are not true, you still cannot see her, and you truly do not know this girl. She's weakening and things may get worse before they get better. She is a loving and beautiful person and she is mistrustful and scared. Do I look hurt by her behaviors toward me? Do I look frustrated? Have I been harmed in some way?"

The group looks about each other and has to come to a conclusion that supports Tobias' argument.

"But" Wilson says. "But, what you do Tobias everyone sees, and they talk and we hear the things they say about you and …"

"Wilson", Tobias interjects. "Does it appear that these things bother me? They don't. Have you ever seen me bothered by what other's do, could, or would say about me?"

The group is challenged to reflect again and their conclusion, again, supports his argument. Tobias continues

---

"Let me share something with you and this is something I share to show you my heart. This is something I want us all to keep in mind as we move into High School as relationships come into play more and more" and Tobias begins:

Love is patient, love is kind. It does not envy, it does not boast, it is not proud. It is not rude, it is not self-seeking, it is not easily angered, it keeps no record of wrongs. Love does not delight in evil but rejoices with the truth. It always protects, always trusts, always hopes, always perseveres".

Tobias falls silent as the group takes in what just occurred. Tobias has, for the first time, quoted something from the bible we think, and he is tearful. He's allowing us time for this message to sink in. This message clarifies Tobias and his pursuit of Ramona and it has brought about an emotion none of us could have foreseen. It is the strength behind all he does with her. It seems to be a resource that is behind his strength, period. We can see this now. Sadie is crying, Wilson and Taylor are wiping a tear or two caused by the proverbial piece of dirt or bug that has infiltrated their eyes and Jimmy J looks off into the distance. Jimmy J has probably never looked so deep into love before. He seems numbed by the moment. After about two minutes, a very long period of silence, especially for this crew, Tobias says,

"OK, you should get it now. Your concerns should not be for me but for Ramona and I really do want you to understand agape love so do some homework".

Wilson asks, "When did you memorize that saying Tobias?"

"What saying?", he responds.

"The one you just told us about 'Love', says Wilson. "I don't know, I always knew that" he responds as if we should, have known it too.

Most of us came to know the Bible was such a part of Tobias' life it just unfolded with his life, and at times it seemed even he was unaware of the lessons and impact it had upon him. And with that moment passed, Tobias begins talking about our sophomore year and our summer plans. We engaged as much as one could engage after this incredible spiritual punch to the heart. Why is it that we can go through life and never have a pastor or priest site the exact bible verse or principal at the exact right time? This was what Tobias could do. It was the perfect time, the perfect situation. He used this lesson in Corinthians to teach his beloved young friends about love, and we got it. This is something else not often to happen amongst a group of 14- year-olds. We listened, we understood, and we began our own journeys to incorporate the gift Tobias offered us today. This was the first time we saw the spiritual power of Tobias present itself directly. We suspected this was in there, yet we never really talked about it. All the goodness we've been exposed to over the past nine years or so with him; is this why? Would this change how we would communicate with him? We did not talk about it, but we wondered and we hoped. We would never again question Tobias' love for Ramona, never. We would now applaud him.

6) *The Dance*

Here we are, May 25th, 1974 Ramona's birthday. The day begins like any other of the school year. Stresses about exams to come within the next two weeks are mixed with the near-to-come excitement of the summer vacation. What a combination; an intense need to focus, with an equally intense need to daydream. But ne'er the two shall meet and certainly not work together for any positive outcome. The lesson to be learned is to "Focus on matters (good grades) at hand", "Good things (good grades) don't come easy", "Keep your eye on the prize (good grades)". The problem --- all these statements all being preached excessively by teachers and parents alike --- we don't necessarily believe them yet. We'll subscribe to our own wisdoms thank you. There just must be balance here as we refuse to believe in complete focus on all things school.

Anyway, Ramona is only in two of Tobias' classes; English and music. Of course, he will do this in the English class as it will stand out more. Yeah, wouldn't want to try and blend it in to the school day within a class that, at least when later defending the action in court, he could say 'It was music and it was in music class". Nope, he would place himself at the mercy of the court and a potential life sentence because there would be no relationship to subject matter for a boy prancing about an English class singing Mony, Mony by Tommy James and the Shondells.

Tobias' teamwork with Ms. Hathway often had Collette in the regular classroom with him; this was the case with this English class. Tobias would tell people how receptive Collette was and how hard she was working on her expressive capabilities. "She's quite talented" he would tell anyone willing to listen. Sadly, most seemed to humor him and even Ms. Hathway much of the time. They seemed to believe no harm, no foul, so they allowed this partnering if Tobias was looking out for her. Collette would be a witness to what was going to happen, as would Wilson. They adored their friend and all that he stood for so they would come to find the patience and compassion for Ramona that he modeled ever so well.

The third period bell rang. The only one not in the classroom as Mrs. Pavlesky called role was Tobias. Already odd, since the boy was almost always the first one in class. Even Ramona was looking about from her back-row seat. This girl tried to stay as far away from any teacher attention. There are historic spots in classrooms in which generations of children have proven relatively sound from such attention; for example, the back row, but not the middle of the back row and either the left or right end seats in the front row. There were, however, some teachers that would purposely go after the hiders. Generally speaking, though, most teachers seemed to either appreciate the privacy of the child who would choose such areas or they would appreciate the opportunity to easily avoid said child. Tobias would usually place himself dead center, but since he needed more space from Ramona due to the perfume thing, he sits front row and center thus making it very easy to observe his presence or absence.

He is about to be noted as absent for the class when he enters the room with his accomplice. He carries his 8-track stereo to the front of the room, plugs it in, goes back outside the door and brings in two speakers. He comes back in and hooks up the speakers and pushes in the tape. Mrs. Pavlesky had to know what he was about to do. She just sat there watching this boy go through the motions of setting up his stage, which seemed to go on forever; probably about five minutes.

"Hi everybody!" Tobias begins. "Today is Ramona's 15th birthday and I have a present for her".

Ramona, has perfected her ability to ignore whatever Tobias tosses at her as if classically trained. From someone in a side row comes,

"Are you going to dance Tobias?"

"Yes, I am, and sing too!"

With that his classmates began to move their seats away from Ramona. Really, you had to feel bad for Ramona. For as much as we observed her rejections of Tobias, no one should have to go through this. The open space in the room now an empty space of a just prior eight-desk area directly in front of her. She really was trapped, but she had her English book and she seemed so much more invested in its contents now than at any other point during the entire school year. All the time, Mrs. Pavlesky just watching. The tape is in, he hits the power and clicks it to the track of "The Song". Tobias had a way of having moments given their own titles. And he's off!

"Here she comes now Mony, Mony
three chords thump
Shoot em down, turn around, Come on Mony

----- ----- -----

Hey, she give me love and I feel alright now

----- ----- -----

You gotta toss and turn in the middle of the night
   And I feel alright,
 I say yeah, (yeah) yeah (yeah) yeah"

And he dances. No, I'll stick with the way it was described before; prancing. He's jumping and twirling and singing along with the music. He's throwing his hands in the air, his legs are doing things like …; they're just doing things. His odd physical stature along with his athletic abilities make this look even odder than it is. And there's Ramona, reading her English book, but her pace appears to be picking up as she is turning the pages a bit quicker.

"Wake me shake me Mony, Mony
three chord thump
Shot gun dead and come on Mony

Tobias is in his heaven. At this point we're not sure he even knows where he is. Prancing, jumping, spinning, kicking and Ramona reads on, but she now appears to be an avid student of Evelyn Wood's speed reading course. The pages are turning faster and harder, close to rip stage. And the singing and the song begins to lead out of its final chorus:

"Come on!
Come on!
…………
Mony, Mony
All right
Mony, Mony
All Right"

And there was to be no reprieve during the base instrumental of this song for Tobias would prance through it as if it were a melodic symphony. His moves did not match the music, rarely did. This can be directly blamed on Herb Alpert and the Tijuana Brass and Ferranti and Teicher. Somewhere around three minutes after it began, it had finished. Even Ramona's expert ability to ignore Tobias had shown cracks in its armor. She appeared to have gone through the book several times and there were some ripped pages, but in the end, she just nestled back into her initial position; total oblivion to what was about to happen and now to what had just happened.

"Happy birthday Ramona!" he says, standing directly in front of her.

She responds and moves not. She sat there, seemingly unaffected, as Tobias began to break down the stereo and speakers and remove them from class. The classmates move their seats back to their proper spaces and Tobias arrives to take his seat front and center. And then Mrs. Pavlesky states,

"Tobias, what happened to the 'simple little happy birthday song'?"

'The Dance" was the gossip of the day. Fortunately, exams were in full review along with project deadlines presenting daily across subject matter. The attention such an act would receive at most points during the school year could not at this time of year. Ramona was saved by this timing. We all met with Tobias after school that day.

"She cracked, she cracked" he proclaimed. "She did not fully ignore me!"

Wilson states, "Tobias, how could she totally ignore you, you were doing that dance thing and singing to her?"

"Exactly! Wilson, Exactly! I believe she still could have ignored me but she did not".

"I don't know Tobias", Jimmy J said, "Maybe what you saw was intense irritation".

"Nope, trust me, she's close to accepting my request for her affections", Tobias offers as his final surmise.

With those words the group moves on. They end their freshman year at Kannot Junior High to begin the excitement of a summer. A summer to play, a summer to plan, and a summer to dream of what comes next at Kannot High School.

Chapter VI

The Summer of '74 — The Love of Friends

Events to unfold during this summer of 1974 lay much of the groundwork for the new world of high school to come soon. Some have jobs; others are in full-time play mode, while another seems imprisoned by a mixture of love and fear. Collette, for all her progress, remains homebound much of the time. Tobias thought he was further along with her parents then what was occurring. Her parents and Tobias would be headed for a confrontation.

A couple weeks into the summer Tobias calls upon the group to meet him at his home one early Saturday afternoon.

"We're going to get Collette out of her house today", he tells them.

Tobias' phone calls to Mr. and Mrs. Adams had not been returned since school ended and they had turned him away from their door repeatedly. They simply tell him Collette is not up for visitors. Tobias believes going to the Adam's home in masse would help move the communication forward.

"Tobias, if her parents won't let us take her out, you really can't make them", Taylor says.

"Not going to make them do anything Taylor, just going to show love", he responds.

Reassured by his motivation for the march to Collette's home, the group goes with him in lockstep fashion. They arrive at the Adams' home and knock. Mrs. Adams comes to the door and inquires to the group's purpose, Tobias tells her,

"We've come to take Collette over to the park with us Mrs. Adams".

"Tobias, Collette is not well, but thank you for thinking of her".

Mrs. Adams is readying to close the door, but Tobias increases in his desire to see her.

"Nope, Mrs. Smith, I want to see my friend today; we want to see our friend today, he tells her with increased firmness.

"Tobias, I said no for today, now please go to the park yourselves and have your fun".

"Nope, we'll stay on the porch until we see her" Tobias says, while the gang affirms their individual commitments to this effort.

The environment begins to intensify as Mr. Adam's now joins the discussion.

"What are you kids doing here?" he says.

Mrs. Adams tells him,

"They say they'll stay on the porch until they see Collette".

"Honey, don't they know?" he says.

Mrs. Adams puts her head down and whisper's,

"No, I have not told Tobias".

"I thought we talked about this after the school year ended and you were going to tell him".

Mrs. Adams is tearful and Mr. Adams explains.

"Collette developed pneumonia right after school ended and she has been in the hospital since. We've been there much of the time. The doctors are not sure Collette is going to make it kids", he says as his tears now begin to flow.

Mrs. Adams is sobbing with her head still hanging low. Then Tobias, in an irritated tone, tells them,

"What if Collette dies thinking her friends must not care about her". He raises his voice higher and says, "What if she dies thinking we did not love her enough to visit her--- to be with her?"

Tobias apparently thinks this is the right time for a scolding. It is uncomfortable, thinking about this moment and what kinds of emotions were being expressed by everyone present. Thinking back on it now, I thought such an approach was quite risky.

"Tobias, we just did not want to upset you kids", Mr. Adam's states and Mrs. Adams nods in affirmation.

"Well it did not work", he tells them. "We are her friends and we are not little children. You should have told us. Your daughter needs love coming into her now. Don't you know that love can help heal people? Don't you know this?" Tobias is escalating again as if in a new round of scolding.

Mr. Adam's stops the Tobias' escalation abruptly and tells his wife,

"Get the keys to the car honey, we're all going to Scranton. Kids, call your parents let them know where you are going".

"Are you sure Bill?" Mrs. Adams says.

"Never more so, let's get going".

It was approximately a one hour ride to Scranton. Mr. and Mrs. Adams in the front and five kids squished in the back. Seatbelts and over loading were not safety matters of the day. The group arrives at the hospital not knowing what they would see. Tobias, very directly told this hurting mother and father that he would tell their daughter why they had not been there to see her. By this point, Mr. and Mrs. Adams were in complete guilt mode for their ill-decision made. This fourteen year-old boy had emerged victorious from verbally spanking a set of parents who were in much pain. He had made his point and they had succumbed to it in remorse. They would do whatever he asked of them at this point. His message of love has given them hope for their daughter's recovery; something they began to lose over the course of the last couple weeks. They are realizing how fear had entrapped their own lives and thus the life of their daughter. Only Tobias could have seen this insight explosion. The rest of us were just mortified by his actions.

The doctor meets with the group and allows everyone to go in to see Collette. He was not worried about germs as we now know he believed Collette was going to die. She had been given last rites by the family's priest.

"Hello Collette" the members of the group begin calmly barking.

She is lying there and looking toward them all.

"We would have been here weeks ago if we only knew, but your parents thought it best we not know. They believed you needed your full rest without having us coming around", Tobias tells her.

With this last phrase, Tobias forgives her parents through presenting a reason that was based upon their love for her. Tobias' eyes meet their eyes and they all smile at each other. Each knows what the other has done. Each knows they all love this person and just want her to be better. Tobias continues,

"OK, time to get better, you've been here long enough. We got things to do this summer and we have to get ready for high school".

Wilson, Jimmy J, Sadie, and Taylor are like Tobias' prayer team. They just affirm whatever he says to Collette. They know Tobias is way ahead of them in these kinds of emotional matters. Tobias is leading the group and Collette's parents' as well. When the doctor re-enters he also witnesses an act of friendship and love he has not seen in his years at Scranton General Hospital.

"Doctor, isn't it true that love can heal wounds too?" Tobias says to him.

"Well son, I don't … "

Hearing a slight bit of doubt coming ---

"Doctor!" Tobias raises his voice, "Isn't it true that love can heal wounds too?"

Getting the point, the doctor seems to think an argument between his science and faith is unnecessary now and relents,

"Yes, I do young man, yes I do".

Collette begins to smile at Tobias and she gives him a little wave.

"Alright then, Tobias states, let's get this love thing going on".

Tobias assembles Collette's "love" team, doctor and a

nurse included, around her bed while the hospital chaplain is beckoned to offer a healing prayer at Tobias' request. Collette's healing begins. The only one convinced of this path is Tobias, though the rest of the team is not in dispute, they are just not as certain. For the next several weeks Collette would get visits and letters by her friends and slowly her health and energy would begin to return. It is reported as some sort of miracle by the medical staff, and even Collette's parents, Tobias does not believe so. He would later tell Mr. and Mrs. Adams,

"If friendship and love is a miracle then yes, a miracle has happened with Collette".

You could tell he really thought it odd people did not fully understand the power of these forces. This was apparent through his scolding of Collette's parents and through his forgiveness for their misguided, but loving decision, to protect their daughter. Throughout life, Tobias would tell people, "Please let sincere love in, let it come through whatever form it manifests; don't judge or question it. In its purest form, love will always translate to good things." He would tell people when it is difficult to trust words, just open yourself to feel it. He was a master of the instillation of hope.

Since Collette arrived back home we were all able to get back to the business of our summer. Sadie and Taylor were spending much more time together. We thought we would see them more this summer but it has been far less than expected. They continue to hang out at Sadie's a lot with little invite to others; only Tobias every now and then, but they did show up for group get-togethers. Tobias is working at Kimberly's Café while also maintaining his support of Collette either with her schooling or their friendship, while Jimmy J and Wilson found some extra cash to be made at Hennessy's Market. None of the group worked full-time so the rendezvous at Jimmy J's yard continued. It was the largest yard of the group and it offered many different places in which to move when an adult got too close. They would alter their meeting times if they had a desire to hear

Mrs. Spagnotti sing the hit songs of the day, or should they desire the culinary treats that would often present at the Greenwood home.

Despite their varying schedules and interests they would meet. The group would remain in touch and enter the next phase of their lives excited and ready, as ready as any teenager can be for the unpredictable, fascinating, electrifying, painful, joyous and terrifying era of high school. Their love and support for each other will be necessary as they would begin the transition into lives that will require much more regard for the decisions they will make. Though the Kannot community would be somewhat protected from the influences of the outside world, the adolescent phase is an equalizer. It is the period when every parent takes a deep breath when their child hits about 15 and holds it with the hope of one giant exhale around 18. It should remind us of another lesson often learned from those with wisdom; we have far more in common with each other than not. We dream, we plan, we like, we love, we explore; we are all prone to the joys and pitfalls of the common life, though uncommon events will visit as well and further challenge our ability and capacity to cope, adjust, resolve, heal; or not.

CHAPTER VII

THE HIGH SCHOOL YEARS: JOYS, PAINS AND EVIL (10TH/12TH '74-'77)

1) A Teacher's Repentance

As fate would have it our high school years began with a bang as did Junior High, only now with Taylor. Within the first two weeks of school, it became evident that a teacher decided to use Taylor as an example for all things bad. Taylor, the boy who never got in trouble or spoke ill of his teachers. The teacher seemed to have a thing about Taylor's intelligence and maybe his color. Jacob Stanton was relatively new to the Kannot Community. He was a young science teacher in his second year at Kannot High, though he had taught elsewhere for several years. Reviews had been mixed from both kids and adults but nothing was pulling either to one side or the other. There were problem signs but not to the extent of any reprimands from school leadership as of yet. When we automatically try to figure out what the student being wronged has done, or what about him is creating the problem, we often don't explore what is going on with the teacher. During class one day the teacher begins his railing of Taylor.

"Taylor, in all your brilliance, can you tell me …..?

"No sir" says Taylor in a near whisper.

"How bout this Taylor, can you tell me ……"

The subject of the questions did not matter and most came to realize this. Taylor probably knew the answers but he would just seem to get rattled and seize up. For whatever reason, Mr. Stanton simply wanted to place Taylor foremost and center, knowing his shy personality would foster him much discomfort.

"I bet if the question had something to do with music you would know it, wouldn't you?"

"I don't know sir" barely responding with any volume.

"Speak up boy! I cannot hear your brilliance".

Tobias waited as patiently as he could; waiting to see if Taylor could muster up the courage to stand up for himself as they had been talking about. He could not.

"Sir, I need you to stop doing that to Taylor", Tobias says.

Mr. Stanton loudly states, "What?"

"I need you to stop disrespecting him, hurting him, making fun of him --- all these things".

"And who do you think you are? Oh yeah, you're the fella we've been hearing about over the years and now you're here at KHS. Well, things are different here, Mr. Greenwood, aren't they? Sometimes, little boy, I will use examples to make points to help the group. Taylor, on many occasions, offers me examples of things even he does not know".

Tobias interrupts, "Let me say they are great examples if your intention is to hurt Taylor and to motivate your students to dislike you and not learn from you".

Mr. Stanton did not know Tobias well enough to know he was not attempting to be disrespectful, but just being very direct with his point.

"You little smart ass!" he yelled. "Go to the office!"

"Thank you, Mr. Stanton, and I will fill out a formal complaint while I'm there".

Tobias leaves the room. The teacher's presentation for the rest of the period was one of utter confusion. We could tell he did not know what had hit him. For us, we could have scripted this scene. We knew Tobias would act at some point. He usually allows time for others to make things right before he intervenes. In this case, he surprised us all at the rapidity of his intervention.

Later in the morning. Mr. Stanton goes to the office

to check on this insubordinate student. He meets the principal, Bill Theison, and asks what will be done with Tobias. Unfortunately for Mr. Smith, this principal used to be a teacher at Tobias' elementary school.

"Mr. Stanton, Tobias has lodged a formal complaint in writing about your treatment of Taylor Hughes".

"Laughable isn't it", he states, as if the principal would join in on the joke.

"Actually, not laughable for you. Tobias has a long-standing reputation of patience, acceptance, goodwill and certainly outstanding school and community citizenship. You, on the other hand, are noted to get into conflicts with kids and word has it you say ugly things at times. It just so happened that no one has stepped forward yet to confront you".

"You can't be serious! This Tobias is just a trouble maker!"

"You were assuming I would brush off his complaint as frivolous, but I can't because it is Tobias and his report supports my thoughts about you. Mr. Stanton, I am going to give you an opportunity to make this right. Sit down with Tobias and hear him out. He obviously thought things were way out of control to do this in class; he usually approaches teachers after class.

"You mean he's done this before?"

"Yes, he's helped many teachers better their careers".

"He's a kid sir".

"You don't think we can learn from kids Mr. Stanton? They can be our best teachers if you allow them. If you meet with Tobias I will shred his complaint regardless of the outcome of your meeting".

Mr. Theison, knew the outcome. He's seen Tobias' work many times and knew there would be a positive outcome; plus, Tobias agreed to the shredding of the document if this meeting took place as well.

"This is crazy Bill, but I'll appease you this time".

He had no idea what such a meeting would entail until he crossed paths with Tobias later in the morning. Tobias stopped by in between classes and gave Mr. Stanton a paper and requested he respond in some manner to it. At this point, Mr. Stanton just rolled with it though he was not pleased. The assignment written on a piece of paper:

1) Please know the other kids love Taylor and are hurt for him, but mostly know you are hurting him.

2) I'm sorry if you were mistreated when you were young.

3) I believe you are a good person and I want to learn from you.

Mr. Stanton briefly looks at the paper and puts it back in his pocket. As the day proceeded, his ability to focus and teach greatly deteriorated; to the point where he had asked for a sub to fill in for the afternoon. Fellow teachers noticed this in the staff lounge. They were not privy to the encounter with Tobias and Mr. Stanton. They just knew Mr. Stanton was very distracted and somber in appearance. It was a long and difficult day and night for this young teacher. His assignment had brought about much pain from his childhood and much shame and embarrassment for what he had been doing with this pain. He did not sleep and found minimal peace for what he had to go through on his next day at school.

Mr. Stanton called in sick the next day and the next. Mr. Theison supported his need for time away from school. He knew this was a make it or break it moment for this young teacher's career. On Friday morning, Mr. Stanton arrives at school early and immediately requests to meet with Tobias. Mr. Theison stated,

"I hope your intentions are good with Tobias, Jake".

The level of discomfort on Mr. Stanton's face was not a recognizable emotion or expression so Mr. Theison had some reservations. Nonetheless, his confidence in Tobias allowed the meeting to move forward. Tobias arrives at school and is immediately called to Mr. Stanton's class. There is approximately 20 minutes of free time before the bell. He enters Mr. Stanton's room and sees a man looking defeated.

"Mr. Stanton, are you OK?"

"Yes, Tobias, I'm OK. Do we need to talk about these statements you wrote for me to ponder?"

"Only if you need to Mr. Stanton, I cannot make a difference from this point, it has to be your difference now. Just do what's in your heart. The kids will hear you".

Most who knew Tobias knew what such a statement meant. Tobias was big on free will and choice. It simply meant you will be heard no matter your message, be it a positive or negative one.

"I'm rooting for you Mr. Stanton; you are a wonderful teacher fighting to overcome something".

And with that he shakes Mr. Stanton's hand, cupping the grasp with his other hand and leaves the room.

The second period class had much tension building as they knew Mr. Stanton has returned to school today. They do not know what to expect, especially Taylor. By now, all the other teachers knew as well. They had long been uncomfortable with many of Mr. Stanton's approaches to children and discipline. Most believe him incapable of change and that bad things were to come today. He enters the class after all the kids were in their seats. Mr. Stanton sits at his desk just glancing around the room at the students in his class. Taylor is attempting to shrink down in his seat to not be seen. Much like the child who is trying not to be called on for a question they don't know. A time-tested strategy that has never worked but prayer and hope seem to keep the possibility alive.

"Taylor Hughes, please come with me for a minute".

And they both go into the hallway; Mr. Smith closes the door behind them.

"Taylor, how are you?"

"I'm fine sir".

"Well, I can't imagine you being fine for what we've been through together. Would it be OK if we both stood at the front of the classroom and I apologized and said a few words with you by my side?"

"You don't have to sir".

"I'm a pretty stubborn guy and if I thought I had to I would probably find a way to protest such a demand. Taylor, I need to for me so I can keep teaching. Will you help me do this?"

"Yes sir, I can do this".

As they re-enter the class and take their place in front of Mr. Stanton's desk, Mr. Theison comes by. He's a bit nervous about Mr. Stanton's resolve in this matter and just as he was going to ask to come into the classroom Mr. Stanton invites him in.

"Students, I am asking you all to forgive me today".

With his eyes becoming glossy, he continues.

"I am ashamed of what I had been doing to Taylor and for that matter many kids since I began teaching. I am ashamed that I've probably hurt fellow teachers as well. My behaviors had nothing to do with Taylor or any other student, ever. It all came down to me and my history. I initially wanted to be a teacher so I could teach kids in a different manner than I was taught. I was not a good student. I was living out how I was taught both at school and home. I never stopped to realize that the strategies used to "teach" me did not work".

Mr. Stanton's eyes are glossy yet he continues.

"I've been teaching for five years now and I feel today is my first day. Today is the day I begin being the teacher I wanted to be, but I need your help and support".

His pleas seem to be touching the hearts of his students and a glance over Mr. Theison's way finds the same. What a cathartic moment. A classroom heals together. The adult ego is left at the door and the fragile egos of children become stronger and all appear sincerely impacted by the level of healing and truth behind this moment. The resilience and the forgiveness of children are lost on most adults. There will be no repeated focus on Mr. Stanton's past by these students, only from fellow teachers at times. These students will live in the here, now, and tomorrow with him, and when they do look back they will look back at the specific day of healing, not events prior. This is usually harder for adults to do.

Tobias never made a big deal out of this as per usual.

Mr. Stanton attempted to thank him several times with the intention of engaging in a dialogue about the event. Tobias would just smile and say, "Really proud of how you handled it Mr. Stanton --- you're a wonderful teacher". And with that, any further recognition was discarded. But Mr. Theison had more to say about this both to Mr. Stanton and the other teachers. Mr. Theison held himself accountable for not addressing these issues much earlier with his young teacher and he told his staff much of the same in a meeting after school.

"I witnessed a beautiful thing between a teacher and his students, but at the same time I/we must acknowledge we turned our backs on this and thus let a teacher struggle and therefore the students in his classes struggle. We all knew it, we heard about it, and ultimately, we decided to let it go. Eventually our children helped resolve this, along with a strong heart of a teacher, a heart we did not know existed because we ruled out the possibility. Ultimately, when we avoid a fellow teacher's limitations, and yes, behavior problems, it hurts our students, it reflects poorly on us all and our school and we may even miss the opportunity to save a teacher's career. So along with the apology Mr. Stanton gave to his students we owe him an apology as well and I will be the first to offer this to him. I hope you will all consider this as well".

And most did so. Mr. Stanton's career, and the quality of his career, blossomed. He became a leader at KHS when it came to matters of teacher accountability for the behaviors and learning struggles of their students. There would be no more casual blame for such matters upon the students. KHS continued to move forward. In a very short period of time, Tobias had set in motion many more good things to come from Kannot High School.

2) Tobias Needs Some Help from His Music Friends

Tobias' history within the Kannot School District and his uncanny ability to interpret lyrics was near iconic. Most were aware of his knowledge of lyrical interpretation and many continued to present him with their questions. The masses really did not believe he consulted with the songwriters. They would ask Tobias for an interpretation and he would say, "I'll get back with you about that as soon as possible". The time was dependent on how quickly his music friends would return his call or connect him to a new lyricist. When he does get back with them and tells them how he knows and/or comes to such a conclusion, i.e. "I ask the author of the song", they laugh it off. Tobias' family and closer friends knew the truth and thus get a kick out of peer and teacher reactions.

Humor abounds for all, but it is the truth behind it that finds the most humor amongst the knowing, especially when the situation receives such public and or school-wide levels. Like the day Mr. Vossman and Mrs. Randall got in a heated argument over a song by Emerson, Lake and Palmer - I Believe in Father Christmas. It was nearing the Christmas vacation and the song was playing often. Mr. Vossman had taken the song as an offense against Christians. Mrs. Randall, in a removed way, simply stated it was such a beautiful melody and dismissed Mr. Vossman's claim. A lesson to be learned about matters of religion --- don't dismiss someone's feelings about their religion. This escalated in front of students to which the principal had to intervene. These were two popular teachers. What unfortunately happened afterwards were students taking sides over the song. We teens love to argue by virtue of being a teen and these teachers handed an argument on our developmental doorstep.

After about a week of problems associated with this incident, Mr. Theison hands the task over to Mr. Franklin, the vice principal. Mr. Franklin was referred to Tobias for assistance.

"Tobias, Mr. Theison says we need you." he began.

"You mean about the song? I'm already on it Mr. Franklin. I'm waiting to hear back from Mr. Lake and Mr. Sinfield as we speak".

"Yeah sure Tobias", he says in dismissive tone. "Just

do what you usually do with these kinds of disagreements; this one has gotten out of hand. People apparently seem to agree with your interpretations. I'll give you control of the intercom when you come up with your response. You'll like this since I know you used the Junior High intercom once".

Tobias was not aware Mr. Franklin knew of this KJH exploit. It was a big deal and administrators would share such situations with fellow administrators. He certainly did not know he was the fodder of so much more than the larger incidents. He was too humble to even consider this. About two weeks had passed since Tobias had alerted his musician contacts to his current need. Finally, one evening the call came.

"Hello Tobias, this is Greg Lake. I hear there is a problem at your school".

"Yes Mr. Lake, there is".

"What do you think the song is about Tobias?"

"I have to admit Mr. Lake, I am torn. I hear some beautiful words in it with this beautiful   melody and then I experience confusion over some statements".

"Which one's Tobias?"

"Well, these three specifically and I think they are the ones that brought about the conflict:

'But instead it just kept on raining, a veil of tears for the Virgin birth'. 'They told me a fairy story, till I believed in the Israelite'. And, 'Hallelujah, Noel be it heaven or hell, the Christmas we get we deserve'Why the tears and the raining? It makes it sound like a sad event. What is the fairy story? The 'Christmas we get we deserve' sounds angry. I think these are the lyrics they need help understanding" Tobias explains.

"Yes Tobias, these are the ones that have received attention over the years. The song was not meant to be a happy Christmas song; one that would bring joy to all who heard it over the Christmas Season. It was meant to go deeper and bring about the idea of commercialism's injustice to Christmas and the loss of innocence and childhood belief. Unfortunately, politics and unintended interpretations were made from the lyrics both I and Peter Sinfield wrote. We soon after recognized when left to one's own interpretation, these gray areas, without more clarification, would create some problems with the song. This happens within music Tobias. We write from our hearts and minds and everyone's hearts and minds express and receive messages differently. I love Christmas and I am a Christian. So that is all I can say Tobias"

"Oh Mr. Lake, would you be able to say this to my school?"

"How Tobias?"

Their conversation went on for another thirty minutes. Mr. Lake was just as enamored with this boy as was all the other writers and musicians to whom he encountered. Into the kitchen walks Maggie.

"Tobias who is that? You've been on the phone a while now".

"It's Greg Lake Mom".

"Who?"

"Greg Lake of the band Emerson, Lake and Palmer. I needed some interpretation".

"OK, you need to get to your homework" Maggie directs.

This was an example of the normalcy in which this boy's exceptionalism would eventually become. She never doubted him after the Paul Simon call.

The following day, Tobias goes to Mr. Franklin's office and tells him he needs the phone and intercom at 9:15.

"It will be 1:15pm in London and this is when Mr. Lake expects my call, Mr. Franklin".

"Tobias, that's enough. Go to class!"

Tobias, not one to argue simply moves on. Mr. Franklin looks at his secretary, Ms. Wyatt, and says,

"All the good things I hear about this kid and he comes to the high school and starts being a goof".

"I don't know Mr. Franklin, he seemed sincere to me".

"That's what he wanted me to think too, but you're not

a vice principal and can't see through this stuff".

Mr. Franklin leaves the office for some hallway rounds. He crosses paths with Mr. Theison.

"Hey Bill, here's one for ya. Tobias Greenwood wants to make a call to London at 9:15 to have Greg Lake of Emerson, Lake and Palmer explain the song that is creating the conflict here".

"What did you tell him?" responds Mr. Theison

"I sent the little wise guy back to class! I don't have to take that".

"George, my wife knew Tobias very well in the junior high school and I knew him in elementary school. He does not have the capacity to lie or tease with malice, and certainly not with adults".

"Are you kidding me Bill? You think I should believe him?" Mr. Franklin states with irritation.

"Yes, I do and what's the harm if you allow the call to see what happens? The conflict we have here suggests you give this a chance".

"Alright Bill, I'll allow Tobias and you all to feel foolish afterwards, no problem. Since you are a fan of him, you can get him at 9:00 or so and bring him up. I just don't want to look like an idiot when this is over".

"Sorry George, but you should prepare yourself for this outcome".

First period passes and Mr. Theison calls for Tobias. A crowd has gathered in the principal's office as word has gotten around. The janitorial staff, the clerical staff, the kitchen staff, a few teachers on free period and Mr. Franklin and Mr. Theison.

"OK, Greenwood, make your call." from a disbelieving Mr. Franklin.

"Can't yet Mr. Franklin. It's not 9:15 yet".

"Oh, Tobias stop this stuff before you embarrass yourself further".

"I'm just trying to help sir".

Tobias tries to reassure him, but he is a stubborn man. He will hold on to his skepticism until the last second. Tobias begins the call at 9:12. A complex call for some, but Tobias has made these international calls before --- he's an old pro. His confidence in the numbers on his paper and the intention of the call is intriguing to most.

"Hello Mr. Lake", he says to the phone. OK, I'm going to put you on the school intercom now so wait just a second and go ahead. If it's not working I'll pick back up.

With the eloquence of the English accent, the man on the phone says,

"Hello to Kannot High School. My name is Greg Lake and I guess I am speaking to the entire school but mostly I will direct my response to Tobias' request to Mr. Vossman and Mrs. Randall".

This voice goes on to say everything that he had shared with Tobias last night. He is eloquent and passionate about his music and his writing, though somewhat sorrowful for the interpretation his song has taken. He speaks of he and Mr. Sinfield's intent and the more in-depth interpretation desired. The people in the office are nodding in agreement with all his words, some of which whom were involved in the taking-of-sides process. Before his speech is ended Mr. Vossman and Mrs. Randall enter the office. Both ask Tobias if they could speak with Mr. Lake when he is finished.

"I'll ask", he tells them.

"Sincerely, I thank this school for the interest in this song so maybe now it has a better, or at least a more understood meaning for you. Tobias, are you there?" says Mr. Lake

"Yes sir".

Tobias shuts down the intercom speakers and talks with Mr. Lake for a minute before he asks,

"Mr. Lake, may I put Mr. Vossman and Mrs. Randall on the line."

He hands the phone to them thus affirming the request.

"We just want to thank you for this and for your time. It really got ahead of us. Yes, yes, we know Tobias can help should such a challenge evolve again" Mr. Vossman states. Mrs. Randall just standing there shaking her head, affirming this statement. He wants you again Tobias".

Tobias takes the phone,

"OK, alright, I'll send Mr. Cocker your best when I talk to him again".

And with that "The Call" as it came to be known, was over. The adults present could only stare at this young man as his unfolding history, present, and future within the world of music both astounds and confuses them. All he could say is,

"I just think it is the best way to get an answer --- to contact the author" and he heads back to class.

It was hard to imagine this to be a gag, but Mr. Franklin attempted to save face by pronouncing the possibility. The believers outnumbered him and he was left to work this one out on his own. He would eventually approach Tobias, albeit a few weeks down the road, to apologize and thank him. The always gracious Tobias would receive it as if offered the moment the phone was set down from "The Call". Mr. Franklin had been Tobiased!

3) Kannot Spartan Football

Spartan football is at hand! In the autumn of every year in Northeastern, Pennsylvania high school football rules the airwaves and discussions at the local bars, barbershops, fire halls and cafes. Not to mention the massive impact upon the high school itself. The expectations are high for this football season, though they are always high in spirit but usually not in outcome. This year is different. Maybe for the first time there is much abuzz about this program outside the boundaries of Kannot. Local sportswriters know about the athletic prowess of two starting sophomores; Tommy and Tobias. They are excited to see if these two boys will dominate games at the high school level as they did at the freshman level. What they cannot know about, however, is the solidarity of this team and how such a strong sense of brotherhood will raise everyone's level. The Kannot High School Spartans are beginning to carve out a new era in

Spartan football; one that will bring forth a saga that will set so many things in motion. This will affect not only the future of Spartan football, but the future of all their sports programs through the truest and purest form of teamwork.

Friday night football is upon us! The familiar chants from the opposing bleachers provoking responsive chants from the home bleachers.

"Kannot Cannot! Kannot Cannot! Kannot Cannot"!

And the home crowd responds.

"Kannot can! Kannot can! Kannot can!", our crowd chants back.

"Kannot Could Not, Kannot Cannot, Kannot Will Not"! They respond

And the home crowd responds with more vigor.

"Kannot Can Do! Kannot Will Do! Kannot Ruins You"!

With a name like 'Kannot' being similar to 'cannot' the battle of the word-play goes on and on and on, but never gets old. Each side believing their chant has won, but ultimately the score at the end of the game will decide the winning chant. Will it be?

"Kannot Could Not! Kannot Did Not!"

Or

"Kannot Could and Kannot Did!"

What a season it was! The Kannot High School Spartans won nine of their eleven games; only losing to the league powerhouse, and again to them in the regional playoffs. This was a Spartan team that went three and seven last season. The attitude of this team was a mature one. Both Tobias and Tommy would not complain about the losses, especially since they knew they played their best and they knew the others on the team did as well. They were congratulatory of their winning rivals and in locker room meetings or when interviewed, they would say such games will only make them better. Recruiters were now aware of the Kannot Spartans. Tobias and Tommy were well in their sights, though the play of other teammates would be raised and some others would come into the view of recruiters as the class of '77 moved forward. Tobias would not get the attention from Division I recruiters because he just didn't have the speed. They simply did not comprehend how quick he was and when he got his paw on you, you were down. His strength and quickness just did not show well to the common eye. Tommy had lots of recruiters interested and he pleaded for them to look at Tobias more, but they were the adults and 'they knew better'.

The ongoing joke around the school regarded the recruiters and their lack of knowledge about Tobias. Most did not know what he looked like and Tobias' teammates and friends went along with it. Sometimes they would be talking to Tobias asking him if he knew Tobias and where he could be found. "Oh, he's close by sir, he was just here a second ago", Tobias would tell them. Those close by could only giggle. Sometimes when Tobias was pointed out the recruiter would say, "C'mon kid, I'm in a hurry here now really, where is this young man?" Sadly, it was the stereotype and judgement made that interfered with a fair assessment of Tobias' football skills. By the end of his high school football career they would all know him, but Tobias' post high school plans did not involve football.

There was not much that could beat the atmosphere a high school football season brings, especially a winning one. The smell of decaying leaves; probably one of the very few things that in death brings forth a comforting odor and also in the process of their death, the unveiling of visual beauty. The ominous nature of autumn is not linked to these factors but to what they represent --- winter looming near. The progressively cooler Friday nights and by season's end maybe even some snow or at least flurries; sometimes giving just cause for the shyest of boys to put their arm around their girlfriend's shoulder; nature's way of saying, 'Can I help?" Though autumn signifies a seasonal end to many things nature, it is a beginning for kids in school from Kindergarten through grade 12.

4) Special Teachers Help Create Special Students

Michael Parker is perhaps the most exciting teacher at Kannot High School. He is definitely the most passionate. He has taught history and geography for tenth, eleventh and twelfth grades for nearly 25 years; all at Kannot High School. He sends a letter home at the beginning of every year to parents. In the letter, he asks parents to sign and provide approval for him "to dance around the world and to different times in the world" with their son or daughter. Many would sign off with a smile since they too, danced with Mr. Parker when they were at Kannot High. You could never be bored in Mr. Parker's class because just when you let your guard down a request would come. "Who wants to dance with me to Poland?" The dance would be a polka.

He had all the music possibilities on hand no matter which place in the world the lesson went or to which era. But he was always ready for a change in direction, which was very impressive since some kids would try to challenge the breadth and depth of his music library --- and dance skills. By the second quarter, he would have many volunteers, boys and girls alike, and those without permission slips to dance would beg their parents for them. It was fun and exciting. The energy level was high as one, two, or even three kids would polka around the room with Mr. Parker, but when they got to Poland the discussion would become serious, interesting and fascinating. Much the same in history class when Mr. Parker would ask someone to dance back in time with him; maybe to a schoolhouse in the Old West, where they would square dance in a classroom birthday celebration. Every day was a new day in this Mr. Parker's class. You never knew what would evolve and who would be dancing. It seemed even the quietest of students wanted to be involved in these trips to other places and times. If there was a place or an era to which a dance was unknown he would beckon Tobias for a freestyle. Tobias' special knack of dance without rhythm would entertain the class every time. Hard to watch, harder to not watch. Tobias loved this role and Mr. Parker capitalized on it. Mr. Parker had some special Tobias music for such events. He had some songs by Yes and Supertramp on hand for such moments.

And the boys were always ready to watch Clarissa Stratham dance. She had been studying ballet and jazz since she was four years old. She had the lines of a beautiful dancer, but of most interest to the boys were not her lines but her curves. She was mesmerizing to watch, but Mr. Parker had to be careful with her. She always wanted to dance but because of her expertise and beauty she frequently had a day dreamy result for boys and sometimes jealousy from the girls. She was known to be a bit snooty in much of her interactions around the school but when it came to dance she would dance with anyone and she would do so with joy. Dance was Clarissa's identity at KHS. She was probably no different than most other teens who had one specific identity; in areas/situations outside of their identity, they and other kids, were uncertain about the course of interaction. I don't know for sure, but I think this may be "snooty's" misinterpretation at this age. Mr. Parker knew how and when to use her for optimal learning results; just as he did so with Tobias. But with Clarissa's presence and presents, as the boys saw them, Mr. Parker's objectives were often challenged by the biological and social development of the boy folk. Sometimes though, it seemed he was after the energy level more than the learning task, for without such a level, the learning would by default be deficit. Whether Clarissa, Tobias, or anyone else was dancing --- the heightened energy level was there.

Mr. Parker could dance but he did have his limitations too. Over the years, he would sustain injuries, i.e. pulled muscles and sprains but he would proudly proclaim he never broke anything. Mr. Theison was worried that sooner or later a broken bone would come.

"Michael, why don't you slow down a bit with the dancing?"

"Oh Bill, can't now, the kids expect it. They are excited to be a part of it. You'll never see a kid with their head down in my class --- only if they are really sick."

"I know Michael, but were you to laup off a finger on the paper cutter or slip on the ice in the parking lot, these things I could explain and cast off as hazards of our industry, but crashing into walls and blackboards --- not so much. Will you ever learn you will not be able to keep up with Clarissa Stratham? You cannot do pirouettes or grand allegros with her."

"Oh, someone is learning about ballet" Mr. Parker says with a snicker. Besides, I don't do them with her, I do them alongside her".

"You do make people want to learn" Mr. Theison responds with a smile. "See, I looked up those ballet terms to present in my discussion with you. Michael, those moves are out of your league and you will get hurt sooner or later".

"I hear you Bill, but it is not about the perfection of the dance, it's about the energy, the energy needed in my classroom to maximize attention and thus, maximize learning".

"You are saying there is no ego involved when you engage in a dance that is well above your skill level?"

"Between you and me Bill, every now and then I am convinced I can do something that appears above my dance skill set. I'll admit, it usually doesn't work out so well but in such cases, my students find humor and this works toward my end goal too. If there is a little ego involved is that so bad? Hey, and by the way, it is far more dangerous to dance with Tobias than Clarissa".

"Oh Michael, just try to be careful. Can you at least back off the air born moves? An injured Mr. Parker will really set us all back, especially your students", says Mr. Theison in summation.

"Alright Bill, I will keep that in mind".

5) God Never Promised a Life Without Pain

Mr. Parker was also a great dresser, probably the best of all the teachers. When asked why, he would say, "I have the most important job in the world therefore I will dress the way I feel". Combine this with his teaching strategies and you have the most popular and best-liked teacher at the school. Just like Tobias' and Tommy's impact upon the football team, Mr. Parker had long raised the teaching level of many fellow teachers. Mr. Parker's passion to teach was even more incredible since he was able to maintain it even after the 1972 death of his son in the war and the recent diagnosis of his wife's leukemia. He comes to school every day with apparent excitement. This would change in the later fall of our sophomore year.

It was the Monday after the Thanksgiving break and we entered Mr. Parker's class ready to be energized about being at school. Mr. Parker was not there, instead a substitute teacher was sitting at his desk. You know you are really attached to a teacher when you are irritated that someone else is sitting at 'your' teacher's desk. Making matters even worse for the substitute was that Mr. Parker was always at the door greeting us. She now has two strikes against her before class even starts; she isn't greeting us and she's in Mr. Parker's seat. She has about fifty minutes to go and only one strike left.

"Class, open you books to page …."

There it was! Strike three! Mr. Parker would never refer to us as 'class', he would never start the class by saying something like 'open your books to page …'; he was way better dressed than this person, and he would have already begun asking us if we traveled to any other parts of the state, country, or world over the weekend! This was his way of seeking that segue. There you have it; she not only hit strike three, but she is well underway of striking out at another at-bat one minute into class time. At this pace, her side would be retired within the first three minutes; that's three strikes per minute. She didn't have a chance as Mr. Parker was a tough act to follow. He had a relationship with every student. He knew us all.

Some of us could not stand for this subpar teaching performance so we went to see Mr. Theison at lunch time. It was not really about the substitute. We did not mind subpar sometimes. Being teenagers, I can honestly say it is OK for teachers to have low expectations at times. It gives us a break and makes the day easier, albeit a bit more boring. We simply wanted to know where Mr. Parker was.

"Mr. Theison, where is Mr. Parker?" Sadie and Wilson asked him as he was sitting at a table in the cafeteria.

"Mr. Parker's wife passed last week. He is currently in Watertown, NY for the funeral," Mr. Theison answered.

Our hearts broke for this man. In a three-year period, he had lost his family. At risk of sounding selfish we had to ask,

"So, when is he coming back?"

"Kids, I don't know if he is coming back to Kannot High School, maybe only to gather his things. He mentioned moving back to his hometown in Watertown. He has a brother, his parents and Mrs. Parker's family there".

"Sir, he has to come back! We can't learn from this substitute!" stated in loud and varied voices.

"Ok, listen to me, the substitute has a name and you all should begin preparing for the possibility Mr. Parker will not be back. I know you all like him very much, but I will make sure you get a good teacher should he not return".

We could tell even Mr. Theison was not convinced by his own words. He knew Mr. Parker was only replaceable in body space. His passion, motivation and love for his students were not likely to be matched. Mr. Theison was sad and he knew we would not be the last to come to him today. Though he tried to speak matter-of-factly to us, he was troubled by this event. Many others would come to him to complain about the substitute. Doubtful such complaints about a teacher trying to take over Mr. Parker's class would ever cease. It was a rough period. Coming to class and not dancing to and from places; it was a boredom fest.

After the second week without Mr. Parker, most of us just wanted a chance to see him again; to say goodbye if he was to leave. We were getting little information. Certainly, he cared about out us and would want to see us too. We would say this often, but we were now intonating at the end of the statement. We never would have questioned Mr. Parker's feelings toward us before. This was awkward; everything changed. We were confused. Mr. Theison saw a group of us hanging out in the school yard after school on Friday and approached us. He knew things were not going well in his classes, but many of us were not doing so well in other classes too. The absence of Mr. Parker was affecting many students across classes. Teachers were doing what they could to be reassuring, while continuing to teach, but they missed their peer too. They missed his energy, his dress, his humor. They are without their favorite team member. It had to be very hard for them too.

"Hello gang" he says.

"Hello Mr. Theison" we respond in unison.

"I want you all to know that if you see Mr. Parker around town you may not see the man you came to know as your favorite teacher. I just don't want you to be hurt. I also want you to remember what he is going through. He did tell me he would let me know if he is coming back to Kannot High School by the end of next week".

Tobias asked the next question.

"Mr. Theison, what are you doing to try and keep Mr. Parker here?"

"Tobias, this is not something any of us can do; it has to be Mr. Parker's decision".

"But, isn't it strange if nobody is letting Mr. Parker know how much we miss him and want him to stay? If he is not hearing this from his fellow teachers and students, of course he will move back to Watertown. Why would he stay? I think we should be fighting for him"

Mr. Theison appeared to be a little stumped by these thoughts. It seemed he had given up on Mr. Theison. He had simply thought the pain too deep to be repaired in Kannot when all along Kannot could be the best place to help this wonderful man begin to put his life back together. Kannot is the place Mr. Parker was most happy, most passionate, most creative, and loved by so many.

"We know he has family away from this place, but he's been in Kannot for over 25 years and I think we are like his family. We should at least try Mr. Theison," says Sadie.

Sadie knew all too well about living a repaired life after the death of family member. She knew her friends and the Kannot community were major players in her and her family's healing. Mr. Theison could not dismiss her thought.

"Well, I will try kids and please let me know should you hatch some kind of plan on your own. I don't want to be ambushed by any craziness at school, OK?"

"That's a deal Mr. Theison," the group responds.

Tobias and friends would have a plan by weekend's end and it would begin early in the week with the sole purpose of opening communication channels with Mr. Parker. Ever the creativity of this group, the communication would involve meticulous restraint; not an easy task for the matter at hand. We had to get Mr. Parker into his classrooms. We felt if we could accomplish this feat the plan would come together.

As the school week began we were having trouble finding Mr. Parker. We would go to his home after school and in the evening and he did not answer the door. Was he not home or just not answering? We were getting nervous since we knew he told Mr. Theison he would have his answer about staying or leaving at the end of the week. It was now Thursday. We had to establish contact today. It was imperative if our plan was to have a chance. Jimmy J had a note from our little group and he ran it over to Mr. Parker's home at lunch time on Thursday. We just had to wait and hope. The note said this:

Dear Mr. Parker,

We are so sorry about your loss of Mrs. Parker. We miss you so much, but we are ready to let you go. We wanted to fight for you but we realize now that you simply cannot stay. We know that at some point you will go back to the classroom and we want to be a part of your healing. Please, Mr. Parker, allow us to be a part of this. Just come back to school on Friday and sit in your classes. You can cry, you can put you head down, and you can even go to sleep; all of this is Ok. We want you to remember us as a part of your healing since our relationship is going to end. We also have some things we want to give you. Please, Mr. Parker, please come by.

With Love, Support and Admiration,
Your Students

There's no way he could avoid our pleas. We tugged at his heartstrings pretty hard. We threw that thing in there about "giving him some things" for added security. We knew what the classroom environment did for Mr. Parker and we were quite sure we would get the desired result if we could only get him back in here. We were banking that his love for teaching, the classroom, his students and his peers was as strong as the pain in his broken heart.

Friday morning comes and we are anxious but hopeful our letter worked. The students in Mr. Parker's other classes are prepared also. If he does come we do not know what classes he will enter. Sure enough, Mr. Theison comes on the school speaker and reports,

"Mr. Parker will be in the building today visiting his classes. Please students do not disrupt the classroom since Mr. Parker will just be sitting in some classes and he is not there to disrupt or socialize with everyone".

Most of our group was in Mr. Parker's afternoon history class. We heard the plan was maintaining itself as Mr. Parker had entered about two classes in the morning and one in the early afternoon. We believe he hung out with his fellow teachers for lunch and suddenly, he arrives at our doorway. Our class with "the sub" is just getting underway.

"Hello, Mr. Parker" the sub says from her desk.

"I was told you may be sitting in our class today".

"Yes, Mrs. Faraday, I would like to if it's Ok."

We are all whispering hellos to Mr. Parker. It was odd. The restraint is horrid. We just wanted to burst out of our skins and swarm him. We previously brought in an extra seat since there were no absences today in our class. We placed it in a maximum observation spot; back of room corner seat should he come to this class. Mr. Parker takes his seat and class resumes. Mrs. Faraday sitting at her desk begins,

"Class, open your books to ...." she says.

Mr. Parker has no doubt already observed the lack of student greetings and is now observing the robotic movements of the students. It's the natural response mode when teachers behave robotically. Ok, so we are stepping it up a notch today, mostly stepping it down, but we have confidence the sub will not even become aware of this.

Sneaked glances at Mr. Parker shows him looking around the classroom. Part of the plan is to avoid eye contact with him. Our peeks are usually through fingers as most of us have our elbows on our desks and the palms of our hands placed on our foreheads; this is the classic boredom and pained learning nonverbal since the beginning of schooling in America and maybe earlier. We have a few kids tapping their pencils on their teeth or chewing their erasers, and the yawns; they are abundant. We even have Mr. Parker yawning. As predicted, the sub has not a clue and this perhaps, is what will make the most critical appeal to Mr. Parker's conscience. Even if he figures out what we were doing, the fact she did not, would speak volumes to him.

Midway through class we could see the discomfort on Mr. Parker's face. He is trying to make eye contact with some of us but we just turn away quickly if our eyes were to meet. He's seems to be trying to 'will' back the passion for learning into us. A few looks on his face suggests he may be onto us. So sorry for Mr. Parker, he'll just have to suffer this out. We haven't even pulled out our ace card yet and he's showing signs of an awakening. Nearing the end of class, while most of us aren't even sure what the lesson is on today, we are sure there is something 'Italy' about it and this is where we drop the bomb. Collette is raising her hand. Mr. Parker smiles because not a hand was raised throughout the entire class. But, the teacher is not seeing her. Collette keeps her hand up though her disability has it flailing about and still the teacher does not see it. Mr. Parker is moving in his seat like a restless student waiting for the end of class or one who needs the restroom and quick. We are getting restless now too because class is nearly over and our ace has not been played. Finally, Sadie yells out rather untypically,

"Mrs. Faraday, Collette has a question".

"Young lady, Collette is old enough to get my attention if she needs it" she responds.

The reprimand did not matter since Sadie's mission was accomplished. Plus, everything was being hyper-observed by Mr. Parker by now.

"Yes, Collette", the sub says.

"Can I yaaaaaaaaance to Itlee wid Mssssssssr. Parker", Collette states.

"What?" the teacher responds.

Collette says again,

"Caaan I yaaaaaaaaance Itlee wid Misssser Parker?"

"Honey, you're going to have to speak clearer for me to understand you," she says in an irritable tone.

And again, Collette labors out,

"Can I yaaaaance wi Parr to Ittttt?" she was tiring herself

Most of Collette's peers and teachers have come to understand her speech patterns and knew exactly what she was saying. Even though it takes some time for her to get the entire question out, we know what she's saying and so does Mr. Parker. You may be thinking, "Oh how pitiful a plan; to use the disability of a child to manipulate the feelings of someone". Yep, we thought about that and we found brilliance in it.

"Mrs. Faraday, Collette wants to dance to Italy with Mr. Parker" --- Jimmy J calls out with restrained irritation.

"What does that mean?" Mrs. Faraday says.

"Well, Mrs. Faraday, that's something I do with my students," Mr. Parker tells her.

"I don't understand. Why would you dance in a history class?" she says.

Mrs. Faraday is strengthening our plight with everything she says and does at this point. We're just letting it roll now.

"I found it to be an excellent way to keep things exciting and fun, " Mr. Parker replies.

"I don't think kids learn about history that way and it sounds like that would be very disruptive Mr. Parker," Mrs. Faraday responds.

Uh Oh! Mr. Parker seems to be taking his gloves off. His demeanor is changing. We got something going on now that we did not anticipate.

"I cannot teach the way you teach Mrs. Faraday. I don't think kids learn best by a teacher sitting at their desk for 50 minutes and the students sitting at their desks for 50 minutes. I just see numb butts and minds".

"Mr. Parker, you were to just come in here to say goodbye or something. I really did not understand why you were coming into these classrooms today, but I did not think you were coming in to disrespect me".

It's way ahead of us now, but it's really good stuff!

"That was not my intention Mrs. Faraday, until …until"

"Until what Mr. Parker?" in a demanding tone.

A tone many a student has heard over the course of their schooling. Especially for those students who were uncertain in their responses to a 'strict' teacher's question.

Mr. Parker is now becoming tearful and he says in a lowered tone,

"Until Collette asked me to dance Mrs. Faraday; she's never asked before".

Mrs. Faraday leaves the class stating,

"I'll be in the office with Mr. Theison until you are done with your silliness Mr. Parker"

And with that she leaves and closes the door. We could not have had a better situation unfold, but we still did not want Mr. Parker to see our entire plan. Then Tobias speaks out,

"I have a tape player and some music Mr. Parker."

"What kind of music Tobias?" he says

"Let me see what's in my bag here. I have some Ferranti and Teischer, Simon and Garfunkle, Joe Cocker, Herb Alpert … Oh, and here's some Italian music".

"Tobias, you just happen to have some Italian music?"

"Yeah, Mr. Parker, I know, isn't that funny."

The cover of our plan has been blown. Mr. Parker begins to sob. He pulls his head up and smiles between sobs. He now has students smiling; some tearing and smiling with him and just at this moment Mr. Theison enters the room.

"I told you guys to let me know what you planned to do and that I did not want to be ambushed by anything crazy at school and look what you went and did. Mrs. Faraday left this class very upset".

What Mr. Theison would tell very few folks over the years was that Mrs. Faraday knew; she was part of his plan. Mr. Theison told the students he would get them a good teacher and he did. This was a woman who stopped teaching in a neighboring school district years ago to raise a family. Mr. Theison talked her into this very special sub assignment, which he believed would be temporary. She was an old friend and she played her part well. She even had to take something off her teaching skills to get the result Mr. Theison thought possible all along. She struggled with the boundaries of adequate teaching, but she did so for all the right reasons. Mrs. Faraday, in the end, was a great sport and a huge factor in what was to happen.

"What's going on in here?" Mr. Theison states with authority. He's having some fun exploring his thespian within.

"Well, Mr. Theison, I'm just getting ready to dance with Collette to Italy".

"Can I turn on the music Mr. Theison?" Tobias asks

"Tobias, please turn on the music" he responds with a laugh.

Those who observed this moment --- Mr. Parker leading a joyful Collette in dance around the room, knew they had achieved their objective. This was the first time Collette danced, but it would not be the last --- Mr. Parker would not let it be so. Collette was the one who started his heart's recovery. Mr. Parker would heal here and he would again find joy here. He would remain a teacher at Kannot High School for many years to come dancing with kids, to and from, all over the world. A wonderful teacher had been saved. The students, staff and community of Kannot were the victors. Mr. Parker's return would come during Holiday Season and it could not be a better gift. Colder days, the snow falling, and joy already in our hearts for Christmas; surely a good recipe for those of many faiths, and for the little ones --- Santa will be coming to town too.

6) Tobias' Other Passion Unveiled

In the kitchen, Tobias' skills continued to evolve. He was organized, clean, and meticulous and he wanted to please. When he served something, anything, he watched the faces of his guest or guests with intensity. He watched for the nonverbal -even the people who did not want him to know he was very good and that his version of the meal was better than theirs or their mother's/etc. He would be reassured by their nonverbal. He would just smile and say thanks for trying my dish. They would eventually come back for more.

Nearing the end of their sophomore year his peers had begun to realize the snacks, sandwiches and even many meals they experienced at the Greenwood home were from the hands of Tobias. Tobias found so much joy in this it was not a surprise to his parents he would not want to go on to college for football, learning, or vocational schooling. He studied on his own. He was an astute observer and learner within his own home and community. He read much, watched the cooking shows, and practiced in his home for many years. Talk of college scholarships for Division II did eventually come for his athletic prowess, yet he was not enticed down that path, which puzzled and even infuriated recruiters and local lovers of sport. The pressures and expectations to prioritize football began as soon as his first high school football season ended. But Tobias operated on a different level. The pressures and expectations were never felt by him or his parents; they were more an issue for his coaches, some teachers, some peers, local sportscasters and many town folk.

Tobias was at peace with the direction he would take post high school. He truly wanted to help people understand this because he felt their angst and confusion about this.

In order to cease this as a topic of distraction for the team, Tobias organized a picnic before school resumed for his junior year. He invited all his teachers, coaches, friends, and a few specific local sportscasters --- the ones who made it known he was "not playing with a full deck" to give up such an opportunity. He would serve them one of his favorite dishes --- apricot pulled pork. He purchased the freshest baked rolls he could find and the best pork and ingredients he could find. He would end the meal with an Oreo cream pie for dessert. Tobias spent much of his savings in doing so, but he believed this would not only answer their questions, but would also be a marketing strategy for his future endeavors. He would tell his coaches and teachers or any adult that challenged his decision,

"Art makes the mind dance. Culinary, paintings, music, theater, it moves people and stimulates the mind to become better!"

Some would say with tongue in cheek,

"Tobias, like you when you dance"?

He didn't get their jest and would say,

"Yes, exactly!"

Ultimately, football lovers still wanted to see Tobias continue his playing days, but after this meal they understood he had another talent that could take him places; they cautiously did not want to give him too many compliments to encourage the career change. After all, they had hoped to keep the football doors open for home. Nonetheless, Tobias, understanding the nonverbals behind their responses to his meal, was quite happy with the result. He knew he planted a seed in their hearts, and stomachs, and that everything would be OK if he did not play football.

7) Ramona Takes a Risk

On another note which went unobserved for a spell, the group would be pleasantly surprised Tobias had made some in-roads with Ramona over the summer. We would be surprised by her new level of tolerance for him. Tobias' neighborhood grass cutting rounds oddly took him by Ramona's home even when the jobs were in opposite directions. Nonetheless, he would happily make the long push of his lawnmower, sometimes three-times longer; all for the glimpse of his princess. Ramona's little brother and sister adored Tobias and while on his rounds he would play with them at times; all under the watchful and increasingly tolerant eyes of Ramona. Ramona began to return the favor by just happening upon/near the Greenwood home at times. Tobias saw her on the other side of the street on a Tuesday evening.

"Hi Ramona!" he called out.

She tried to ignore him but couldn't. He was persistent, but she was also more willing to acknowledge him. They had been doing well in school, but outside school was still different.

"What are you doing over this way?" he asks

"I'm going to the store" she tells him.

"Yeah, but the store is over that way" Tobias reminds her.

"Just shut up Tobias. I'm going this way because there are some dogs I don't like to go by on the other way."

"What dogs? I know all the dogs in the neighborhood" he innocently proclaims.

"Tobias, you think you know everything. There's a couple dogs and that's it, so leave me alone".

Tobias, finally realizing what he had done says,

"Oh yeah, I think I know the area. Yes, a couple new dogs and they do look a little scary too."

Unlike Ramona's typical communication pattern. She does not leave. She accepts Tobias' veiled regret to the insensitivity of her fragile relational nature.

"Tobias, who is that over there with you?" calls out Maggie Greenwood.

"It's Ramona, Mom!"

"Oh, I have been waiting and wanting to meet you Ramona. Please come over here".

Ramona was not one for much attention from adults. She would later tell us she believed they all knew everything about her Mom and therefore, did not like her either. Having this underlying feeling would certainly help people understand why her communication with other adults was generally hesitant, suspicious, and usually very brief. It would be different with Mrs. Greenwood though.

"Come on in for a bit Ramona" Maggie directs.

"Just for a little bit Mrs. Greenwood" Ramona states in a very soft tone.

Tobias had not heard this tone before. She was like a sweet little girl toward his Mom. He had only known the 'school' Ramona and the 'in-her-own-home' Ramona. Ramona appeared very relaxed and calm around Maggie and even she may not have been able to describe why. But she was immediately attracted to Maggie. She saw her as a beautiful and gentle woman. Ramona also knew on a much deeper level, that Tobias' goodness must have something to do with her. Yet the thing she was most mesmerized by was Maggie's lack of make-up, yet still so much beauty. This was foreign to Ramona.

"Don't you wear make-up Mrs. Greenwood?"

"Yes Ramona, I do".

"How come I can't see it?" Ramona replies.

"I guess I just got good at covering up my make-up." Maggie says with a smile.

"What do you mean?"

Ramona is intrigued and does not appear ready to end this interaction as briefly as would be her pattern.

"Well, I just learned exactly how much to use, where to use it, and even when to use it so that I feel good about myself and my appearance. When a girl is able to figure this out you can hardly tell they are wearing make-up" Maggie proclaims.

"I never heard anything like that before. How do you think I look?"

Ramona was putting many of her vulnerabilities out there, yet in a matter of minutes she knew Maggie was safe. Understanding the plight of the adolescent female in general, and some of the things Tobias had said about Ramona, Maggie knew this was very sensitive territory as she proceeded. She knew the mask Ramona wore was more than make-up covering a face; it was a mask to cover pain, it was a mask to project something even Ramona did not fully understand, and it was the mask her mother taught her to wear --- this question posed was truly an emotional mine-field.

"Ramona, it took me until I was 18 to begin to understand this and probably a year or so later before I really got it".

"You mean I could still learn how to do what you do?" she asks with sincerity.

"Well, sure. You could ask your Mom more questions about it and .."

Maggie stopped speaking as she saw Ramona's demeanor change. Ramona's head went down with total loss of eye contact. Maggie immediately knew she went down the wrong path. Ms. Evan's would have no interest in addressing this with Ramona. Ms. Evan's existence at this point in their lives had very little to do with Ramona's general well-being, let alone with such sensitive and developmental matters.

"Or, I could show you a couple things when you have the time".

Maggie barely got the last word out of her mouth before Ramona was back to full attention.

"Ok, I have the time. Can you show me some now?" she asks with restrained excitement.

Tobias is observing all of this. He is internally ecstatic because he knows Maggie is what Ramona needs so much. An adult female caring about her; not passing judgment, not in a rush to do something else, not angry, not drunk. One of Maggie's gifts in life was that when you had her attention, you had her full attention. Right now, here is this young, scared, abused and vulnerable girl, letting all her defenses down, possibly for the first time. Tobias and Maggie knew the power of this moment as they had communicated through eye contact on a few occasions during this exchange. Maggie noticed this too, but it did not matter, these were two people she trusted therefore their glances at each other were not deemed suspicious and she had completely given herself up for any risk. To Maggie and Tobias their glances meant ----keep going.

"Alright, what would you like to know first?" Ramona says

"I'd like to take off what I have and have you do my face like yours".

Maggie was not ready for that and Tobias was a bit stunned too. Tobias had known Ramona for over two years and never saw her place herself in the hands of another person like this. She has relinquished herself to Maggie whom she has known all but seven minutes. The physical change Tobias is about to see does not matter to him. He has seen and loved Ramona for who she truly is; he has never focused on her make-up; he may have never seen it. But he is being affected by her willingness to become emotionally nude in front of both he and Maggie.

"Well first, I can't do you just like me because we girls are all different. What works for me may not work for you and what works for you may not work with me. We have different skin tones and facial features. Let's start from the beginning. Are you sure you have the time? This may take a little while".

Time was the last thing on Ramona's mind. She only needed to know her little brother and sister were Ok and since it was early evening she had already fed them and she believed her Mom would not be drinking yet. Ramona's life revolved around such considerations.

"Yes Mrs. Greenwood, I have the time!" Ramona proclaimed loudly, surprising even herself with some slipped excitement.

Maggie asks,

"Would you like Tobias to stay or leave?"

Without hesitation she replies,

"No, I want Tobias to stay".

Maggie knew what this meant. This little girl did not just like Tobias, or love as most teens love, she was in-love with him. She may not be able to say this, but for such a young and vulnerable girl to allow a boy to be part of this --- Wow! she thought. She could now see Tobias' feelings and his desire for Ramona in his young life. They were soul mates. Their outer shells were so different very few gave them a chance; Maggie was the first to see the matching souls, that is, other than Tobias.

"Tobias, I am going to get some of my make-up. Would you please get me a little pan of warm water, a rag, and the witch hazel from the medicine cabinet?"

"Sure Mom."

For a brief period, Ramona remained in the kitchen area by herself. If she was to run, this was the time. She could retract and regress from everything stated and implied over the last ten minutes or so and be none the worse --- like it never happened and then, between a heartbeat's moment, she was out the door. Tobias and Maggie re-enter the room with gear in hand, but they re-enter to the absence of Ramona. Before their hearts could complete the sinking, she runs back through the door and scares them with her crashing-like movement.

"Sorry, I left my jacket on the gate and it's starting to sprinkle" she laughs as she notices what her excited pace has done to them.

Tobias and Maggie, could only giggle. All within a matter of seconds they experienced a range of emotions they will gladly relinquish to giggles. Even if attempted they could no longer grasp the sadness of the second and a half just passed.

"Let's get comfortable in the living room Ramona. First, I want you to lay back on the couch. We should take the make-up you have on off, OK? asks Maggie.

"Sure, whatever you want me to do Mrs. Greenwood" she answers.

"Ramona, may I help?" Tobias asks in tender tone.

In-kind, Ramona responds, "Sure Tobias, I've gone this far".

Maybe for the first time since they've met they are locked in full attention to each other. Seeing past the face, deep behind the eyes, both doing so at the same time. They are now feeling the intensity of what they are engaged in. Without the mask, everyone will be able to see Ramona. They will now get a glimpse of what Tobias has seen all along. A new beginning is unfolding. Tobias and Ramona have tears in their eyes as he gently wipes away the layers of make-up away from Ramona's life. Maggie joins them. The three people in this room know this is so much more than a make-up lesson, yet they all know words about it cannot be spoken. Their communication has gone by way of love, faith and trust without the English language --- words would only ruin the moment.

"Tobias, change the water" Maggie directs.

They proceed and the true beauty and innocence of this little girl unfolds. Maggie is petite though one would not have used this word to describe her before this moment. Her persona was big. She was cocky and often seemed angry. Just like her make-up added a few years to her physical presentation, her lack of it has taken some away. We have gone from a vision of 17 years of age to 13 in a matter of minutes. We've also gone from the big persona with the cockiness and anger to a girl appearing less her age of 15 who is non-threatening, innocent and seemingly at peace.

Maggie asks,

"Are you ready to see the cleared stage? As she raises a large mirror in front of her.

Ramona shakes her head affirmatively but slowly. She is scared. This is the first time since this process began in which she has shown hesitation. She places the rag Tobias was using over her face and begins to sob. Both Maggie and Tobias just wait it out. Tobias slides his hand under the towel and begins to gently rub the side of Ramona's head. Maggie in the meantime is gently rubbing her leg as she is sitting down now beside her. After a few minutes, Ramona speaks.

"Hey, Tobias, what are you doing?"

"Just comforting you" he responds.

"Where did you learn that?" she says

"I don't know I just did it"

"Well, I don't like it. It's like you're scratching at my ear or something" still with the rag over her face.

Tobias and Maggie look at each other and smile. Ramona's coming back. She is showing us some strength and may be ready to proceed.

"I'll stop then Ramona" he tells her.

"I didn't say to stop, I just don't like it there right now. Could you do that on the back of my neck for a little bit?"

Maggie did all she could to not tease these young teens in love. She knew Ramona could not turn back now. Certainly, she would regain some hutzpah. She could not walk around like the emotional wet noodle she had turned into during this process. She had crossed the boundary and let Tobias see her fully.

"Sure Ramona, how's that?" he questions

"That's good Tobias. That's really nice".

The recovery took about another half hour so Maggie went about some other things while Tobias attended to Ramona's directions as to where to rub, scratch and for how long and how hard. Maggie reappears to begin the next phase.

"How are you feeling Ramona? Ready to try some new make-up?

"I can't stop now Mrs. Greenwood"

"Sure, you can if you want" Maggie says with a smile

"You know what I mean; I don't want to stop now" smiling back at Maggie.

Tobias became lost during this phase. Tobias being Tobias he got all the emotional stuff building up to this but he did not get the actual make-up lesson. Ramona and Maggie became so invested in this process and their talk while doing so, Tobias just began doing other things around the house. He also inherently knew this was something they needed to do without him. By the time they were finished, a new girl appeared before them. Ramona was a beautiful girl. Though Tobias would prefer her without any make-up, he certainly preferred this level of make-up over the previous. Even though he could see past this before, he was fully aware of how others could not. As they parted ways, Maggie reassured Ramona she could come by anytime for tips and such about these matters. Ramona was so excited and in her own excitement she began to believe it possible her Mom would be excited as well.

Ramona's excitement of the moment fostered an expectation of a normal, loving maternal response. Things were not going well in Ramona's home. Ms. Evans had begun drinking more and more and the conflicts within the home had been increasing since early fall. Ramona seemed used to the cycle but for Tobias, her new friends, and the town's people, it was very new. Despite this, Ramona seemed to persevere.

Tobias and Ramona had been doing well. The girl now smiles at Tobias and even at others sometimes. Seems like his feelings toward her have been accepted, while Maggie Greenwood was becoming the maternal figure Ramona so desperately sought. Tobias and Ramona do not appear to have many out-right dates, yet they do hang out a lot at school. Word has it Ramona's mom has been limiting their time together. Ms. Evans' addiction has been no secret; it is too small of a community. There are increasingly public incidents to which many locals are aware. Ramona has been seen numerous times helping her Mom walk home from the local tavern and all the while her Mom cusses and degrades her. Ramona appears accustomed to this role. It has become easier to see why she looks out for her little brother and sister so --- she tries to protect them from their mother. The love of this mother's daughter --- to take such verbal abuse and disappointment yet be there for her whenever someone would call the home and tell her that her Mom needs help getting home; not uncommon for families dealing with the demons of addiction. The children are held emotionally hostage to a person who sometimes loves them, sometimes not, and then the adult-child roles become reversed. This role reversal only benefits the adult; the children will suffer great consequences.

8) *A Mother's Influence Gone Awry*

It is later in the evening and Ramona enters her home. She can't wait to see the reactions from her Mom, little brother and sister. Within moments after opening the front door, Ms. Evans appears. There is a silence and she just stares at Ramona. Ramona is so proud and ready to burst with joy. She is so wanting to share this feeling with her Mom.

"What the hell did you do?" Ms. Evans inquires

"Mommy, what do you think? Tobias' Mom helped me do this.

"What was wrong with the way you looked?"

"Nothing Mommy, I just wanted to try something dif… her Mom cut her off and said,

"Shut your mouth. Does that lady think she can change you by doing this to you? You still look like a tramp and you or I can't change that. I'm going out, go watch you brother and sister".

Devastation by her Mom's reaction for the rest of that evening was slowly replaced by a steady boiling anger and deep, deep sadness --- by recognizing she and her Mom may never have shared moments of joy. Her Mom may never be the Mom she was supposed to be or the one Ramona so wished her to be. Ramona had begun convincing herself her life situation was one of permanence; it would never change.

The fall of 1976 brings with it great expectations for the Kannot High School Spartans. Tobias and Tommy are co-captains. They are natural leaders and their teammates willingly and merrily follow. They have earned their trust since their freshman year and now they are ready for another hopeful run at the league championship.

Some kids in Kannot planned a keg party before game night. Those old coal drags created mazes amongst the column dumps and provided the cover for such activities, but for the teens these areas were well known for their party and parking potential. The local cops seemed to stay away from the area even when we believed they knew what was going on. It was like they didn't want to interfere with tradition as they frequented these areas as teens as well.

Tobias did not partake and he requested others not too as well but he knew the limits of his directives when it came to matters like this. Despite Tobias' sense of maturity and influence even he was no match at times for the intrigue and excitement of some wrongdoings of the adolescent landscape.

The first three games of the season came and went with the expectations of the community being reached. Kannot is 3 and 0 and had won each game decisively. The fourth game of the year was a tougher match. It was with a traditional powerhouse in the league --- one to whom they had only came out the victors a few times in their fifteen-year history. But, it was a close one last year and because of this, it is expected to be a great game this year with many of the same players on both sides leading the charge.

Word made its way around town, at least through the teen underground, that the party was a go at Sky's Clearing for Friday night; the night before a rare Saturday game. Sky's Clearing was an area well up the side of Sunrise Mountain, only accessible through the mazes of the column dumps near the bottom of the mountain. There was only one road up and down, but it was so grown in it was well hidden from those unfamiliar with the area. Local teens had convinced themselves only they knew of this road, however, it had been traveled before by their parents, town officials, town business folks and town police as well during their high school years. It was so exciting to believe it was a secretive place. Nobody openly discussed it and it seemed as if this level of anonymity was respected by those in which the teen years had long passed.

It's Thursday night and Ramona's Mom has not come home. Her Mom usually got drunk very early. She would eventually receive calls from a bar patron or bar owner as to her whereabouts. On this night, no calls came and it was late. Ramona made sure her siblings were asleep and then took to her walk downtown to find her Mom. She looked for her at all the usual places but nothing. If not for a loud laugh she never would have gave a car parked in the back corner of an unfamiliar bar her attention. She knew her Mom's loud laugh; it only happened when she was drunk. In the home her Mom's laughter was never of joy but of some sort of sarcasm or mean spirited jest. Ramona approached the car and was deeply saddened by what she saw. She couldn't help but yell to her Mom.

"Mommy, Mommy, please stop and come home!" she cried.

"Woos out there!" yelled her Mom

"Mommy, it's me, Ramona, please come with me Mommy and we'll go home".

By this time, the man had gathered himself and was telling Ms. Evans to get out of his car. Ramona's Mom crawls out of the car, wardrobe unkempt, and begins her attack on Ramona. There were some witnesses by this time. Ramona's yells for her Mom were heard by some neighbors and some patrons on the way to their cars.

"You little whore!" she yelled to Ramona. "Who zhink you are coming here! I'm mother you little whore".

"Mommy, please stop and come home" was all Ramona would say.

Ms. Evans ramped up her verbal assault.

"You zhink youuuu better than me? You think you pretty more than me? You bother me. I wish I never had zhoo, you tramp."

"Mommy, please stop"

"Zhstop wha? The twuth. You know you done more of this than me, whore!"

Those words came out clearer and louder than anything

her mother was saying. It was as if she sobered up for a moment to spew the most possible hate-filled message onto her daughter. And with that, she began slapping Ramona in the face and head. She pulled her hair as well. Ramona, crying out "Mommy, mommy please stop and come home with me" between verbal and physical assaults. Her Mom would not stop. By the time the police arrived, Ramona had blood streaming out of her nose and on to her jacket and pajama bottoms. Her face was scratched and swollen, yet she begged the police officer to let her take her Mom home. She had been through this before, but not since her arrival in Kannot. It would become clear to many that the behaviors Ramona presented at her previous school were calculated. Her expulsion would prompt another move, this time to Kannot. This was Ramona's way of protecting her mother from public shaming and confrontations.

The police would not let Ramona's Mom go home. She would sleep it off in the county jail; a situation well-known by law enforcement and Camille Evans. By the time most people began hearing of this event, it was late morning at school. Ramona was not there yet. Her Mom would be released from jail early and taken home. After Ramona got her cleaned up and put in bed she began to get her brother and sister ready for school and then prepare herself for a day she has experienced before. But this time Ramona responded differently. She seemed to let the drunken words and assault by her mother rip to her core, she seemed to believe them. Ramona would not come to school on this day as the Ramona she wanted to be; the way she risked being since her beautiful day at the Greenwood home just a few days past. She would come to school the way her Mom projected her to be.

By mid-morning Ramona arrives in full make-up mode. She was ignoring all who called out to her. Tobias was stunned by her appearance. Her makeup could not fully cover the marks on her face or the pains in her eyes and heart and it was those pains he saw clearly. As soon as the third period ends Tobias tries to stop her from walking past him.

"Ramona, Ramona" Tobias calls to her.

"Tobias, leave me alone. It's over. I can't be what you all want me to be. Just leave me alone" as she walks away.

Everyone had heard about the events in the bar parking lot by the afternoon. Most had been seeing the positive changes in Ramona over the past year as her progress on the social front had really picked up, but especially since Tuesday, Ramona's appearance was much the chatter --- good chatter. But now, their hearts break for Ramona; she is cold and distant, even more so than when she first arrived in Kannot. The school day will end with Ramona speaking with no one and briskly walking home. Tobias attempted the walk with her but she was heard to scream at him.

"Get away from me!"

Tobias' facial expressions rarely include one of worry. He almost always showed a calm confidence things would be Ok. On this day, he did not have this look. He looked like a lost puppy. He did not seem to have an answer. The pain he was feeling for Ramona transferred into him a sense of helplessness. Another brief glimpse into the humanness of Tobias. Tobias saw his only option was to keep an eye on Ramona's home. He thought he could at least do this to protect her from, from ... even he did not know.

The party was beginning to blossom at Sky's Clearing. At about dusk time, 7:30 or so, Tobias sees Ramona leave her house. Ramona is going to the party to rebel against all things good and to confirm her mother's perception of her.

He begins to follow her. She is the painted lady again and her wardrobe is more like her mother's. She is making her way to the party and is aware Tobias is following her. Tobias simply resigns to the fact he will protect her from a distance as she is simply too angry to talk with him. He is hopeful she will come around but he intends to protect her until that time comes. The other kids are surprised to see Tobias at the party.

"Hey Tobias!" they call out. "Glad you could make it man" he hears repeatedly, all the while as he watches Ramona from a distance.

She is breaking his heart as she also begins to drink. This party is a bit different. It is bigger than usual and there are quite a few unfamiliar faces; perhaps friends of friends and with the big game on Saturday night maybe it's billed as some kind of informal pep rally. There will be very few players here and they will not be drinking, especially now that Tobias has shown up. They are a disciplined lot.

About two hours pass and Tobias has not taken his eyes off Ramona. She now has a few guys around her. They are amongst some of the strangers at the party. Tobias asks a few of his peers about them but no one seems to know them.

"Tobias, what are you doing here man?" from a familiar voice and teammate.

"Hi Tommy. Just making sure our teammates are behaving"

"Me too, that's why I showed up but I did not expect to see you".

"Well, you know, I guess I am unpredictable sometimes"

"Tobias, you and unpredictable don't belong in the same sentence. You are one of the most predictable people I know and what's up with the hand- why is it turned like that?"

"I'm fine Tommy".

"So, you ready for the game?" Tommy says.

"Always Tommy, always" Tobias responds as they begin talking for a bit about some of the particulars for the Saturday night show.

"Hey, get that hand checked out by coach tomorrow" Tommy replies as he walks away.

9) Evil Enters Tobias' World

After about 10 minutes Tobias realizes he has taken his concentration off Ramona and begins to look for her. She has moved from the area last seen. He spends the next five minutes looking for her. He moves from person to person asking if they had seen her. Finally, someone tells him she had left a while ago with some guys. Tobias hears of the direction they went and begins his pursuit. It's dark but the moon is bright and provides enough glow to see the road and pathways. He hears a commotion off to the right and takes the pathway toward it. He sees the boys tearing at Ramona's clothes. He charges them. While wrestling with two boys he gets hit on the head from behind. He is knocked unconscious and placed on top of Ramona. He regains consciousness as they are trying to pull him off her to further rape her. He clutches on to her as they beat him; he is a concussive–like state and is fighting to do the best he can for the moment --- protect Ramona. He will not let them on her. They pull his pants down and run as they hear others coming down the road. Someone else leaving the party hears Ramona's cries. There are now several other teens there and what they see is Tobias on top of Ramona; both half naked. Her clothes are ripped and he seems drunk. They cannot believe what they are seeing. It appears as if Tobias attempted to rape Ramona. The police are called, the party is broken up and the town of Kannot's favorite son is receiving their judgement. Ramona was in shock through that night and into the next day. She was not aware of what was being said.

Throughout the town: "Our Tobias! No way" but then they would say something like, "I guess you never really know anyone". When Ramona became able to speak, the truth was heard. The town of Kannot was devastated for at least 24 hours until Ramona's story could get out to the public. Nonetheless, the confusion is cleared up and Tobias is vindicated, but he ceases communication with Ramona and most others. He appears a different person; still loving, just different --- much quieter. At this point in their lives, Jonathan and Maggie are relieved to see one of Tobias' hands turned backward. Over the years, they recognized the pattern just never spoke openly about it.

Tobias was unable to play for four weeks after the attack. He suffered some head trauma and had a severe laceration requiring 33 stitches and a concussion, but even more visible was the change in his demeanor. His pursuits of Ramona had come to a halt. She did not know how to handle this. She had become accustomed to this and without it she seemed lost. She had guilt too. After all, it was her decision to go off with those boys. She just remembers them howling like wolves when they first got her off the path and tore at her clothes. They almost raped her but could not because of Tobias' will to protect her despite his concussive state, but they beat Tobias badly. No one, two or even three people could do this on most days, but for him not knowing there was a third person behind him, it happened on that night. Our group was also suffering from this change. He would not talk much with us. The doctors told the Greenwoods Tobias may be "out of kilter a bit" for a while but further stated he would be fine in a couple weeks. A couple weeks passed and he was still not the Tobias we knew.

Tobias began to practice nearing the late part of the season. The team had done well without him; Tommy made sure of it. They won the biggest game of the season the night after the attack. They are 7 and 0 and they have been playing with Tobias in their hearts. Tobias was on the sidelines but without his usual passion for the game. With Tobias back on the team they would cruise to two more league wins and win the league championship outright --- A championship the Valley Cats had won the five years prior. The Kannot High School Spartans would move on toward the district championship and Tobias was again playing at his best. The district championship game was at the Scranton Memorial Stadium. It was by far the largest venue this team played in. They would be playing the Mountain High School Wolves. A fierce team in its' own right and also undefeated.

All of Kannot is there and it appears the same for the fans of the Mountain High Wolves. The atmosphere smells of cigars, in contrast with the health and well- being the beautiful evening clear sky presents, though on such a night the olfactory and visual senses work together and help create this incredible football atmosphere. Many clad in their high school class year jackets that maybe shouldn't be as there are some tight fits out there. The hustle and bustle of the crowd movement, the cheerleaders; it's just a crazy beautiful atmosphere! It's so much more than just a game for Kannot. We've never been here before; our football legacy just started within the past few years. We are the new kids on the block and it is fun. It's a cool late November evening though and the blankets are out in the bleachers just waiting for the umpire's whistle to get this game underway.

The way we've been playing we thought we'd have this in the bag early, but there is a reason the Wolves have been here before. They are good and have more players playing at a higher level than our small-town team. On paper, this should not be much of a match, but we have Tobias and Tommy and their leadership will give us a great game, win or lose.

The first quarter goes by in a flash and Kannot held its own for the most part; only down 10 to 3. You can tell this high-powered dynasty is surprised by Kannot. They are frustrated and can't seem to make sense why they're not rolling over Kannot like they did to most of their competition this past year or probably more. Tobias and Tommy have the team performing at a high level, thus the coaches have the faith to stick with the game plan they've worked on for this team.

The second quarter starts and Kannot gets a quick score behind the pancake blocking of Tommy and Tobias all the way down the field. The Wolves are now tied and they don't like it. I would say they are not a team that knows good sportsmanship. They've been on a high for so long, they don't know how to handle any diversity. They've just been called for a personal foul which occurred well after the play was over --- and it's their ball. Several of the players start to howl like wolves. What seemed like poor sportsmanship is turning quickly into something else. Ramona is a few seats to my right and she starts sobbing violently and cannot talk. On the field, Tobias is looking for us. He's trying to find Ramona. He appears to look at her, then at the howlers, then starts pacing. The referees are trying to start the game again after the foul but Tobias is pacing in their backfield. He then makes an aggressive turn and run toward the three players that were howling. Tobias lifts the one in the air and throws him like a rag doll and picks him up two more times and does the same. Ramona now starts screaming for Tobias. She is screaming to us to help him, to stop him. She knows what's happening but as of yet no one else does. The one player is down. The referees are signaling for Tobias to get off the field and he won't. Flags are all over the place and he seems not to care. Tommy goes to hold him back and he pulls away as if not even touched. He goes after another player and body slams him with a couple punches to anywhere they would land. The crowd is silent and scared on both sides. You could hear the third boy yelling,

"It wasn't me, it was them, it was them!"

Now, we look at Ramona and she is saying they are the boys who tried to rape her. She leaves the seat and she's running and screaming for Tobias. In the meantime, he's after the third boy. The coaches, the refs, the players --- no one wants to get in Tobias' way at this point. He is strong and out of control. The police are on their way to the field. Fortunately, Ramona runs onto the field at the same time and runs to Tobias. She is the only one he does not seem able to hurt at this moment. She is holding on to him. He is staring off, nose running, red-faced and in a state not seen before. She is talking to him.

"Tobias, Tobias, it's me honey, It's Ramona. Please stop Tobias, it's over".

By this time, the teams have figured out what happened because the third boy has confessed to his coaches. The night of the party at Sky's Clearing they were initially there just to check out their potential opponents no doubt. The police are letting Ramona try to settle Tobias down before they approach and in the meantime, learn of his motivation. Tobias drops to his knees and lets out some screams that sends shivers down everyone's spines. He's holding his head in his hands as Ramona holds him. She is now gently rocking him like a baby. "I love you Tobias, I love you. It's over honey. Please talk to me, look at me". Tobias couldn't look at anyone and didn't move. The game was held up for 25 minutes. Finally, the refs inform the Kannot coaches he had to leave the field, while the Wolves' coaches were told the police would be taking their three players to the station, along with Tobias, though due to Tobias' aggression they also had to cuff him. They had some difficulty with this task because of Tobias' 'deformed' hand they would write in their report. This was a heartbreaking moment for those who knew Tobias. Tobias' teammates, coaches, Ramona, his parents and a few friends from the bleachers were able to get Tobias to stand up and move with them. He knew his game was over, but his peers vowed to play on and fight for the win; to which they did to the score of 28 to 13. Many upset fans left and the win did not have its intended effect on Kannot. It did in the media because they love a good story being further affected by the emotions surrounding the story. But Kannot was worried about their favorite son. They witnessed an aggression from a young man they never knew possible. Tobias moves about his school, classes and home quietly for a couple of weeks. He has still stayed away from Ramona as well. He's never stayed away from Ramona so long since the day he first saw her. He keeps his head down at school so he makes little eye contact with anyone. His coaches, teachers, parents and friends all support him and tell him it's OK and that they understand why he did what he did. But Tobias doesn't seem to understand. This young man who loves life and cares for others so deeply, is troubled over his reactions. Jonathan and Maggie are encouraging him to read his bible, specifically on areas of forgiveness, while Ramona is heartbroken at his shuns.

10) Recovery

By February Tobias starts to change. Seems he is forgiving himself and beginning to look at people again. The looks of love and support he is now seeing is helping. Ramona is walking around lost. Tobias is told about her by Wilson and Jimmy J and he says,
"She still wants me?"

"Yes, you big goof, she was telling you that on the field that night too. She must have said she loved you a dozen times" they tell him.

"I didn't hear any of it. I couldn't hear anyone. I thought it was over. I couldn't look her in the eye, couldn't answer her calls, would avoid her whenever possible because I thought she was going to yell at me or tell me I'm some kind of animal"

"No way man! She's just been waiting for you to come around, you need to find her and tell her what you told us because she has no idea and is really hurt" they tell Tobias.

Now Tobias begins searching the school and he finds the class Ramona is in. He walks right in to the middle of the class and extends his hand to her --- she takes it. He walks her out of the classroom and they leave the building and sit and talk on the picnic tables for the rest of the day. No angry teachers, no student interference; they were all happy at the change of events and wanted to move forward too. This had been bothering the adults and students for quite some time. The healing begins.

Tobias would often speak of forgiveness. He would say it was such a beautiful word, a God-created word. A word delivered with the simplest of breaths and if you try it with too much volume it just doesn't work. He would say it was made that way so anyone could say it. It is clear even in a whisper. It can only be asked for in the most beautiful ways, but he initially struggled with offering it to himself.

The tragedy and triumphs of the first half of the school year are behind us. The Holiday Season has come and gone and life has settled back down in Kannot and at the high school. It seemed as if a catharsis was necessary for Ramona to truly break free from the emotional bondage of her Mother's addiction. Ms. Evan's may never recover; she may not want to, but we found out her daughter does.

CHAPTER VIII

THE SURPRISE:
OTHERS HAVE GIFTS TOO

It was a long and cold winter in the mountains of Northeastern, Pennsylvania; cold snaps of below zero are not uncommon, nor are some major snow storms. The best part about which are the snow days. Days of either sleeping in, playing in the snow, or just hanging out with friends on a gifted day off. Notice no mention of studying or work, henceforth the foreseeable joy of such days.

With the end of winter comes the excitement of spring, mostly because the end of the school year is in sight. This is only matched by the excitement as the end of a summer nears; most kids are bored and ready for a new school year; excited to be in a higher grade, especially the former 6th, 9th and 11th graders. They're moving on to Junior High, High School or senior year. But that excitement is short-lived, probably by the second or third week when everyone gets settled in they are reminded about schoolwork. Unlike spring, when there is a steady building crescendo to the finish line.

Along with spring time comes the annual High School talent show. Taylor is so musical --- you could be in a deep conversation with him but still see his body moving in some sort of rhythm to some far-off music; sometimes you may not even hear it. It could be from a radio four doors down in the staff lounge or it could be from a car stopped in a gas station at the end of the block. His body seems to seek it. He could be in a non-musical activity yet this rhythmic movement is still there, though barely noticeable or even unnoticeable at times to others. To the untrained eye or ear, he just seems fidgety I guess.

The end of the year talent show is upon us. Taylor usually runs the sound system and he has, on occasion, played some back up instrumentals for varying performances. He's never been one for crowds let alone be front and center on a stage. He certainly has the talent. The boy seems able to play whatever instrument is placed in front of him. I believe at last count, he could play eighteen instruments and that number has probably stagnated since this may be all the instruments we have in Kannot.

Taylor's out-of-the-limelight personality is only matched by his closest friend in the group, Sadie --- apparently till now. The school paper is out and guess who's performing together, but after their names it simply states, "performance unspecified". Being that acts are not always easy to come by, or maybe better said, good acts are not easy to come by, the talent show committee has allowed this mystery performance. Plus, everyone knows Taylor is a musician so we are quite sure he can entertain us with an instrument. But Sadie? I guess we'll see come April. The questioning however has begun.

"Hey Sadie, what are you and Taylor going to do at the talent show?" asks Jimmy J.

"Taylor, what instrument will you be playing?" asks Wilson.

The questions were coming from many angles though always met with a low energy and voice.

"I don't know ", says Sadie; "Not sure yet" says Taylor.

After a week or so of this it became clear there was only one of us not asking any questions ---- Tobias.

And there could be only one reason for that --- He Knows! Collette approaches Tobias.

"Tobias, what are Taylor and Sadie going to do at the show?" she asks.

The group put her up to it. Collette is sometimes used as the innocent child, one with a severe disability. A child that certainly could not have any particular motive in search of such a simple answer. Unfortunately, the team forgets Tobias' relationship with Collette is not based upon her disability. He really doesn't see it anymore.

"Did you ask them, Collette?" Tobias responds.

"No, I really haven't seen them much lately and when I do I guess I forget to ask".

"Good try Collette." Tobias says

"Tobias, that's not fair!" Collette yells.

"What's not fair? I think being nosey is not fair" Tobias says

And the two begin to argue. When the dust settles, the group has once again been reminded about Tobias and Collette's relationship and recognizes using Collette was not a wise choice. But what they did surmise is that he knows.

The "Talent Show" is upon us. There are mostly seniors involved; every year they seem to figure they have nothing to lose. They'll just get crazy on stage and not worry about making fools of themselves. From teacher impersonations, to acting out commercials, or giving a shot at something they themselves deem funny; it's a senior thing. Funny how public performance is perceived. Some are terrified, yet others take the opportunity to make complete fools of themselves --- and not even care. But, we are worried for Taylor and Sadie as they would fall in the "terrified" group. They are fragile and could come out of this devastated. Most of us are ill at ease with this, that is, except the usual cast of characters and their acts, along with a few new ones. Nonetheless, the seniors enter and leave the stage; some with great laughter, some with none, some with applause, some with none --- awkward moments indeed. But now, the announcement from the MC,

"Ladies and gentlemen, Taylor Hughes and Sadie Spagnolia, singing and playing together for the first time in public".

Oh, I can still hear those words and I relive the angst that fell upon most of our crew --- 'for the first time in public'. I remember picking that statement apart --- so they've been doing this but not in public? Somebody had to know! Of course, I look over at Tobias and he's as comfortable as a kitten on a cool pillow.

"Tobias, you knew something about this!" and he just smiles.

And the MC cuts into my confusion,

"Taylor and Sadie, or as they prefer to be called, Ladies and Gentlemen, Agape's Call!"

See, this is what I was worried about, the bunch of goofs in this room, minimal applause, and their eagerness to eat these two alive and then the curtains begin to slowly open. Oh my, the stage is beautiful! Where did the elegance come from? As stream of purple, blues and pinks shimmering across blankets of white sheets in a half-moon shape around the performance area of the stage. There's a piano and there's a mic at the piano and one standing from the floor near the piano, but where are …

"See Tobias! They just couldn't do it and I blame you! Now we have to put Humpty Dumpty and Humpty Dumptess back together again"

"Yee of little Faith", Tobias whispers. "They're just making the crowd want to see more".

He knows something. I don't know what's getting me more upset --- "Agape's Call" or Tobias knowing something. And suddenly, this beautiful woman walks upon the stage to the mic. She is in a silver sequenced gown with the colors of the beautiful lighting exploding onto her. Her hair is gorgeous and …. Hey! That's Sadie! The crowd is reacting as I. No one could imagine it was her until they realized IT WAS HER. And then the other half comes out in a white tuxedo, and again, the colors are working for him too. He takes his seat at the High School's grand piano and Sadie positions herself at the microphone and who are they looking at and smiling? Tobias! Everyone in the audience is stunned at the sheer beauty of the visuals and the apparent professionalism of the stage and humor décor. But they think as I am certain --- Oh no! They over did the entry! There cannot be a follow-up that will match. We are back to me being even more upset with Tobias.

"Hey, one of big Faith", I say to him. "Are you happy now?" Everyone is expecting a great performance of something and they already got it with the stage and the dress. Now what are we going to do?"

"OK, what is the name of their group?" Tobias says to me.

"Agape's Call"? I questioned back to him

"That's right, so get ready to see and hear something really lovely" he says.

Sadie approaches the mic,

"First, let us thank the Lord for what we are about to share with you and we hope you'll like it".

And she's standing there with a smile on her face, all the confidence in the world, looking the pro, and then winks at Tobias! What is going on here? Then Tobias reminds me of something.

"You do know Sadie's Mom was a performer once, and a very good one. You have heard her sing before" he tells me.

"Yes, I do remember her singing sometimes and it was beautiful" I respond.

"Then relax and just know God gave her child the gift of song and performance too".

"Yes, but both of them are so quiet and shy in front of others" Collette quips.

"Don't let that ever fool you my friend," he says. When you have a gift and the Holy Spirit wants you to share it with others you will see people do phenomenal things and that is what will happen today"

And the keys of the piano begin the moment.

The group is all sitting together and Collette says, "I know it, I know it"! excitedly.

And Taylor starts to sing first.

"You can come as you are with just your heart ….."

Collette loudly proclaims, "Yes, Marilyn McCoo and Billy Davis Jr"!

And I'll take you in though
You're rejected and hurt
To me you're worth
Girl, what you have within
And then Sadie kicks it in,
Oh honey, boy
I don't need no superstar
Cause I'll accept you as you are
You won't be denied
Cause I'm satisfied
With the love that you can inspire
Back to Taylor
You don't have to be a star, baby
To be in my show
Oh, honey
You don't have to be a star, baby
To be in my show

And they're trading off lines now. No piccolo or flutey
thing in the background, no back-up singers, but what Taylor
is doing to those keys you would think an entire band is
playing.

Somebody nobody knows
Could steal the tune that you want to hear
So stop your running around
Cause now you've found what was cloudy is clear
Oh honey, there'll be no cheering from the crowds
Just two hearts beating out loud
There'll be no parade
No TV or stage
Only me till your dying day

And then the harmonies! They are incredible!

You don't have to be a star, baby
To be in my show, Oh, honey You…

And they bring the song to an end and the crowd finds itself stunned. I knew they could do it all along! But there is silence and a moment of uncertainty regarding reaction. OK, there it is, some teachers start clapping and the entire crowd erupts.

"Thank You, thank you so much" the two pros applaud back to their classmates --- now fans. The chants for "More, More, More" start and as fate would have it, Agape's Call has more.

"Thank you" Sadie tells them and she says this; Without the Father's Graces we could not be doing this today so here we go. Let's thank Him Taylor".

And the keys start it again. It's familiar and I think we are going to church this time.

Amazing grace, How sweet the sound
That saved a wretch like me.
I once was lost, but now I am found,
Was blind, but now I see.

'Twas grace that taught my heart to fear,
And grace my fears relieved.
How precious did that grace appear
The hour I first believed.

And again, they trade off vocally like pros and bring in their harmonies for the highest of emotional impact.

Through many dangers, toils and snares
I have already come,
'Tis grace has brought me safe thus far
And grace will lead me home.

The Lord has promised good to me
His word my hope secures;
He will my shield and portion be,
As long as life endures.

Yea, when this flesh and heart shall fail,
And mortal life shall cease
I shall possess within the veil,
A life of joy and peace.

When we've been there ten thousand years
Bright shining as the sun,
We've no less days to sing God's praise
Than when we've first begun.

And they finish their two-song set and the world is a different place, or at least the school is. But guess who just sits there and appreciates and always knew? I'm telling you this young man knows things and sometimes it seems he knows too many things. I'll get over it. I'm just jealous of the way he moves about the world. There is no way Taylor and Sadie did this without Tobias; I just don't know, and probably never will know, how this unfolded. Oh, and holding hands as they left the stage and I saw a kiss and hug off to the side of the stage --- they are also a couple?!. Should I have known this or saw this coming? In retrospect, apparently. They had some townspeople gossiping and saying some racial things but they were the minority. The friends made through school and this special group of friends made them an adoring couple. In this case, as in many, the kids at school educated their parents on things like this, not the other way around. Maybe this was just in Kannot. Tough to know how other communities learn. Time flies now. Life seems to have picked up speed. Our high school years have ended and everyone has gone their own way.

Chapter IX

The Class of '77 Moves On and the Christian Light Reigns

Life after high school was greatly different. Most of us were still getting up early to address the challenges we now face, i.e. college or work. Jimmy J was off to Penn State, Wilson to Keystone Community College and no doubt to start his first classes there with,

"Wilson Willson – that's first name one L, second two!"

Wilson would start his trek to become a social worker with a focus on grieving children and families. Amen! How lives may be impacted at such early ages. Belinda's life **MATTERED** and Wilson's work would prove it.

Jimmy J seeking a major but living it up at PSU while trying to remain the practicing Christian he had become over the years.

Sadie and Taylor committed to Agape's Call and their performances together across the state, Tobias to his Diner now, and Collette to her vocational rehabilitation program, which by the way, just happened to end up at the Diner with Tobias. Kimberly was still in the picture at the diner, but only on a part time basis. We would still find a way to support each other and to get together whenever possible. Holidays offered the best times since everyone would be home. We maintained our group identity through Jimmy J's, Wilson's and Collette's graduation, through Sadie and Taylor's increased notoriety, and through Tobias' success as a restaurateur. During the summer of 1982 life was a joy. Tobias and Ramona married after high school. They have two little sweethearts; a four-year-old, Tobias Theodore

Greenwood or, as fate would have it, Teddy, and a two-year-old girl named after Ramona's Mom, Camille or Cammi as she was often called. And, yes, Ms. Evans' heart was changed by her grandchildren and was then able to understand what Tobias meant way back when he said "eventually".

1) Raymond's First Call for Help

We decided to have a fifth year KHS reunion at a local hotspot with Sadie and Taylor, married now, also offering some performances. The night was well underway when Mrs. Gilbrandt came running into the Auditorium looking for Tobias.

"Tobias please come and help Raymond, please Tobias"

"What's going on Mrs. Gilbrandt?"

"I think he wants to kill himself. He just started talking about this reunion and how he hates himself. Please Tobias, please come, he is very drunk and is trying to get my keys".

Tobias would never turn down a plea for help. He had witnessed Raymond's deterioration since elementary school and he was aware of his drinking and drug abuse since high school. Tobias left the club with purpose. Since Mrs. Gilbrandt made her pleas in front of our group we would all leave with Tobias and make our way toward the Gilbrandt home. The last thing Tobias said as we departed was,

"Raymond's conflict begins to end tonight"

As we pull up to the driveway and get out of the car, Raymond was jumping into his mother's car. Tobias began yelling,

"Raymond stop! Please, Raymond stop! I'm so sorry Raymond"!

Raymond stopped for a moment and stared at Tobias.

"You saw what he did! You saw what he did!" yelled Raymond. "I was little Raymond. I didn't know what I was seeing" Tobias yelled back.

Something was being communicated but only Tobias and Raymond seemed to know. What did Tobias apologize for? This was all happening so fast. Off Raymond went, speeding away down Rabbit Road; named so for its frequent hops and turns. It was not a friendly road for those of sound mind and body and Raymond had neither tonight. Before we could gather our senses to determine our next move, we heard a loud crash. It had to be Raymond. There was no way he could have made that first turn.

Tobias began running down the road. He knew he would be there before the time it took everyone to get back into the car. By the time the rest of us pulled up, Tobias was already at the overturned car. It was smoking badly and we could see Raymond. He seemed barely conscious and there was lots of blood. The smoke was getting thicker and thicker yet Tobias remained at the driver side door trying to get at Raymond. The police and fire stations weren't but five minutes away and we could already hear the sirens coming. As they were pulling in, the car began to blaze. It was a chaotic scene as we were all yelling for Tobias to get away. The police and fire crew were not initially aware Tobias was on the other side of the car. When they realize this, they tried to get near.

"Tobias! Son, let it go! Tobias, let it go! cried the fire chief

"No sir" he yelled back. "I cannot desert my friend again"

"Tobias, you can't help him now, get out of there now!"

The flames were coming out of the engine and starting to come in through the dashboard. The fire chief could not get near and he did not know how Tobias was still able to communicate. Then he notices,

"Oh my God, Tobias let go, let go!

He sees Tobias's skin dripping off his arm and the side of his face. The fire chief sees Tobias' right hand and believes his deformed hand cannot help him get free he later reports.

"Tobias, Tobias! Oh my God Tobias, let go!

Within a fraction of a second the door is ripped open and Tobias throws Raymond away from the car, but he himself collapses within the fire's breath. The fire chief and one of the officers are able to grab Tobias' feet and pull him away from the burning car.

"John! Get his friends back. They cannot see him like this".

Tobias is smoldering so much his body is barely visible.

"Tobias! Tobias"! We scream.

"Ok, Ok, I need you all to stay away from him" says the chief. Help is on the way, just please don't look at him, stay away".

This all happened so fast we were right there. There were no blockades or other officers to keep people away. We saw our friend melting. We could only scream his name and cry.

Within an hour, the town of Kannot was in crisis. Its favorite son may not make it along with another young man as well. Everything went into slow motion for the rest of that night. It took about an hour before we all ended up at the Scranton General Hospital. We were in shock by what we saw. We were being attended to at the hospital, while we had no idea about the status of Tobias or Raymond.

The Greenwoods arrive and they have Mrs. Gilbrandt with them.

"How is Raymond?" asks Mrs. Gilbrandt.

"We think he is doing OK. He was not burned but was unconscious. We heard them saying he regained consciousness on the way here. Tobias got him out before the fire got to him" Sadie told her.

"How is Tobias?" asks the Greenwoods

"What about Tobias Jimmy J? asks Maggie

"Mrs. Greenwood, Mrs. Greenwood, he, he .."

That's all Jimmy J could say before he began to sob. He, nor any of us, could tell them they watched their son's skin melting off his body. We knew we could not say this to them. If it was to be said it would come from the chief, one of the officers, or the doctors. Maggie and Jonathan begin to frantically search for any of these people to tell them about Tobias.

"John, John, you were there! What do you know?"

asks Jonathan

"Jonathan, it is really bad. He is burnt badly. That's all I can say. We have to wait for the doctors to know more"

"But John, you should know more, How badly John, How badly?" cries Maggie

"Maggie, please don't make me say anything. Please don't make me say anything" as his head falls into a silent slumber.

"Oh God, No, No Jonathan" Maggie screams.

Now they know the severity and all Jonathan could do was hold up his falling wife. He would hold her on the floor of the emergency room until someone came out with answers. They were not alone. The childhood group of friends that watched their son grow up were with them. They were all there, except Ramona and their two little children. In the craziness of the last hour we had forgotten Ramona was not in Kannot. She was visiting a friend for the day in Scranton with her children. We know her friend and make the call.

"Please no, please no, not Tobias", Ramona shrieks in pain.

"I'll come and get you. Don't you drive here. I'm on my way" Wilson tells her.

Within twenty minutes Ramona and the children are with us.

Chapter X

The Healing

In a year since the accident, Tobias is surviving with significant injuries. He lost his left arm and had severe nerve damage in his right leg. His right hand now has a permanent twist. When this was mentioned, he would only smile. Jonathan and Maggie would also. No one understood their light apparent humor about this. Nonetheless, Tobias was still surprisingly solid in his presence and movement. His face was disfigured, but no one in Kannot saw that. They came to know Tobias' heart so the typical staring and such did not happen from the townspeople; only from others when they first met him, but shortly after they got to know him they also became blind to the physical injuries. Despite his abilities to overcome these limitations, the truth was still known; the ongoing surgeries and infections would eventually take his life. He was very fragile to the outside world. He knew it, we all knew, but we moved forward within his strength for his walking mate, Jesus, who in turn became our walking mate as well. I'm not sure if there is a non-Christian in Kannot today. Possibly a few. Tobias' life pretty much solved that riddle. Kimberly had come back to the Diner to help Tobias and Collette continue the Diner's success. It was all Tobias' recipes now and he had to teach them to Kimberly and Collette. They were taught well and the operation moved forward without a glitch, despite Tobias' rare appearance at the Diner.

About a year after the accident in the summer of '83, Mrs. Gilbrandt calls upon Tobias again. The Diner phone rings and she tells Collette about the problem. Collette knows where Tobias is and calls him. Raymond is once again held up in his home with a gun and Mrs. Gilbrandt believes he's going to kill himself. The mood that beset us was similar to the mood from the outcome one year earlier. But the weather has presented more discomfort as it is a hot and rainy mud-muck kind of day. The group is largely in town and Collette calls them all as Tobias and she are on their way to Raymond's home.

They pull up and Tobias says something different from what he said last year. Last year I strictly remember him saying 'Raymond's conflict begins to end tonight'.

Today he says, "This ends today with Raymond".

He gets out of the car to be met by Mrs. Gilbrandt who offers her physical support to help him. Tobias can see Raymond looking out from his bedroom window.

"Raymond, get down here, I have something to tell you!" – Tobias yells.

"Leave Tobias, there is nothing anyone can do for me. I'm sorry Mom" – he yells out the window".

"I love you Raymond! You have to hear what I need to say" Tobias yells back.

"Look what I did to you and I still hate you and now everyone even hates me more! I have no life here Tobias! I have no life anywhere! I can never be forgiven!"

"Raymond, please come down here to me" Tobias yells

Tobias then uses self-pity, which I never saw him use before. It was the only time in my life I knew he was insincere. But he knew this would get Raymond down close to him so he went for it.

"Raymond, look what you did to me – you owe me some last words before you do this. I know you hate me, but look at me --- look at my face, my arm that is not here, and my leg that doesn't work so well. And I'm not going to be around too much longer. I promise I won't take your gun, just come down here so I can tell you something".

Silence befalls the lips of all. And by now Jimmy J, Wilson, Ramona, Maggie and Jonathan, Sadie and Taylor have all pulled up. The only noise is coming from the downpour of rain that everyone outside is standing in. It's a lake of mud. One cannot hear unless one yells. Up to this point it has been Tobias and Raymond yelling back and forth. And now, stillness and silence of words ---only the roar of a downpour to be heard. Raymond is not near his window, yet in a moment he comes out the front door, walks down the steps and right up to Tobias.

"You're pitiful Tobias!"

With gun in hand, everyone has backed away except Tobias.

"You are right my friend."

And within a half second of those words, Tobias has the gun from Raymond's hand.

"Another lie, another deception from Kannot's favorite burnt up son!" he yells, as Tobias hands the gun to Wilson.

"Raymond, I'm sorry for what I saw, I'm sorry for what I didn't do my friend" Tobias says while beginning to sob.

"You want to cry about this now, 19 years later. You bastard Tobias"

After those words, Tobias grabs Raymond and they begin to struggle. Tobias remains strong despite the injuries and Raymond is no match. They fall to the ground and are rolling in the mud.

"Raymond, my brother, please forgive me, please forgive me. I was young too. I didn't know what I saw, what to say, or what to do.

Sobbing, holding and now hugging Raymond as they lay motionless in the mud under and around them.

"Tobias, I had to hate someone, I just had to hate."

Though there are people around it is hard to hear the dialogue but I'm catching most of it. Tobias has asked for forgiveness about something and it's looking like Raymond may be ready. Fortunately, on this day Raymond is not drunk. The last year took its toll on him. Having the town feel the way they do about him because of Tobias' injuries. He knows they blame him. Even the alcohol could no longer numb his pain. He truly was ready to die today. But it is looking like he heard what he needed from Tobias and Tobias heard what he needed from Raymond. They forgave each other in the mud fest on this day. No one yet knew what each were forgiving the other for until a few months later.

During their childhood when Tobias broke his arm falling off the ladder --- his fall was not from a slip. His fall was from another little boy's eyes gazing into his as an adult was sexually assaulting him. Raymond's heart at that time relied on Tobias to fix it. But, Tobias was a little boy. and though walking with Jesus and having the Holy Spirit, even Tobias did not know how to handle it, so he pretended it did not happen as so many children do when they don't understand things, really bad things. But, pretending makes nothing go away; an evil act became a 19-year hate fest from Raymond and unequalled patience by everyone watching Tobias handle this over the years. No one could imagine the level of forgiveness that both boys needed from each other. And the man? Who knows where his life went or if he continued to hurt others. He was a passerby in Mrs. Gilbrandt's lonely years post her husband's early death we later learned. He wasn't there long, but long enough to do so much damage. Such moments can happen in heartbeat measurements, yet so too can forgiveness.

So, when Tobias said, "This ends today", he meant it and it did. Raymond's life turned for the better. He was now unburdened and able to feel the love that was always there for him, but was hijacked by evil on a day long past. Now, he has the love of the group and Kannot to help him heal further. As the story circulates the town, Raymond begins to live again. He's not embarrassed; he's allowing the love to overcome. Don't know if this man or his Mom has smiled in years. They look like different people now. Raymond, is also enjoying his discovery of Jesus and oh, what changes can occur.

Chapter XI

The Meaning of
a Christian Life Well-Lived

So, here I am, at the foot of the stairs leading to the stage. I'm already shaking and tearful, knowing Tobias' words have been falling true to me as they have been for this entire year. I don't remember being called up, but my next memory places me at the podium as if lifted there void of time, when in fact it would have been Tommy Hollister and Wilson who lifted me there. Sadie will be my voice because I still know the world is not ready for a three-hour introduction. We got into a rhythm over the years; Tommy, Jimmy J, Taylor, Wilson, Sadie and me. They have been great scribes as I put Tobias' story together. And always, they would read back my words so I could hear it read in everyone else's normal time. The boys came to peace about the dialogue Tobias shared with me on their Sunset Mountain hike way back them. They would always remind me,

"Hey, we didn't admit anything, we were just talking about it".

I could only smile and say,

"Sure fellas".

They were never upset with Tobias about the breach of confidence. I think they realized Tobias was my world back then and that I needed to be in on all of it. It made me feel so special; so included. I would have been truly alone without him. I had self-pity back then and I nailed Tobias with it every opportunity I could, at least in our younger years. I have no self-pity now. I am a confident, happy, loved and loving person in this world.

I look around the rows in front of me and see familiar

and unfamiliar faces. The familiar with glossy eyes because they know and those without soon to be. I try to begin to say hello and want to hand over the reading task to Sadie but I choke on air. Of course, everyone worries thinking I am having some sort of Cerebral Palsy (CP) related trauma. I put my hands up to acknowledge good health, let my head hang down for a few seconds and take in some air. I try again.

"Hhhiiiiiiiiiiiii, moooooooooI naaaaaaaaaame Collette Aaaaaadams and IIIIIIII rode de torrry uv my freeeend Tubbbbbbbbias life and disspeech tooooo night. Sadie will ggtell youuu.

"Thank you, Collette, and all the hard work you put into this".

Colette's parents are in the audience proud as peacocks.

"This was Collette's speech and story of Tobias' life. She did what he asked her to do and this is the culmination of a friendship that did not see disability but ability and love. But mostly, it was about patience. This is what Tobias wanted people to know about Collette and others afflicted with CP; just be patient and give them time. We know many may be surprised by Collette's ability, but let us remind you when you know one child with CP, you know one child with CP. Everyone is different, whether afflicted with some form of ailment, disability or not, everyone is different. We suggest you work out an arrangement to communicate with people who have difficulty communicating. Look what we would have missed in Collette --- a beautiful person, friend, and talented storyteller and writer. So, as I go on here, please know I am Collette talking".

"Ladies and gentlemen, I am here today to honor a special person. A man whose life involved lots and lots of love and compassion along with tragedy and triumph. These stories have been well-embedded in this community's history and need not all receive specific attention tonight. Ours is a special community. I know of no other that attained what we have been able to attain in our little place on this earth. We have experienced the profoundness of the impact of true forgiveness --- not just in word as often so --- but in truth. We function as a community like no other. We succeeded as an exceptional community together because we first understood we would stand together even in failure. We have Tobias to thank for this message and many others. The forgivers and the forgiven have moved on together and have done great things together. Our voting process for this event had been agreed upon by our community 11 years ago. When we began the award process for Theodore Tobias Greenwood, we set forth the rules we wanted to hand down to future generations. Open, respectful, non-political dialogues about candidates may begin two years before the choosing. We agreed that anyone being discussed in such distinction would be a good person who has totally committed themselves to the betterment of our community.

The discussions began two years ago in our diners, barber shops, salons, teacher and staff lounges, etc. Unbeknownst to this man, I've been a part of his life for about 29 years --- About 9 years ago, I was there when two men, lying in mud and tears, forgave each other --- I had this moment confirmed by both. Where many only saw the tussle, some of us observed so much more. We saw the sharing and handing over of Grace to a seemingly unlikely candidate. A person that since has led a life of love and giving to others. A man who has led this community to be one of the most charitable communities in our country. His volunteer work as a fireman has saved the lives of two children in our community. His leadership of charities for burn victims, victims of spousal and child abuse, and addictions are unmatched. One needs to look no further than this community to understand the choice of charities. It is with great pleasure and pride I present a wonderful man; a son, husband, father and friend to us all and perhaps most importantly, a link to the goodness and Godliness to our passed brother, Tobias. A link this man will no doubt pass on to the next Person of the Decade. Ladies and gentlemen, Raymond Gilbrandt".

Raymond is in the audience and near collapsing in his mother's arms. For so many years he was a beaten young man. He hated the world and wanted to die. He would later tell people how many times he was going to end his life, but the thought of hurting his mom more would stop him. However, he would then admit, he was at his life's end the night his mom called the Diner for Tobias. Even the love of his mother was not enough anymore. To get to that point, he told us he also had to find blame for what happened to him on her as well. On that night, he was able to do so.

Mrs. Gilbrandt walks Raymond up to the foot of the stairs and releases him to the audience. She claps for her fully forgiven son and this incredible new life he has brought to himself, her, and the Kannot community family. The audience is on their feet, the balloting wasn't even close. The community witnessed a boy's pain, a young man's pain, and then an adult's pain all in one person for nearly 25 years. They then witnessed a recovery like no other. How could they not vote for such a man? Since the moment-in-the-mud back in 1983 he has evolved into a wonderful Christian man.

"Thank You, Thank You" Raymond announces to the crowd. "Please, let me tell you that my healing came through a man who walked with Jesus.. Please know, when we forgave each other, it was as if the Holy Spirit was rolling around in the mud with us. He took advantage of the moment and rescued us. We will never know how much Tobias needed to be forgiven for just being a little boy and not understanding what he saw or what to do about it. Please know I realized at that moment Tobias did not need to be forgiven by me, but only for himself. He was leading the fight for my soul for so many years, I just couldn't see it through my own pain. I am so fortunate that I loved Tobias when I first came to Kannot and I loved him when he left us. In between was what evil can do if we allow it to take hold. But evil did not win!"

Raymond raises his voice with that last comment and the crowd explodes with applause and Amens.

"Love will always win when given the choice, but sometimes someone has to help you see the choice. Tobias was my 'someone' and Jesus led him to me. I sometimes wonder what would have happened if Tobias was not on that ladder on that afternoon. Who would I have vented my anger at over all those years? How long would I have made it? I tremble at the thought. Just by Tobias being there that day I was saved. If ever there was someone who could take the verbal abuse and threats I made for so many years, it would be the Father, actually, The Trinity. I'm sure they needed to support each other with me"

--- as Raymond and the crowd chuckle and just laugh for a bit.

"They knew Tobias on a level we cannot understand in this life. They knew Tobias could be their conduit for this outcome. Right now, right here, what is happening tonight and since the moment-in-the-mud"!

Raymond, raising his voice again in praise; the crowd erupts again in support.

"Well, I'm going to keep doing what I'm doing. It's the best path for me to choose and I had a lot of help finding this choice. My Mom, my family, my Kannot family, and most of all The Father.

He said, **But, the fruit of the Spirit is love, joy, peace, patience, kindness, self-control; against such things there is no law.**

"Oh yes, that is scripture, but like Tobias, he said scripture every now and then, but you would have to look in the Bible for it yourself --- It's in there and maybe you'll read more while you're looking. Thank You, Thank You, Praise Be to God".

And with that, a near 32-year history with Tobias came to an end in Kannot and started anew; his influence to never end, just be handed down.

After the program was over and I got to reflect on the accomplishment of my book, my speech, and Raymond's transformation, it all came to me. When Tobias said, "you'll know when I know....." This is what he meant; Raymond's transformation and my identity, my real self, and how people and communities can be impacted by love and The Truth. I have never experienced what normal could feel like until this moment. I can now feel my words. I even feel special, not because of my CP but because of my gift to write. Most importantly though, I was a witness of a loving Father through my pen and through my friend. Such outcomes must be what Tobias believed he and I would find out together. I must thank you God. It was because of Tobias I could tell the story of Grace and whilst doing so, get a taste of it myself. Oh my God, Oh my God ---- Thank You. I am normal and with a gift of my own. I was a witness to the power of the Lord and Love.

The last question one could pose about Tobias - Did his faith bring him to wisdom or did his wisdom bring him to faith? Which came first? He was so young. How did he get on either side of this equation? We know he knew the Bible, yet he never talked of reading it much. Even Maggie and Jonathan did not see that. It's like the boy had a direct line to The Teacher. And that hand and its position during different times and situations throughout his life? He told me at his bedside that it happened when Jesus was holding it. He told me Jonathan, Maggie, and Ramona were the only other people who knew this. He just did what Jesus asks of all Believers. Walk with HIM through this life on earth. Live and behave as you believe Jesus would have you. This was the greatest gift Tobias could give us; this example, and this is the gift our community of family and friends will forever be thankful for. The beautiful circle of living a Christian life has been witnessed in Kannot, Pennsylvania and its impact is immeasurable.

- And now there is Faith , Hope and Love, and The Greatest of these is Love. God Bless You All and Good Night.

An Author Exercise

1) Can the Christian influence read about in this story be manifested in public schools today? Remember, Tobias did little to bring attention to his Christian foundation outside of his special friends.

2) When most of us talk about Jesus walking us through hard times, we may speak in metaphor about his holding of our hands. Do you think it is possible for people to know this happens?

3) When you look at people with special needs, what do you see first, a disability or ability? Does this story incline you to look more for the abilities? If you choose this path, how will you know what to look for? Did the big kid with black wavy hair and pear-shaped body help you in this area?

4) What are your thoughts on the influence of evil based upon this story?

5) The story of Tobias did not present much in the realm of the Supernatural with the exception of the handholding with Jesus. Were you able to see possible ways you could live your Christian life better and how this may impact the lives of others?

6) Were there parts of this story that were just too unbelievable for you as the reader to see happening in "real life"? If so, Why? This question is perhaps the most important of all.

7)What can you do beginning today, to MATTER as a practicing Christian in this world, and where will you seek the Fellowship for the knowledge necessary to garner this spiritual strength?

219

PUBLISHED by PARABLES
Earthly Stories with a Heavenly Meaning